The
Eidolon
LIBBY McGUGAN

First published 2013 by Solaris
an imprint of Rebellion Publishing Ltd,
Riverside House, Osney Mead,
Oxford, OX2 0ES, UK

www.solarisbooks.com

ISBN: 978 1 78108 157 0

10 9 8 7 6 5 4 3 2 1

A CIP catalogue record for this book is available
from the British Library.

Designed & typeset by Rebellion Publishing

Printed in the US

The
Eidolon
LIBBY McGUGAN

SOLARIS

Prologue

I DON'T REMEMBER the beginning. Only a vague dawning of being, fragmented lakes of feelings and thoughts. Somehow, over eons, they coalesced like the primordial ooze that gathers in the murky pond, gradually finding form. The sound of the orchestra tuning up, slowly, over huge swathes of time, discordant notes sliding into one until from them a single, clear tone is born. And in perfect synchrony, it vibrates as one being. I am. Purity, born of the minds of men. They gave me life, and for that I am indebted.

With that life came a hunger that has nothing to do with the stomach. It became a need, a voracity, that for an age nothing would satisfy, until I found the answer lay in my creators. There, in the darkest recesses of the mind, that place where men are afraid to go, is where it germinates. A seed that takes root in thought and sends its tendrils out into experience to blossom. They are the incubators, I am the harvester. It is the perfect symbiosis.

Chapter One

IT'S FUNNY HOW everything changes when a couple of bricks fall out of your wall; those things that shored you up without you realising it. You only notice when they go and the rest of your life starts crumbling away.

Six weeks ago I had a job, I had a partner; I had a life. Now I have a headache from the altitude. I also have one of the best views you could ask for. Below, sheep on the slopes blend with the grey earth and the muffled tinkling of yak bells comes and goes on the breeze as the beasts lumber across the pastures. Ahead, the sun glints on the lakes, one round, one crescent shaped. Above, white purity shrouds the mountains, becoming the sky. Unspoiled wilderness. Barren beauty. I still have a headache.

The soft snow makes walking tricky. You don't walk in this; you trudge. *Look on the bright side – it's not Middlesbrough*, that's what she would say. Cora. Always positive, always the optimist. Always with her head in the clouds. And then she'd say something like, *Look at where you are – the Tibetan Plateau, the rooftop of the planet, where you can look down on the*

madness of the world and wonder what it's all about.
See how lucky you are? She'd be right, I suppose. Up
here, nothing really matters, just that your steps are
small enough to let your lungs catch up with the rest
of you, and that you keep drinking through the rubber
straw from your CamelBak. It seemed like a good idea
at the time. Something to take my mind off redundancy
and our dissolving relationship. Something to help me
get my head straight. You know what, Cora? So far,
it's not working. Christ, Robert, if you can't clear your
mind in nine hundred thousand square miles of nothing,
there's no hope for you. It still hurts to think of her.

Danny pauses ahead of me and I almost bump into
him. His cheeks crinkle as he scans the skies. Blue-
eyed, wiry, unconventional, Danny Mitchell has been
a trekking buddy since we were students at Cambridge.
He was doing politics, I was doing physics and computer
science, and we met in the bar after an evening talk by
the climber Joe Simpson. So would you cut the rope?
Save yourself and drop your friend to certain death,
when not cutting it means you both die? It made for
an interesting opener to conversation. Danny knocked
back a whisky. He would have done it, he said, and he
meant it. Always so black and white. His philosophy
is simple: work to live, and then only until you have
enough to fund your next trip. Over the years we've
climbed in the Andes, the Pyrenees, the mountains of
Sarawak, the Cuillins of Skye; and when we do, the
differences between us don't matter.

"I think we should pitch here for the night," he says,
still studying the clouds. "It's getting dark."

"Good idea." Whatever you say, Danny. I'm struggling
to make decisions, however trivial they might be.

We drop the packs and raise the tent. The wind's beginning to strengthen but we work silently, familiar with the routine. For some reason, erecting a tent was like lighting the blue touch paper with Cora. Every time. It could be sunny, on the shores of a glassy loch, warm grass, no midges, a case of wine, and still we'd find ourselves bickering about the best way to anchor the guy ropes. It never lasted, though. Once we sat down and opened the first bottle, and felt the breeze on our skin, we'd remember why we were there. I'm going to miss that.

Danny crawls inside and hangs the torch from the hook in the roof, and the orange fabric lights up. A small glowing refuge in a wild, unforgiving place. We get the stove going at the entrance to the tent, take off the waterproofs, unpack the sleeping bags, and soon we're spooning mouthfuls of steaming rehydrated food into our mouths. Chilli con carne tonight, followed by plum duff. Stodge fit for a king. I didn't know how cold my insides were.

"Do you reckon we'll make the summit tomorrow?"

"The wind's picked up a bit, but I think we'll make it," says Danny, the food still steaming on his tongue, as he tips the boiled water into two mugs of powdered chocolate. The sweet smell competes with the odour of damp socks. "If we get another clear day like today, we'll be fine, but the weather's due to turn after tomorrow." He passes me a mug.

I take a sip. "Everything tastes better when you're camping."

"Yeah. You forget, don't you? By the end of the trip you won't want to go back."

"Not a whole lot to go back to, now."

He stares at his mug and stirs it slowly. After a moment he says, "It might not look like it yet, but maybe it's an opportunity."

"An opportunity." Why is it that when you're in a bad place people who've never been there feel compelled to offer you advice on how to get out?

"Yeah, you know, a blank slate. Start again."

"I loved the job."

"And what about Cora?"

I don't answer.

He glances up from his stirring.

"We were too different."

"So what's with the ring, then?"

He nods towards my left hand, which is absentmindedly rolling the small silver ring looped through a black leather thread. My fingers close round it and I return it to my pocket.

He stares at me expectantly.

"I gave it to her for her birthday a couple of years ago. She gave it back to me before I left. It's nothing."

"Uh-huh." He takes a sip then heaps another spoonful of chocolate into his mug. "You really loved the job? Cramped down some mineshaft looking for... what was it again?"

"Dark matter."

"Dark matter, whatever that is. That's not a job; that's a sentence. I couldn't do it."

"No, you couldn't. You're not bright enough."

He snorts. "Really? You spend your time studying life. I spend my time living it. Who's the smart one? You tell me."

He has a point, but I'm not going to concede. I stab the air with my spoon. "It's people like me who make it

12

possible for layabouts like you to bum around for your whole life, with your storm-proof tents and your gas stoves and your torches."

He grins and unscrews the cap of a hipflask, toasting me. "Well, here's to you and all the other specky scientists who keep the rest of us in good times." He takes a swig and hands me the flask. The wind keens and rumbles against the sides of the tent, bowing them inwards. Everything tastes better when you're camping, especially the whisky.

Danny wriggles into his sleeping bag, stuffing a pile of unwashed clothes underneath the top end to make a lumpy pillow. I lie back, my hands behind my head. The wind drops until it's only a breath on the tent. Beyond its breathing is the silence of the mountain.

"Listen to that," says Danny.

I stare at the roof, listening. "No traffic."

"Bet you're glad you came along."

"Yeah. I'll be even more glad if the weather holds for tomorrow."

"We'll be fine." He turns his gaze back to the space above him, one corner of his mouth smiling. "Picture it – looking down at the planet from up there. Nothing else comes close."

"If people knew what it was like..."

He snorts again, reaching behind his head to plump up his pillow. "Just as well they don't. They can stick to their mortgages and their pension funds and all that shit and stay out of the way, as far as I'm concerned."

The wind carries a howl from a distant place.

"I tell you," he says, "that mountain will sort your head out for you. You'll be a changed man."

* * *

WE SET OFF at a good pace, leaving the tent where it stands. The sky is clear and it looks like the weather might hold, but it's not long before we're trudging again. The air's thinner here, a lot thinner. My lungs are sucking it in, in the hope that it contains a passing oxygen molecule. Our breaths rise in icy puffs, and underfoot the snow groans and rasps as our boots sink into it. We don't talk much; there's not enough air. I thought I'd use this time to work things out in my head, or just to forget, but it's not like that. There's not enough air to walk and think – it's one or the other – so my brain elects to concentrate on breathing and trudging, leaving me with a vague awareness that I'll still have a shitload of baggage to offload when I get home. Not what I had planned.

Danny stops and drops his pack, breathless. We take a break, panting like we've run uphill, and sip hot sweet coffee from the flask. White peaks stretch out in all directions, like crested waves on a frozen sea, and the water in the lakes below glistens in the sunlight. Above, a buzzard calls, circling between tatters of inky cloud.

"This is what it's all about," says Danny. He draws a slow, deep breath and closes his eyes, savouring the freedom. "This is real."

I nod, but say nothing as the wind slinks round us. My head's thumping.

"To life." Danny gulps from the flask and hands it to me.

"To life." I down the remnants, then wipe my lips with the back of my glove. The wind has picked up, drawing in a mist that shrouds the distant peaks. "The weather's turning," I say, eyeing the changing sky. Wisps of snow billow in the icy air.

"Yeah. We'd better get moving." He stuffs the flask into his pack. "It's not far now."

I frown at the sky, where fragmented clouds are coalescing, churning out from a grisly horizon. "Maybe we should head down and try again tomorrow."

Danny slings his pack over his shoulder. "It's not too bad. Where's your sense of adventure?" He grins and sets off again, in the lead.

THE WIND'S PICKING up in bursts, moaning, whipping, splintering the snowdrifts into puffs of white mist that rise into the air and settle on our footprints, concealing them. When I turn to look back, it's like we were never there. A fierce gust whips up from the lower slopes, and I stagger against it. It's making me uneasy, this wind. I glance down the slope, but it's all veiled in white. There's no sign of the lakes. Turning into the wind, through the flurry of snowflakes, I peer up at the faceless ascent and it stares back at me – cold, unmerciful. The fear grips me for a moment. The kind of fear I've read about, when men who undertake this pilgrimage – anticipated it, planned for it, made friends with it – realise that they're nobody to the mountain; that it doesn't care if they live or die. It would be so easy to give in to it, but there's no way back from that. *Get a grip, Robert. Just keep your mind on your feet.* Danny toils ahead, his head bent.

Those clouds are moving in too fast. The sky blackens, pressing down on the white, squeezing the brightness from it. Snow gusts about in thick, fat flakes and dark clouds weigh heavily on the horizon, obscuring the peak. The wind is wailing like a tortured cat and it won't let up, not for a moment. You could go mad with this wind. It's almost as if it's become personal, buffeting our steps into staggers. Mountain weather, like its mood, changes swiftly and with little warning. I know what she'd say. *Can't you read the signs? The mountain doesn't want you here.*

Another blast knocks me sideways, shaking my balance and my confidence. Alright. Enough. There's a point when pride needs to step aside for instinct, and it's right here. "Danny! We won't make it in this! We need to turn back!"

He stops and turns towards me, from his place further up the slope, then looks up to the summit, or where it should be somewhere behind the thick, grey mist. "But we're nearly there!" The wind keens and wheezes and he stumbles back a few steps. It's making a point.

"No, Danny, we won't make it. We need to get down!"

He stares through the cloud towards the peak, then turns his face to the sky. He drops his head and stands looking at his feet as the snow whips around him. I know how much this means to him. Eighteen months in a kitchen with an arsehole of a chef and a daily barrage of verbal abuse just to raise the cash for the flights. He held down the job because he knew it was a means to an end. The weather reports said it's due to get worse, so it may be that we don't get the break tomorrow or the next day, or at all. But it's all relative. *Let it go, Danny. Don't be a fool.* When he lifts his head again, he nods. He turns and tramps down the mountainside, passing me without meeting my eye.

The descent is clumsy against the rising wind, and our footing uncertain; the snow has devoured the tracks and there's nothing left. I catch glimpses of the plain below between the shifting white curtains, but there's still no sign of the lakes. There should be lakes, below. This isn't the way we came up.

"Wait, Danny, we're off track!"

I catch his voice in a break between gusts. "No, this'll take us down!" He ploughs on down the slope, head bent, undeterred. He's so bloody pigheaded.

I stop dead. Ahead, just beyond Danny, the cliff face disappears into a crevasse, white emptiness. He hasn't seen it. "Stop! Danny, Stop!"

He looks back up at me from under his thick, fur hood, then turns, glancing down the slope. The mountain mist closes the door on its secret, but not before he sees the drop. He stumbles onto his back. "Shit!" His voice is muffled through the scissoring snow as he scrambles to his feet and back up the slope, ungainly like a toddler wrapped in too many puffy winter clothes. I wade towards him and catch his arm, steadying him.

"We'll not make it down in this!" I yell, hoping he can hear over the din. It's getting dark, beyond the clouds. Nightfall in the wings. "We'll have to shelter till it blows over!"

He nods and casts around, then points higher up the face to a place where the edge of the mountain rises steeply beside a level bank of snow. It might offer some shelter from the wind. Crouching into the storm, we tramp towards the bank, take the snow shovel from my pack, sink to our knees and begin to dig.

I can't feel my hands. I glance up at Danny. His lips are cracked, the colour of slate, and his cheeks are scorched red beneath his hood. He screws up his eyes inside his goggles. This fucking wind, it won't stop. It just blows harder. "Keep digging," he shouts.

Slowly, he disappears inside the snow hole, his boots still visible between the sprays of snow he flicks out. We take turns. When it's done, I sit back on my heels, dizzy, hot in my core, cold in my limbs, as Danny wriggles inside. I glance up at the sky. The clouds have leaked away with the light. I've never seen the sky like this. Millions of tiny, distant suns riddling the black in great trailing swathes. Tibet must be higher than I thought; closer to the heavens.

Inside the cramped, dark hole, the sound of the wind dies a little. Thank God for small mercies. We loosen our laces, letting the blood back into our feet. A ski pole pokes through a small hole in the roof, enough to let some air inside. I struggle to light the small candle, my fingers frozen and clumsy, but finally it catches. Such a small thing – a tiny, yellow, flickering flame, a symbol of hope.

Danny fumbles with his wrist and pulls off his watch. "We'll take turns to sleep. Keep an eye on the candle." If it starts to sputter, we're running out of air.

I'm dying for a drink, but we've nothing left, so I stuff some snow into my mouth.

"No," says Danny, catching my arm. "It'll just make you colder. Get some sleep. I'll wake you in an hour. God willing."

I've never heard him say anything like that before. He's not religious. Like me, he's an unabashed atheist. Damn right he'll wake me in an hour. I'm not dying in some snow pit in the middle of nowhere. "Make sure you do." I reach for Cora's ring, still in my pocket. I wish I hadn't been such an arsehole.

MY INSIDES ARE cold now that I'm lying still. It feels like my limbs are only vaguely attached to the rest of me, like they've all been to the dentist for a jag then left in the deep freeze. Even my guts feel cold, and my lungs when I breathe in, and my headache's changed from thumping to that feeling you get when you bite into ice-cream. Brainfreeze. Maybe there's a neural pathway connecting ice-cream to the lining of the brain. An ice-cream-neuron, waiting to be discovered. The shivering hurts, but at least it's a sign that I'm still here.

Sometime after that, I don't know how long, I give in to sleep.

I WAKE TO a sound. I hush my breathing, as much as I can in the thin air. The candle's still yellow, it's not sputtering, so we must be alive. So much for waking me in an hour. Danny's lying, eyes closed, shivering. From the candlelight I can see his lips flubbering in a soft snore. What was that sound? The wind? Through the vent in the roof I can see it's still dark.

I check my watch. It takes a while to focus on the numbers and even longer to work out what they mean. 3.14.

There it is again. Am I imagining it? It sounds like a voice. If the wind had a voice, it would sound like this, resonant and commanding. No, I was wrong; it's not a voice, because there aren't any words. So why do I know what it means?

GET UP.

God, Robert. You must be hypothermic. Voices in the head can't be a good sign. A voice with no words. Like a thought, but coming from somewhere outside of me.

GET UP NOW.

I need to get up. Irrational or not, there's no disputing it. I don't know why but every fibre in me knows it's right. From some reserve I didn't know I had, I find the will. It takes over, becoming an urgency, an edge. I kick the wall of snow at my feet, toppling the candle and snuffing it out, then wriggle from the hole. It's snowing again, the clouds inking out the stars.

Something makes me turn, something over my right shoulder. A little higher up the mountain there's something in the darkness, just visible through the blizzard. It's insubstantial, like the shadow of steam on a wall, but something else is there. I rub my eyes, and when I look again, there's nothing. But it feels like...

Sudden certainty seizes me. I've got to get Danny out. I reach into the remains of the hole and grasp his ankles, tugging, dragging him into the open. "Wake up, Danny! Get up!"

He mumbles, eyes still closed, and turns his face from the driving snow. "Danny!" I kneel over him and slap him hard across the cheek. "Come on, come on! Get up, dammit!"

A low groaning sound issues from the mountain, as though something that lies beneath is awakening. Something enormous. We sink, suddenly a few inches lower, jolting downwards as though...

"*Move!*" I'm on my feet, grasping Danny by the hood. His feet flail under him as I try to pull him away, but he's fighting me, trying to free himself from my grip. "What the hell are you..."

The ground creaks and groans and shifts. The shelter breaks apart and disappears, leaving nothing but frozen gusts of air as we scramble back from the collapsing edge, kicking furiously, the ground crumbling and falling away in great chunks that tumble into emptiness. It gains on us, ripping at more of the mountain until it reaches the snow under Danny's feet.

He slides away from me, his arms flapping wildly, groping for a hold. I catch his hood again with one hand and with the other, grasp his wrist. The groaning stops and the ground steadies as he hangs there, suspended, the wind gusting up from below, teasing. A block of ice breaks away and bounces into the darkness and Danny's gaze follows it as he sways from the precipice. He looks up at me and for a moment our eyes meet.

"You know what I'd do," he says.

Should I? My arms are beginning to quiver. I can hold on for a bit, but then... I'm not sure how long until... what am I thinking? "No. Hold on!" I dig my heels into the snow, jerking with his weight beneath me, and lean back. Nothing happens; he's still dangling from the end of my arms, a dead weight. My legs are shaking now. I don't know if it's the shivering or the strain they're under.

"Robert..." Danny holds my eye. "You can't... Just let go!"

He slips a little, only a few inches, but each of them closing the gap to death. My limbs are on fire. It would be so easy to let go, just relax, release the grip and the pain will stop...

And then what? From somewhere, I don't know where, the certainty grips me again. It's like when you look through the lens of a camera and adjust the focus until everything comes into sharp relief. A clarity, or absence of doubt. Something so obvious you wonder why you didn't see it before. "No!" I clench my teeth, my eyes squeezed shut, my arms trembling with the effort, and with one last painful heave I haul Danny onto the ledge.

He's face down in the snow, gasping, quivering, hugging the mountain. A shard of moonlight slices through the snowflakes, the mountain quietens and the snow is still. We lie there, panting, staring through the blizzard at the abyss.

"Thanks," begins Danny. "I don't know how you..."

"Come on," I get to my feet, facing into the wind. "We need to get down." It still has me, that unwavering certainty.

"Wait, Robert!" He sways to his knees. "There's not enough light. We can't walk in this!"

"We can't stay here." I grasp his arm, hauling him upright.

"Look what just happened! We could go over the edge!"

"We won't. We have to go down."

Danny flaps his arms like a toddler having a tantrum. "What makes you so sure?"

I glance over my right shoulder, towards the place where I saw... I don't hear any anything and I don't see anything, but I don't have to. It's a feeling, more than a sound or an image, the memory of a shadow. Something else announces it, something undefined. It is like walking into a dark room and knowing, in that inexplicable visceral sense, that someone else is there with you, before you see them. I'm not frightened, I'm calm. Calmer than I've ever been. It's watching.

But there's no point in telling Danny, he won't get it. I turn back to him. "I just know." I lead the way down the mountain, surefooted and confident in the descent, Danny stumbling behind, and something else, almost beyond sight, but not beyond perception. It follows us into the white noise.

*   *   *

As THE STEEP slopes surrender to a gentler gradient, the wind begins to die away and my steps slow. I turn back to Danny, waiting for him to wade closer, watching him sink into the powdery snow, bluish now in the fading night. Each step is laboured, like his boots are filled with lead. As he draws level, his harsh breaths score the air with steamy puffs and blend with the thick mist. I point ahead. The mist parts and moonlight glimmers on the shores of a vast lake. I put a hand on Danny's shoulder, my lips cracking as I try to smile. I turn back, over my shoulder, eyes narrowing as I peer into the nothingness.

And then, as a candle flame snuffs out with a breath, it's gone, and with it the sense of stillness. The moonlight reflects on the snowy shores, but the lake itself is a deep black – not a ripple of light on its surface. A black hole in the tundra. A cloud consumes the moon, darkening the land again. I collapse face-down in the snow.

Chapter Two

THIRSTY. THERE'S A forest fire in your throat. Feel that by your left cheek? It's wet. Turn your head, that's it. Slurp it up. Cold, burning your lips, hot ice. Look around – white space everywhere, endless stellar brightness, fierce wind. A place to hunt yourself. Don't eat snow. Remember? *It'll just make you colder.* Danny told you, before. Where is he? Rest your head down, just sleep, it's alright.

No! No sleeping! Fuck! You want to die here? Then focus! The lake, remember? See that, ahead? Liquid water, mirror-smooth, black beneath the mist...

Nectar. Dark, cold, nectar, trickling down inside. You're colder now, the shivering hurts. And dizzy. You hate dizzy. You've never seen water like this. The sun's glare hurts your eyes but there's not a glimmer of light on its surface. The mist is parting, and there's something behind it. Something dark. Why are you uneasy? You want to get away from it but you don't have the strength or the will to move.

Then rest your head, just for a moment. That's it. Just for a moment.

WHAT HAPPENED AGAIN? There was a storm, wasn't there? Digging in the snow, the blizzard eating my face, a dark hole, a voice with no words. Danny dangling from a cliff edge – oh, God did he drop? Did I let him drop? What the hell will I tell his parents?

No, no, he didn't drop. We had to go down, even in the dark. No question. Great feeling, certainty. Besides, the other man agreed with me.

Who did? It was just me and Danny. Wasn't it?

Cold's made me crazy, that's all. Best lie still, a bit longer. Think of home.

Not much left there for me, not now. When did it all change, again?

IT WAS RAINING and cold, a typical February in England. I was late for work – my bike was still at the garage getting repaired, so I hitched a ride in a truck. Thank God for truckers. This trucker's belly was an appendage on which to rest the steering wheel, and the cabin reeked of smoke.

"You work at the mine?" he asked after I told him where I was going.

"Yeah."

His eyes narrowed as he glanced from my face to my hands. "You don't look like a miner."

"No. I'm not a miner."

"You some kind of manager, then?"

Maybe I should have walked. A stroll through Middle England in the pissing rain might have been easier. "No, I work in the Dark Matter Research Lab."

He frowned.

"It's down a mineshaft." I hoped this might help, but it didn't. If anything, judging by the way his face folded in on itself, it only made things worse. "So where are you headed?"

"Whitby, then have to be in Scarborough by ten."

"Right." I watched the fields and woods whip past and yawned. My head felt thick, and it ached.

"So, what's dark matter, then?"

I knew it was coming, and I didn't have it in me to explain. "It's the missing piece of the universe."

He snorted, "Missing piece? Haven't we got enough problems already? Sounds like a wild goose chase, if you ask me."

Well, I didn't.

He shook his head, like people do when they think it's all a colossal waste of taxpayers' money. "This do you?" he said, pulling into the lay-by. He peered at the sign that read: *Middlesbrough 12 miles* and, underneath, *Potash Mine ½ mile*, with an arrow pointing to the left.

"Thanks a lot – I appreciate it."

I jumped down from the truck and waved as he pulled away, then ran the half-mile down the road that led to nowhere but the mine.

Tall, grey chimneys puffing out smoke struck into the sky, a collage of drab buildings huddled low around them. The hum of machinery quivered on the air and the smell of diesel was thick that day. It used to make me feel queasy, but you get used to it. The changing rooms were empty – I was really late – and after donning the orange suit and helmet – *safety first* – I headed for the entrance to the lab. It's not a very grand entrance, given what goes on down there. It's nothing short of a disappointment. If it weren't for the sign above it which reads:

DARK MATTER RESEARCH LABORATORY
RESTRICTED ACCESS
AUTHORISED PERSONEL ONLY

you'd walk right past it. It's always dim in the entranceway. I used to think of all the people who work in the finance sector in somewhere like London or New York whenever I pulled back the caged door to the lift-shaft. They'd be wearing suits as they walked up those broad, smooth steps and disappeared through revolving doors into a building made of glass. And inside there would be an escalator to take them to the main foyer. Here, you had to grapple with the cage door just to get it to open. No lift attendant to tip his hat at you. Why did I choose this job again?

I clanged the door shut and pushed the green button on the control box that dangled from a thick wire in the corner. *I swear, one of these days it would drop off and I'd be stuck a kilometre under the planet in a bloody lift shaft.* The cage shuddered and began its descent, and the earth exhaled its hot breath on me, its morning salute. I adjusted my helmet, fumbling with the headlamp, and a pool of tepid light spilled onto my palm. I tapped the torch, and the light stuttered and went out. Bollocks.

The descent took several minutes, and the air grew stuffier with each of them. Lights set into the rock face swept from my feet to my head in slow, regular pulses.

I ran my hand over my stubbled jaw, and yawned again. Glancing at my watch, I winced. Zimmer was going to be pissed off. He wanted an early start – today of all days. Given all the hours I'd put in, he couldn't really pull me up on it, especially since they didn't pay overtime. Ever since we got the scent that we were on to something, about a year ago, I'd spent most of my time at the mine, probably more than Zimmer himself. Not when things were really bad for Cora, though. Then I would take some time off to be with her, even though it didn't seem to help. I think she found it easier when I wasn't around. She needed her own space, she'd said. I didn't want to think too much then about what that meant, so I threw myself back into work. Before long, if I got home before nine on a week night I was doing well. And the weekends were almost as bad. It was like a drug, like gambling: the thought that it's there, that we almost have it, and if we put one more coin into the slot, the next run might be the one that pays off. We were close. We knew that from the preliminary results, all we needed was to verify them. And if we found the nature of dark matter? If we solved the mystery of what's all around us? That's what kept me going. Zimmer and I had already been invited to speak at the Annual Conference on Astroparticle and Underground Physics the following week to present our findings and I'd had provisional acceptance of a paper I'd submitted to the *Journal of Physics*. I had a call last month from the physics lead at the University of Manchester, offering me a temporary lecturer's post covering for a computer scientist on long term sick. "Between you and me," he'd said, "we need some fresh input, someone who's on the cutting edge. It could lead to a full time post." There was growing interest in the scientific community. Ears were pricking up, and it fuelled the drive to reach the finish line. It would change everything.

THE CAGE BUMPED to a halt and I dragged the whining doors open, this time in the bowels of the salt mine where the air smelled of scorched rock. I pushed the doors closed behind me and walked down the corridor, my boots echoing on the concrete floor. A man shuffled towards me from the other end of the corridor, pulling a large trolley. He wore a safety suit and helmet like everyone down here, but his were blue and I didn't recognise him.

The man glanced up then lowered his eyes without smiling as he passed. I glanced back. Piles of cardboard boxes overburdened the trolley, full of books and paper files and bits of electrical kit. Maybe Zimmer had decided to clear out some of his mess, I thought. About time.

Ahead of me, a door. Someone had amended the sign reading:

**RESEARCH LABORATORY CONTROL ROOM
ACCESS RESTRICTED**

with the word 'MOTHERSHIP'.

I suppose that the bottom of a pit is an odd place to study anything.

I pushed open the door and froze. It was all wrong. Five men I didn't know were dismantling computers and packing them into cardboard boxes. They picked files from shelves and thumbed through their clipboard lists and none of them would meet my eye.

"What the hell's going on?" I strode towards Chris, lounging back on a swivel-chair, his feet perched on an empty desk as he watched the men pack. Nothing winds him up, I've always thought, and this confirmed my suspicions. He twirled a pen between the fingers of his right hand and observed the scene as though he was watching a TV show. His short dark hair was just visible beneath his helmet and he ran his left thumb over a carefully sculpted beard. Two men moved to either side of his table and began to pull it out from under him. He lifted his legs free, but in his own time. When he planted his feet on the floor, he looked up at me.

"Nice of you to show up. But you shouldn't have bothered."

"Why? What's happening?"

"They pulled the funding."

"What? You're kidding me."

"Does he look like he's kidding?" Chris glanced at a man standing in the shadows. He was lean, in his late thirties and dressed in a suit that would cost me several months' wages and then some. He stood with his back straight and his hands clasped in front of him, watching with a detached air. His eyes briefly settled on me.

"What do you mean, they pulled it? Who pulled it?"

"It came from the top."

"They can't just take all this stuff! All of our data..." I snatched a file from the top of a nearby box and glared at the man carrying it. The business man took four long strides towards me.

"Mr Strong, that file is no longer your property."

"And who the hell are you?"

From behind me, three other men in suits closed in. Not slim, like the first, but bulked out and standing several inches above the rest of us. They didn't speak – they didn't have to. Chris's pen stopped twirling.

The lean man's eyes were still on me. "I'm Steven Ryan from Organol Security. I realise this is unexpected, but we've been tasked with taking possession of the contents of this laboratory."

"Tasked by whom?"

"Her Majesty's Government."

"What?" I glanced at Chris, who nodded.

Ryan continued. "It's my duty to remind you that we require any files you may have on these premises. We appreciate your cooperation." He spoke with the reassurance of a priest but there was no doubt he was comfortable with violence. "Do you have any other files?"

I caught Chris's eye. "No. I have backups, but they're all here."

Ryan watched me for a moment, without speaking. I wanted to punch him hard in the face.

"Leave it, Robert," breathed Chris.

All those months we spent at the edge, fine tuning it, pushing through disappointment after disappointment, and just when we can see the finish line, some little shit in a suit says it's over? My fists clenched and the muscle man nearest me inched closer.

Chris gripped my arm. "Let it go."

I tossed the file back into the box. The lean man smiled thinly and nodded to the others.

I turned back to Chris, my insides burning. "Where's Zimmer?"

The door at the other end of the room crashed open and Zimmer stormed in, right on cue. His face matched the scarlet of his helmet and he barked at the phone held to his ear. The veins on his neck stood out like purple ropes.

"Well interrupt his call! This is an urgent... you tell him that it's Geoff Zimmer... YOU!" He covered the mouthpiece with his free hand as he bellowed at one of the intruders lifting a sheaf of paper from a shelf at the other side of the room. "PUT THAT BACK! ...No, no, I'm sorry, not you... wait... no, wait... Ah, *shit!*" He hurled the phone to the concrete floor and it smashed into pieces.

"Don't worry about it, boss," says Chris. "We won't be needing it anymore."

Geoff Zimmer took off his helmet and spectacles and pinched the bridge of his nose between his finger and thumb.

"What the hell happened here, Geoff?"

Zimmer sighed and slumped into an empty chair next to Chris. When he lifted his eyes, he looked beaten. "They didn't even phone me. The first I knew about it was when I got here this morning. They're closing the whole project down. They have it in writing."

"For fuck's sake! When we're this close? How can they stop it this far down the line?"

"I don't know..."

"What about Norris? Have you spoken to the Science Minister?"

"He signed the letter, Robert."

"But he endorsed the project!"

"He seems to have changed his mind. I'm sorry, boys, there's nothing I can do. This is way above our heads now. The others have already gone. They're taking everything – I mean *everything*: programmes, discs, scrap paper, anything relating to the research." He sat back. "They're giving us one more month's pay. If anything else comes up, you'll be the first to know."

I turned to Chris. "Let's get out of here."

CHRIS DROVE ME home in his dented red Mini. I stared out of the window at the grey buildings and sodden streets, frowning, and chewing my left thumbnail. I turned to Chris. "You've got back-up, right?"

"Yeah. You?"

"Uh-huh."

We drove on in silence.

"So, what will you do?" I said eventually.

Chris shrugged. "Dunno. See what else is out there, I suppose. If they can't finance this project, the chances aren't good of something else coming up. Not in this line of work. I know times are hard, but I'd didn't think they'd pull the plug."

My teeth ground together as I thought about it. "You don't buy that it's just about the funding?"

Chris shook his head. "No, I don't. Maybe it's better we don't know." He snorted. "Kay keeps on at me to take a break, so maybe this is the right time. What about you? What'll you do?"

"I don't know. Maybe I'll try to get into Romfield Labs again, go back to doing some work on the Grid. Or maybe do some lecturing work. There's a temporary post going in Manchester." I shrugged. "And I can always do some web design to tide things over." It was how I got by as a student.

"You won't have any trouble. Not with your track record."

Of the two of us, I was in a far stronger position than Chris, and we both knew it. And of the two of us, he would be under more pressure to sort things out, with an eighteen-month-old child to consider. I don't know how he stayed so level about the whole thing. I felt like I was on the edge. The slightest trigger and I'd detonate.

The grey streets flashed past: glum mothers pushing prams, youths in baseball caps leaning against the walls of seedy pubs, puffing out smoke and waiting for life to happen, shuffling old men with nowhere left to go. Disillusionment festered where optimism once might have been.

"How's Cora?" Chris asked. "Is she, you know... okay?"

"She still cries some nights, and she's still not sleeping much. She's back teaching yoga, at least, and she's getting out a bit more." I glanced at my watch. She'd be home from her lunchtime class soon. What the hell was I going to tell her?

"How long's it been now?"

"Seven months." God, had it really been that long? I couldn't believe that Sarah had been dead for seven months.

"They must have been pretty close. If Kay lost her sister, she'd cry for half an hour and then go shopping."

I snorted as the car pulled to a stop beside the tenement building. Fresh graffiti decorated the metal shutters of the shop beneath our flat; I stared at the frustration vented on them, feeling a mix of anger and empathy towards whoever had left their mark. I got out and leaned my forearm on the roof of the car. "Thanks for the lift. Let me know if you hear anything."

"No problem. See you... whenever."

I swung the door shut. The Mini chugged off and splashed a puddle of muddy water onto my legs. I stepped back, then stood for a moment looking up at the sky. The rain washed down in sheets.

I CLIMBED THE stairwell, passing the door of Jenny and Arthur Randle, who were bawling at each other, again. Why the hell don't they just give it up? Put it down to experience, move on, go their own separate ways and give the rest of us a break. On the second floor, a small pot of violet pansies sat by the red doorway – Cora's idea; she'd painted it herself. I entered the flat, took off my coat and tossed it onto the chair next to the table with the lamp and the photograph of Cora and me on some Munro. We'd set the camera on a rock and rushed back to pose in time for the shot, giving us a slightly manic look, with Cora's dark red hair whipping across her face and me with a crazed, half-fixed smile that made me look like the Joker. The almond-shaped face and messy, slightly spiky sandy coloured hair haven't changed much, but my eyes have. Laughter lines, they call them, but the laughter seeped away without me noticing.

I made myself an extra strong mug of black coffee and walked into the living room where Cora had concealed the tear in the brown couch with a blue rug. White candles of different sizes stood in the unused fireplace. Cora would light them every night when she came home. The place reeked of incense. She'd taken to burning it when she meditated, and even my clothes were beginning to stink of the stuff, to the point where Chris accused me of being a dopehead. Reminders of her time in India decorated the room: a large wall tapestry, faded rugs on the bare floorboards, a Buddha on the bookcase, squeezed between my books on climbing and her books on philosophy, Taoism and other weird stuff. My contribution to our home was the laptop on the wooden desk in front of the long, thin window – which rattled whenever the wind picked up – and the stack of journals on the floor; last night's empty beer can sat on top of it. I sat down at the desk and checked for phone messages while the laptop booted up.

Two messages. The first, the man from the garage. "Hi Robert, it's Alf Barlow here. 'Fraid it's not good news with the bike – the frame's cracked the whole way through. If I could weld it together, I would, but it wouldn't hold. It's a death trap. It'd be cheaper to buy a new bike. Anyway, eh, give me a call when you get this."

Great.

The second, Danny's voice. "Robert, can you take your snow shovel? I can't find mine. Think we'll be okay with one between us. Only four weeks to go!"

Four weeks till Tibet and he's already packing. Only four weeks.

I opened my inbox. The first message didn't help. It was a knock-back from the *Journal of Physics* about my recent submission.

Unfortunately, we feel that your research needs to be further forward before it justifies publication in this journal. However we would welcome a resubmission when you have validated your results.

Well, that's not happening now, is it? What a fucking day.

Things got worse. The next email was from the lab, untitled. Maybe some kind of explanation. All the text said was 'Update'. I clicked open the attachment as the phone rang.

"Robert, is that you?" It was Chris.

"Yeah, I'm just logging..."

"Don't open it!"

"What?"

"The email from the lab – don't open it!"

Too late. The screen flashed and flickered as fleeting programs and documents and files haemorrhaged down some invisible plughole. I dropped the phone. "No..." I punched into the settings and found the remote access enabled, and not listening to commands to turn it off.

"Shit!" The chair toppled over behind me as I shot to my feet. I pressed and held the power key, but not before the curser blinked, having completed its task. I picked up the phone.

"Robert?"

"This happen to you?"

"Yeah."

"Could you trace it?"

"No, it's fixed the boot sector and overwritten the files. They got my backup, too."

"What?"

"I had them on File-Safe."

"The commercial server?"

"Yeah, but they got into it. My guess is they keylogged my login." Do you have anything else?"

"I'll call you back." I hung up.

I BOLTED DOWN the stairwell and pushed through the door leading to the small strip of garden which we shared with the Randles. At the far end was a small shed. It's well built and full of rusty tools left by the old man who was here before us. I unlocked the heavy padlock and the door creaked as I swung it open. A few years ago I had fixed a metal lock-box against the wall, and I kept my backup discs and keys in there. It's cheaper than storage on a remote electronic server, and although it's old fashioned, it feels like I have more control. I opened the box and took out the contents, then knocked on Jenny Randle's door and asked if I could use her computer.

All of the discs were blank.

"WIPED?" SAID CHRIS when I called him back. "And you're sure the box was locked?"

"It must have been an electromagnet on the outside wall."

I heard Chris blow out a long breath.

"No one knew about that locker, Chris. No one. Who the hell's doing this?"

"I called Zimmer. He says we need to let it go. No police, he said. It wouldn't get us anywhere."

I ran my hand through my hair. "Oh, come on. We can't just let this go! This isn't just shutting down a project – it's wiping out any evidence that it ever happened!"

"Let it go, Robert. Whatever it is, it sounds like you don't want it in your life. Look, call Zimmer yourself if you like. But you won't get anywhere."

I did, and Chris was right. Zimmer was a wall. I don't think he really knew what was going on, but he sounded scared. "It's above our heads, Robert," he said. "This is right from the top. It's not worth it."

"It's not worth it? It's not worth everything we did for that project, for all those years? Come on, Zimmer! What happened to you?"

"Leave it, Robert. Please. You won't win this one. Let it go."

He said he'd do what he could to get me a place at Cavendish, but he couldn't promise.

I hung up in disgust, but I was shaken, more than I wanted to admit. I knew he was right.

I HEARD THE front door open. Cora walked in, pulling a scarf laced with sparkly strands from around her neck.

"What are you doing home so early?" she asked.

She was dressed in jeans and a purple top that was too big for her and her hair was swept up on her head in the way that it usually was. Her jewellery was unchanged – plain leather bands around her slender wrist, a single, broad, silver ring on her thumb and the silver ring I bought her which she wore on a cord round her neck. She used to wear it on her index finger until she stopped eating well and it became too big for her. For all of her shiny accessories, her face still had a haunted look that had been there since her sister died.

"What's wrong?" She regarded me through narrowed green eyes beneath dark lashes.

"I... eh. I got some bad news today."

"What's happened?"

"They've closed down the lab."

"What?"

"No warning – even Zimmer didn't know till this morning."

"Why, was it dangerous?"

"No, nothing like that. We don't know what's going on. All we know is that we get a month's pay, but the project's finished."

"But can they do that? I mean, after everything you've done?"

"They just did, Cora."

"Oh, Robert, I'm sorry..." Being bitter about it all was easy, but when she put arms around me, and held me tight, I felt like a child. For a moment, I was anchorless, like I couldn't remember who I was any more. "After all your work," she whispered. She stroked my hair. The fury melted into despair and threatened to spill onto my cheeks; I pulled away from her before it did.

She held onto my hand, squeezing it gently. Her palm was cool and delicate in mine. "We'll work it out, Robert. I'll get some shifts in a café or something. There's a waiting list for my class, so I'm sure I could run another one."

"It's not going to be enough, though."

"Well, maybe you could go back to web design for a while, just until something else comes up."

I nodded and turned to the window where grey rain pattered on the glass.

"Listen, let me make a phone call. I was going to go out tonight with Jacqui and Liz – I'll let them know I won't make it."

"Who?"

"From my class."

"Oh. I didn't know you socialised with them."

She shrugged, stooped to light a few candles. "You're always late home." Then she flushed and said, "Sorry."

"It's okay."

She sat on the sofa, watching me, and I turned to look out of the window to the sodden street below. Jenny Randle's Fiat Punto was parked below, like it always was. The car hadn't moved since I saw it this morning, but my whole life had. And I had no say in any of it.

"Maybe we should go away for a while," said Cora.

"I need to get some work, Cora. I've no income now, remember?"

"We've got some savings."

"Yeah, as a last resort. I need to get another job."

"Well," she said, patiently, "you might be in a better place to deal with things if you take a break."

"I've already paid for the trip to Tibet. That'll be enough of a break."

"I meant with me. We could go back to the cottage."

A few weeks after Sarah died, I had taken Cora to a cottage on the coast. I thought the change of scene would help, and it did, a little. We had some walks on the beach, drank a lot of wine and I held her each night as she cried herself to sleep. Watching her suffer was almost unbearable. I kept wishing I could take it all for her, but there's nothing you can do with invisible wounds. We were closer then than we had been in a while, but when we got home, we fell back into our separate lives.

"Or we could go up to the pottery," she continued. "It won't cost us anything, apart from the travel. My parents won't be back till next month."

Cora's parents, Evelyn and Frank, had bought the old pottery along the glen from where I grew up, on the west coast of Scotland. He was an engineer and she was a social worker who had taken a pottery evening class one autumn at the local polytechnic. They saw the light, as they said, and packed it all in, in exchange for the simple life. Grow your own veg, brew your own cider, summer solstice parties. You get the picture. One harsh winter without running water made them realise that cities aren't so bad and now they spend most of their time on city breaks. The longest they've been home since Sarah died is four weeks. Probably too quiet up there; nowhere to hide from their thoughts. I met Cora there seven years ago when I was up visiting my mum and she was helping set up the pottery. There was something about her that I couldn't put my finger on, but we just clicked. We laughed a lot. She had a vibrancy about her that was infectious, mixed in with an intoxicating sense of calm. She had me hooked. It seemed like a long time ago.

"Where are they off to this time?"

"Barcelona. You know, we could go walking again, like we used to."

It was the first sign that she was in a better place, something I'd been hoping for, for seven months. Just in time for me to pass her on the way down.

"That sounds good."

GRADUALLY WE SEEMED to switch roles. Now it was me who would wake up in the small hours, and she'd get up and sit with me, or make me a drink. She still carried her grief around with her, and sometimes her eyes would glisten whenever something triggered it, like a reference to family on the TV or a piece of music on the radio. But she seemed to box it away, in the way that a parent who's hurting might box away their pain from their child, and smile as if everything is okay, and those tears on their cheeks don't mean anything. I knew she was trying – she did get some extra shifts and took on another class, but I began to find it easier when I was on my own.

"I don't have a solution to all this, Robert," she said once, "but I know there is one. You'll find a job."

"And what if I don't?"

"You will. Just trust that it'll work out."

I took her hand and tried to smile. I didn't know you could feel lonely in your own home.

The lecturer post had been filled and nothing came up with Zimmer's plan for Cavendish, not that I expected it to. Zimmer cancelled our presentation at the conference, and I was copied into the reply.

From: sjpickard@aup.ac.uk
Sent: 21st February 11:27
To: geoff.zimmer@sightlabs.ac
cc: robert.strong@sightlabs.ac
Re: Presention at Annual Conference on Astroparticle and Underground Physics
Priority: High

Dear Professor Zimmer,

Thank you for your correspondence updating me on the situation with SightLabs. I understand your reluctance to proceed with your presentation at the upcoming conference, given that your results are preliminary and the ability to validate them has been taken from you. I am deeply dismayed at the decision to close SightLabs and I suggest we raise it at the AGM. I am certain that you will find a body of physicists to back your appeal. You certainly have my support.

Sincerely,
Prof Simon Pickard

At least Zimmer was showing some spine in tackling this. I went to the conference with him and sat in on the AGM. The Chief Executive of the Institute of Physics was chairing and drafted a document to the Minister of Science, outlining the objections to the closure of SightLabs and the cack-handed way it was handled. Everyone at the meeting signed their support and it made me feel better for a bit.

But I still didn't have a job. I advertised to do web design and got some interest – from a furniture removal business called Packit Up and a health food shop in Surrey. It wasn't much, but it brought in some cash.

I didn't realise how much time Cora spent meditating. The flat was beginning to feel like a prison, and I'd go out to the library with my laptop to work when the smell of incense got to me. I was becoming more and more irritable, easily affected by small things, like finding a flier on the hall table for a music festival; the book on transcendental meditation that she was half way through reading, lying open on the couch; the calendar on the kitchen table, the one I couldn't help reading, that gave a new quote every day, with some namby-pamby non-advice like, 'Whatever has happened is the perfect reason to keep going. Keep going and create the life you have chosen to live.' *You know what? I didn't choose any of this. And I don't need some airhead to tell me I need to be happy about it.*

But what was worse than the anger was the indifference. That feeling of nothingness. Like I'd been cored out and I was existing in a pointless shell, going through the motions for the sake of it. Cora's attempts to help just frustrated me, and I'd snap at her whenever she asked questions, like if I'd had any word from Cavendish or if I'd thought of going out for a beer with Chris. "I'm only trying to help," she'd say. "I know how difficult this is for you."

No you don't. You've no idea how this feels. And your treating me like a victim is just making things worse. But I didn't say any of it. I'd make an excuse to go back to my laptop.

A couple of weeks later when I came back from the library she looked different. Not what she was wearing, but her expression, her demeanour had changed. She was sitting at the kitchen table writing something in a notebook.

"Hi." She smiled fully, for the first time in ages.

"Hi." I put my laptop down on the chair.

"How did it go?"

"Same as usual."

She got up. "You want a coffee?"

"Yeah, okay. How are things with you?"

She closed the cupboard door and spooned the coffee into the mugs. She glanced at me, as though trying to read my mood. "Well, actually... something happened to me today."

"What?"

She leaned on the worktop and looked down at the mugs while the kettle chugged steam onto the green tiled wall.

"I saw Sarah."

"Sarah who?"

"My sister."

"What do you mean – you had a dream about her?"

"No, I was awake."

"Well, what do you mean you saw her?"

She bit her lower lip, but the smile crept out on either side. "Robert, you're not going to believe this. Just after you left, I felt really low – I mean worse than I've felt in a long time. I just wanted to know she was okay, you know? And then... then she was there, standing at the window. Smiling at me." *Sweet Jesus, was I hearing this?* "She looked like she used to look. No bright lights, not like a ghost or anything. Just like you look, right now... and when she left, I felt this really strong sense of peace, right here." She pointed to the left of her breastbone then shrugged. "I just know she's okay now." She stared at nothing for a moment then found her focus on me. "Isn't that amazing?"

What do you say to something like that? Pass it off as casual conversation? "That's... well... that's great you feel better, Cora."

She stepped closer to me. "But don't you see how incredible it is? She was right here, Robert, as real as you are."

"That's great." *God, she really means it.* I smiled a forced smile. *Do something. Something normal.* I turned to fill the mugs with boiling water.

"That's it? It's '*great*'? Robert, don't you see what this means?"

"It means you're happy, that's all that matters." I tried to make it sound light-hearted, but it didn't come out like that. She took a step back, her eyes searching my face.

"You don't believe me."

I let out a sigh. "I believe that you believe it."

"That's not the same. I need you to believe this. What do you think I saw?"

"Cora, you're exhausted... after what we've both been through... you hardly sleep, you're not eating... Your mind can do all kinds of things to you when you're stressed."

"You think I imagined it?"

"A lot of people who've been through what you have must see things that..."

"That what? Aren't there?"

"Cora, Sarah is dead." I put my hands on her shoulders and said it again, gently. "She's dead."

"I know that – I watched her die, remember? But I'm telling you I saw her."

"Oh come on, Cora." This was getting stupid. "Maybe it was just..."

"No. It was her." She shook her head. "Why do you always react like this?"

"What do you mean?"

"I know you think that this life is all there is, but why can't you just admit that maybe you're wrong? What are you afraid of?"

Oh, please. "I'm not afraid. Come on, let's leave it, Cora." I picked up my laptop and walked out of the kitchen. I could feel the bubble of irritation swelling and I didn't want it to burst.

She followed me into the living room. "No, let's not leave it. Why can't you just open your mind?"

I couldn't help it. Something snapped in me. "Open my mind? *Open* my mind? My mind is wide open! No, I don't lap up whatever the latest beardie-weirdie bastard is telling me – I don't buy it – but don't tell me my mind isn't open! I spend my life looking for something that no-one can see, but I deal in facts, Cora, not wild assumptions."

"Just because you haven't found a name for it doesn't mean it isn't there!"

"If someone could give me a shred of evidence, just a shred" – I picked up the Buddha statue from the bookcase and slammed it down again – "that any of this woo-woo shite is right, I'd believe it. I really would. But there's nothing! There never has been. All this..." – I waved my hand around at the room – "...this new-age crap is just filling a hole. It's blind faith, Cora – if you choose it, go ahead, but not me. I need proof, not fantasy."

"You can't prove everything."

"Yes, you can, Cora."

"Really?" She reached for the silver ring that hung from the black leather cord around her neck. "What about love?"

She held my stare for a moment, waiting for me to answer, and when I couldn't, she lowered her eyes and left the room.

A leaden silence rang out between us that night. I hated it, the edge that hung in the air after we argued. It flaunts the side of me I don't want to know. It leaves me feeling deflated and irritated. I wish I could have let go of it, but I didn't know how. I scowled for most of the evening and banged things when I put them down, frustrated with Cora and bitter with myself. Why couldn't she just accept that I see things differently? She passed the evening reading a book by the window, although she seemed to spend more time staring at the rain on the glass than at the pages on her lap.

That night when I lay next to her, I couldn't sleep. The anger dissolved into guilt and it clawed at my insides. Still, in the darkness, our exchanges played over in my mind. I turned to watch her, as she lay sleeping, her skin pale and smooth against the pillow, and brushed a strand of hair from her cheek. *Couldn't you just have let it go, let her think you believed her? Would that have been so difficult?* The truth was something I didn't want to face, and there, in the silence of the darkened room, it was surfacing. When did we become so different? It wasn't always this way, was it? Or did I just dismiss it before; think it didn't really matter? A part of me, somewhere deep and unsettled within, wondered who she was, and how we ever ended up together. I rolled away from her and closed my eyes. It would be alright in the morning.

BUT IT WASN'T alright. We barely spoke for the next few days. She stayed out more and more, and Tibet became the escape route I was aiming for. Until then, I was marking time. I hated myself for it. Sometimes I'd catch her crying, then she'd brush the tears away in angry shame and push past me, and I knew it wasn't about Sarah. We slept in different rooms, each making the excuse that we didn't want to keep the other awake. If it weren't for that picture on the hall table, I'd have said we were flatmates who barely knew each other. I couldn't think of anything we had in common anymore. Not a single thing. Is that what happens to people?

But the day I left for Tibet, I got a glimpse of something that was there before. She kissed me on the cheek, and that kiss, soft and simple, had more tenderness than all the others we'd shared before. She took the ring on the leather cord from around her neck and handed it to me. She was letting me go. I needed to go, and she knew it; that kiss was her permission. She wouldn't be there when I got back.

SOMETHING SHARP IS needling my face. A taste of copper in my mouth, a throbbing upper lip. Ignore it, it'll go away.

Nope, it's still there, pushing against my cheek. Is it pushing me or is it the other way round? Either way it feels like I'm bouncing. How odd. *Open your eyes.*

What the...

The whole earth is bouncing nearer and further away, nearer and further away. What way is up? Below, something black and furry, the smell of musty leather. A thudding sound – hooves beneath me. What the hell? A man's lined, weathered face, dark pebbles for eyes peering in; grey rocks and shingles on the hard ground below. If I lift my head a little. Shit, it hurts – a nail in the skull with each bounce. Sunlight floods in, sets my eyes streaming again, as I squint up. Is that a lake? Why so black, in all this light? Not even a glimmer on it. I remember it, black water with no light. Uneasiness crawls under my skin as the thick grey mist parts for a moment, and behind it... what is that? A dark sphere where the sun should be, not yellow but black, a seething dark orb. I don't want to, but I can't help but look, it's drawing my eyes back to it, draining me, sapping me from the inside. There's a sound. A soft whispering, a breathing of indiscernible words, and something else is behind the whisper, like the sound of an out-of-tune bagpipe. It hurts – I'm feeling actual pain in my head with it. *God, make it stop. Please...*

Blackness falls.

Quiet, the absence of wind and snow, a cup of warm liquid held to my lips, the smell of incense, and blackness once more.

WHAT DID I dream? It was a ramble, a rant in the caverns of my dizzy mind. I dreamt that Cora was wiping the blood from my face, soothing me. She stared down at me, unsmiling, and dropped a stick of incense into a bowl of water, extinguishing it, then walked away. I dreamt I was in Michael Casimir's garden with him, like I used to be when I was young. The old man, the next best thing to the father I never had, and probably better in many ways, was crouched down, staring at his empty beehive, and I was reassuring him that his bees would come back, some day, even though I knew they wouldn't. A dream about a black sun behind the mist and voices I couldn't understand.

The smell of incense comes to me, but not from the dreams. Men's voices in a strange language, whispering nearby. I don't understand what they're saying. I try to call out, but nothing comes from my mouth. The sound of a door creaking, and silence.

I DREAMT THAT something I could neither see nor hear was behind me on a snowy hill.

Chapter Three

EVERYTHING ACHES, ESPECIALLY my head. My tongue is stuck to the roof of my mouth and the stench of my own breath as it hits my nostrils makes me want to vomit. My body is drenched in sweat, my clothes sticking to me as though I've been doused in a bucket of oily water. I lie back on the hard mat and stare at the wooden beams overhead. Don't know them. I turn to the door, closed only a moment ago, I think, but it doesn't help. There's a sound in my head, the echo of a memory, whispers slithering on the fragments of a dream. I reach for Cora's ring. It's still there, in my pocket.

I sit up on the mat, resting my feet on a cold stone floor, my elbows on my knees. I clutch my temples again, trying to squeeze out the last of the sound. It dwindles and dies away but my brain still thumps inside my skull. My lips are stuck together and it hurts to swallow. The wooden beams around me swim in and out of focus. Where the hell am I? Beside me, a wooden bowl half-filled with water sits on the floor next to my boots. My hand trembles as I lift it to my mouth, and the water spills over my shirt.

A different sound drifts in on a wave of incense: the sound of deep, resonant chanting, almost too deep to be human; the low vibration of a gong, the labyrinthine rumble of horns. In a funny way, it's calming. I lean down and pull on my boots, sweat collecting in the nape of my neck, the nail driving deeper into my head with the effort.

I take a deep breath and stand, swaying a little, then follow the sound and the smell of incense out of the room, my footsteps echoing in an unlit, empty, wooden corridor. Half way along, I pass a door that stands ajar. I peek round to see if I can find someone. The room is deserted. At one end is an altar with a large golden Buddha sitting on a red cloth. Incense sticks trickle smoke trails into the air. So, I'm in a monastery.

I follow the passageway to a huge hall with a long, wooden table down one side, lined with wooden benches. Several monks are gathered at one end, dressed in orange and red robes, their heads shaved. They're playing an assortment of weird instruments – huge long horns held to their lips that scoop down to the floor and produce a noise that makes the floorboards tremble, shorter ones which bleat a harsh woody tone like a goat, singing bowls that ring out crystal harmonies. One monk stands over a large, hide drum beating it slowly, almost lazily. They look up at me, and carrying on playing. The largest of the monks sits with his eyes closed and his voice sounds like it's coming from the caverns of the earth, as the syllables roll slowly from one rumble to the next.

All of it is strange – no, downright weird. There's nothing familiar here, except... I stop. He stands out like a tourist as he walks towards me, wearing trousers, not a robe, his head not shaved, but a matt of tangled fair hair that falls over his eyes. He's grinning at me.

"Danny?" I whisper. My voice is weak and scrapes my throat.

Danny nods and the grin widens across his broad face, a bit thinner than I remember, the hollow of his cheeks a little more pronounced. He throws his arms around me and the force of his slaps on my back makes me cough.

"Thought you'd never wake up, mate," he whispers. "You had me worried."

"How long?"

"Three days. They've been bringing you water, but they wouldn't let me see you for too long. You feeling okay?"

Three days? That long? "I've felt better, but at least I'm here. It was a close one, for both of us."

"You're not kidding."

"How about you? You okay?"

"Fine, I was just waiting for you to wake up." He throws a sideways glance at the monks. "This is no holiday camp. They get you up at four, to eat with the rest of them. I mean, who's hungry at four o'clock in the morning?"

Small cracks stab at my lips as I smile.

"And the tea..." Danny pulls a face. "If you weren't sick before, you will be after that."

"You're an ungrateful bastard," I say in a low voice.

"Maybe. They've looked after you, alright. One of them keeps asking questions – like he wants to know everything there is to know about you."

"Really? Which one?"

"Ssh," says Danny. "Here he comes now."

An old monk with a round face like crumpled leather smiles and nods as he shuffles towards us, his red robes trailing on the floor. He seems friendly. I smile back. "Thanks for looking after me," I say.

He presses his palms together and bows a little. The chanting stops and the old monk, still smiling, ushers us to a seat on one of the benches. The other monks gather, and when they sit down, four boys dressed in orange robes, who can't be much older then ten, bring out wooden bowls of tsampa and butter tea.

"Thank you," I say to the smallest one as he hands me my bowl. The boy looks about seven years old and stares at me with wide eyes, his mouth open. "Thanks," I say again, not sure what else he's expecting, but the boy just stares back until the old monk prods him and he trots off to get more bowls. When all the bowls are placed, the monks bow their heads, saying what must be a prayer. I catch Danny's eye and he grins. I wait till the monks begin to eat, then pick up my spoon. Danny steels himself, then takes a sip of tea, struggling to keep control of his face. Sometimes he's got the sensitivity of a doormat.

"Like this," says a young monk sitting next to Danny. He breaks off a piece of tsampa, a rough sort of bread, and puts it in the bowl of butter tea. Then he stirs and kneads it with his hand, turning the bowl, until it forms a dumpling. He nods at Danny, his eyes twinkling like dark beads. Danny takes some tsampa, concentrating hard as he tries to make his dumpling. The young monks stop eating, their eyes on him, exchanging furtive glances. When his dumpling turns into a thick paste that sticks to his fingers and stretches into a long, clay-coloured goo, they lower their heads, trying to stifle sniggers. He's making a real mess of it. One of them, who'd been struggling more than the others to suppress the giggles, keels sideways, his eyes squeezed shut, threatening to fall off the bench until the monk sitting next to him props him upright again. I grin at Danny. "I thought you'd have got the hang of it after three days." He glowers at me, flicking the goo back into his bowl.

WHEN THE SMALL monks clear the bowls, the rest of the group begins filing from the room and we join the tail of the line.

"So, are you up to a long walk tomorrow?" asks Danny. "The lakes should be something."

"Ask me tomorrow," I say. At the moment, I'm focusing on walking back to my room.

"Mr Robert?" I turn back. It is the leather-faced monk. "Can I speak?"

"Of course."

The monk smiles and looks at Danny but says nothing.

"Oh," says Danny. "Sorry, I'll leave you to it." And he joins the line leaving the hall.

"Please," says the old monk, gesturing to a bench. I sit down and the monk settles beside me, a wizened old face with sparkling eyes.

"You are well now?"

"Yes," I say. "Thank you for everything you've done."

The monk's eyes smile. Then he says, "You came to Tibet for something, isn't it?"

"I'm not sure what you mean."

"Why you came here?"

I shrug. "To get away from my life for a while."

The monk nods and chuckles. "Running away."

"Well, more just taking a break. I lost my job, you see, and my..."

"And your wife?" says the monk. "I am sorry, your friend tells me."

"She wasn't my wife."

"I am still sorry."

"That's okay."

"Your friend say you are a scientist."

"My friend talks too much," I mumble, and his face wrinkles into a grin. "Yes, I'm a scientist."

"What kind of scientist?"

"Physics and computer science. I work... I used to work in research."

The old monk raises his eyebrows and nods. "Very important work. What is it you researching?"

"We were looking for something called dark matter."

The old monk frowns and nods, his face serious. "Many matters are dark." When he looks up, he says, "Which one is it you looking for?"

"No," I shake my head. How the hell do I explain this to a Tibetan monk? "No, it's... eh... you know when you look around you and you see things like..." – I cast around for inspiration – "...like the table or the bench or a tree – anything that is solid matter?"

"Yes?"

"Well, we've found something else in the universe – something that isn't solid matter."

"Yes?"

"Most of the universe is made up of something else, something we don't fully understand. We're looking for the missing piece of the universe."

The monk chuckles and shakes his head.

"What?" It's difficult not to smile even though I've no idea what's tickling him.

"The scientists are catching up."

He settles, eventually, and raises his eyebrows, creasing his forehead into a stack of ridges. "Your parents are very proud, I think."

"Well, I guess my mum is – my dad died when I was three. He was a physicist too, so I suppose he would have been."

"I am sorry."

"It was a long time ago."

The monk stares at the floor then asks, "Did you find what you come for?"

I got more than I bargained for, but let's not go into that. "Yeah, you know, the peace and tranquillity and all that. Where I live, we don't have that much."

"It is very busy place, your world. But you found your peace on the mountain?"

I hesitate. The memory, the ridiculous memory of the voice comes to me, and the certainty I had then that something else came down the mountain with us, something I found myself trusting. Hypothermia can do strange things to you. "I suppose you could say that."

"Good. It is a good place to find peace."

We sit together and neither speaks until the old monk says, "But you are still going back? To your life?"

"Yeah. Of course." What's left of it.

"Hmmm. So you run away and you run back again." He chuckles. "Maybe your life is not something out there." He waves his arm vaguely to the side. "Maybe it is something in here." He holds a fist against my chest. "And when you run you take it with you. Sometimes you have to let go the life you planned, to make room for the life that is waiting for you."

"Is that a Tibetan saying?"

"No. But it is the words of a wise man."

We sit in companionable silence for a while longer, before the monk says, "Do you remember the lake?"

"The lake?"

"We found you by the Crescent Lake. Do you remember this?"

"I remember seeing a lake when we came down the mountain." Mirror smooth, black. Not a ripple or reflection on its surface. And that feeling...

The old man's eyes narrow. "You remember nothing else?"

"No."

"Hmm." He leans closer, peering into my face; a small, curious creature. "What did you feel?"

I wipe away the beads of sweat that have gathered on my forehead, feeling my lips dry again. "I felt, eh... kind of uneasy." I shake my head as I think of it. "I thought the sun had gone black, and the sound, it was..."

But he's frowning at me in a way that's making me nervous. "You *heard* it?"

"It was like voices, whispering. It felt almost... dark."

The old monk sags, his face crumpling even further. He stares at me for a long moment as if I've disappointed him somehow.

"Listen, I was dry and cold and hallucinating. That's all."

"No."

"Well, what was it, then?"

He takes a long, slow breath. "There are two lakes on the mountain. One, Lake Manasarovar, is shaped like the sun; it is called the Lake of Consciousness. The other, the one shaped like the crescent moon, we call Rakshastal, the Lake of Demons. These two lakes are joined by a thin channel of water. When waters flow from the Lake of Consciousness to the Lake of Demons, all is well. But the signs that came to you tell us the waters are flowing the other way, and this is very bad."

"So, what does that mean?"

"It means the energies are changing – they are shifting between the worlds."

I hear a soft scuttling and a shiny black cockroach appears from under the bench. I think about stepping on it, but remember where I am. It scuttles past the monk's foot, claiming sanctuary.

"You believe that there are other worlds? Like other dimensions?" I don't know much about Buddhism, only what I've picked up from Cora, but I didn't think this was part of it.

"They are here, right next to us, only a breath away. Very few can sense them, and even fewer understand it when they manifest. You are one of those people, and you believe they are there, I think."

Don't drag me into your superstitious folklore. "No," I say, shaking my head. "That's not what I believe."

"Then what do you look for, in your work?"

"Dark matter? No, that's completely different."

He snorts.

"It's nothing to do with other worlds."

"You seem very certain."

Well, old man, I am. But right now, I don't have it in me to explain. I just smile.

He nods. "Perhaps one day you will see for yourself. But I hope you do not see the World you sensed here. I would not wish that on you, or anyone."

I hear the whispering in my head again and feel a sickening clamminess on my skin as I catch a flash of a black sphere. My mind playing tricks. "So, what's supposed to happen when these energies shift?"

"The world you sensed will leak into ours; what you felt will become our world, until that is all there is to feel. Unless people like you choose to stop it."

"What?"

He gets up, slowly. There's something else in his eyes. Is it fear? "Tell no one, until you listen to it and understand." He lowers his eyes to the floor. "I am sorry, but you must leave at sunrise." He bows and turns, then shuffles away and doesn't look back.

"YOU ALRIGHT?" SAYS Danny when I find him waiting in the empty corridor. "You don't look well."

"I'm still recovering, remember?" But there's something inside me that has nothing to do with physical weakness.

"What was all that about, anyway?"

The monk's words gnaw at me. Bad juju. "Nothing. I'm leaving tomorrow."

Chapter Four

MY CARRIAGE PULLS up in front of the monastery – a small, battered, dark green truck which stutters to a halt with a shudder that rattles its doors. The chances of it making it down the mountain intact are slim. The chances of it making it to Lhasa Airport, which lies several days to the southeast? It would be a safer bet that Danny Mitchell will end up working on Wall Street.

I sling my rucksack into the back, beside some old rugs and faded bundles tied together with ropes. The driver takes the cigarette stub from the corner of his mouth and flashes me a toothless grin, pulling the canvas flap down over the cargo. The wind and sun have left their signature in the creases and texture of his face. There's mischief in the small, dark eyes that peer out above high cheekbones. He pulls his fur jacket up round his neck and places the cigarette stub in the edge of his mouth, blinking as the smoke rises into his eyes.

"Are you sure you don't want to stay on? Even for another week?" says Danny. "The trek round the lakes should be something."

There's no question of staying here. I haven't slept properly since... I glance up at the mountain looming in the middle distance. "I just need to get home." Behind me, on the steps of the monastery, the old monk is watching.

"I'll let you know about the next trip, whenever it comes up," says Danny. "Take care of yourself." He holds out a hand.

"You too." I grip his hand and shake it. "Keep out of trouble, okay?" I know he won't, but saying it absolves me of responsibility when he doesn't.

Danny grins. I get into the truck, where the leather seats are worn through so that the springs are just visible at the edges. They squeak in protest when I sit on them. It smells of cigarettes and damp clothes, and there's a crack at the bottom left corner of the windscreen.

The driver jumps in, grinning his gums at me as his cigarette wobbles. He scrapes the long gearstick into neutral and turns the key. He mumbles something I don't catch, and wheezes at his own joke as the engine growls to life, a puff of smoke chugging from the back, the smell of diesel suffusing the icy air. Danny's waving figure retreats as we pull away from the monastery, dwarfed by the white mountain. I'm itching to get away from here, back to reality. I thought about little else during another night of sleeplessness, and the memory of that black lake. I don't do ghost stories, especially ones that gatecrash your subconscience. But I didn't bank on feeling a sense of loss. Something about losing that feeling of certainty I had on the mountain. That life would never be so clear again.

The truck bounces over the shingle-strewn ground, the springs squeaking their objections like a pen of frustrated piglets. The driver is in his element, hooting and grinning each time we shudder over the bumpy ground. Six years ago I spent three months on the back of a Suzuki DR350, negotiating the rubble trails of Mongolia that are passed off as roads. I *like* off-road driving, preferably on two wheels – it's the stuff of adventure. I love the purity, the freedom, the danger. But my fingers close round the roof handle of the truck and my other hand grips the patchy leather of the seat. There's no-one else on the road for us to hit, but his driving is making me nervous.

We pass through several small towns, where men and women sit on the side of the road selling yak meat from coloured rugs, and children dressed in bright, grubby clothes, with unruly dark hair and running noses, crouch in the street playing games in the dust or running, waving after the fair-haired stranger in the truck. The towns give way to valleys of green splashed with snow, and great canyons spanned by metal bridges; the kiss of industrialisation, even out here in the wilderness.

The miles bounce away under the tyres and each one of them carries me further away from the mountain and the black lake. For four days we travel towards the southeast, stopping in the small villages to eat and to try to sleep. The driver, Jinpa, knows someone in each of the settlements and finds us rooms for a few yuan. I'm not sleeping well. I don't know what happened on the mountain. Part of me just wants to forget.

THE FLIGHT IS on time. We take off from one of the highest airports in the world, over the sandy razor-peaked mountains and turquoise rivers meandering

65

through the dusty valley basins. One day away from home, thank God. One day away from a pint of beer, a hot shower. Chips and curry sauce. Anything that's not tsampa and sodding butter tea. The gloss will wear off before I've unpacked my rucksack, I know, but until then, I'll savour it all.

The wilderness becomes patchy, obscured by blotches of white cloud, succumbing to dense, grey fog. The engines whine and shudder over some invisible bumps in the sky. Nothing out of the ordinary. A ping announces the seatbelt sign is switched off. A couple of people make their way up the central aisle to the toilets. One of them is a monk, not unlike the one with the crumpled face from the monastery. I get a sinking feeling in my stomach that has nothing to do with turbulence.

Other worlds. Some physicists believe in an infinitely expanding cosmos full of parallel universes, all budding off every time we make a choice about anything. Just another theory, and not one that's cost me any sleep. So how come the monk's superstition is getting to me? It's ridiculous. One fairytale with a bad ending and I want to keep the light on. I look down. My fingertips are gripping the armrest. The seatbelt sign is switched off, but mine is still tight around my waist. This is the third time I've checked that it's secure. What the hell's wrong with me?

"Are you alright, sir?" The air stewardess is frowning at me. Her perfume announced her approach five seats away. Her face is the colour of a tangerine, and quite distinct from the colour of her neck.

"What? Eh, I'm fine, thanks."

"Not keen on flying?" She purses her scarlet lips and inclines her head, giving me that look that mums learn to give to children when they graze their knees.

"No, I don't know what's got into me this time. I'm usually fine with it."

"Just relax and try to get some sleep. We'll be there in no time."

I can't wait. What for, I'm not quite sure.

I WALK AMONGST the droves of people striding through the corridors of Manchester Airport, yawning and rubbing my eyes. My muscles feel like they've been locked in a dusty cupboard for a month. Outside, the early morning light bulges between grey clouds on the other side of the large panelled windows. We arrive in a foyer with shops – shops that sell things you didn't realise you had to have until they reminded you, like miniature bottles of shampoo and shower gel in case you feel compelled to wash your hair on the plane. There's something about entering an airport that plays on the idea that you're escaping to something better – leather bags to give you that executive look, perfume to make you smell like a film star, whatever that scent may be, jewellery modelled by some heroin-chic stick insect. Maybe, if you're here long enough, you have a party in your own head, where you are that executive, or film star or stick insect. And all at a price that's a snip if you move in circles where having second homes in Paris or New York is commonplace. And if you don't? Well, why not just pretend, for a little while? Make the most of the daydream.

I don't like daydreamers. This is Manchester, for fuck's sake.

I make for the coffee stand and join the queue. My watch, a genuine 1993 Swatch watch, tells me I've got two

hours until the next train. I pay for my coffee and walk
to an empty table. The chair scrapes on the tiled floor as
I pull it back, making the skin on my arms prickle. I drop
my pack and slump into the seat, before the obligatory
mobile phone check-in. *Maybe she sent you a message.*
Its screen stares up, blank and unapologetic, telling me
she hasn't. What was I expecting?

There's a bald man in a suit sitting at the table across
from me, tapping feverishly on his laptop. He keeps
sighing at it as though annoyed by its fickle performance.
A mobile phone sits on the seat next to him. Armani
suit, Rolex, cufflinks. An executive. A real one. Why's
he frowning then? What's he so worried about? He's
meant to have it made.

At the next table sits a teenager, with purple hair that
sticks out in all directions over her button earphones.
She's blowing pink bubbles, her head bent over her
phone, texting at a speed that makes my thumb ache
just watching her.

People bustle past. They're right when they say that
airports are great places to people-watch. Most of them
look like they're late for something because they walk
at a pace just short of a run and almost none of them
smile. They do their best to avoid eye contact, locked in
their own worlds. I think back to the kids running after
the truck in the dusty villages, smiling and waving.

Should I call her? Maybe I should tell her about what
happened – it's crazy enough for her to understand.

There's a *pop* and a pink bubble explodes over the
teenager's face. She peels it off, then stuffs in back in her
mouth and carries on chewing.

I select Cora's number and my finger hovers over the
dial button. Absence makes the heart grow fonder, they

say. Whoever they are, I hope they are right. I suspect, though, that all absence does is give you time to forget the stuff that pissed you off before. I cancel the number and it disappears from the screen.

THREE HOURS LATER I'm standing outside our flat in the drizzle. There are no lights on, at least none that I can see from outside. My heart picks up pace as I climb the stairs, and not just from the exertion. What if she's home? God, I don't know if I'm ready for another round. It would be easier if she wasn't.

The pansies have wilted. Their purple heads are drooped over the edge of the pot and the soil is dusty. I turn the key and stand in the dim doorway. The flat is empty; I don't have to go inside to know. It feels like a shell, like I did before I left. I flick on the light as I walk inside. The photo still sits on the hall table, like someone else's memory. The living room seems bigger than it did before, barer. Some of her books and the Buddha have gone from the bookshelf, along with the tapestry. Something else is missing too, but I'm not sure what. I walk over to the computer and draw my index finger along the top of the keyboard, collecting a small pile of dust. That's what's missing. There's no scent. No incense.

She's left me a note in the kitchen.

I'll pick up the rest of my stuff in a couple of weeks when I get back from the pottery. Hope you had a good trip.

Hope you had a good trip.

I stared at the scrap of paper in my hand. If she were here now I'd tell her what happened on the mountain, and she'd believe that it did. She'd believe that it wasn't the cold, it wasn't the dehydration or the altitude. Part of me wants to hear her say that I didn't imagine it, but that's the reason she's gone, because I couldn't deal with her thinking like that.

No. It's for the best. But it was never going to be easy.

I make myself a coffee and turn to read the feel-good quote on the kitchen calendar, but she took that too. I could use one of those quotes just now, even if it is all just bull.

I go back to the living room. It feels like I'm in someone else's house – someone who just died. It's too quiet. Not just normal silence; it's the kind of silence you get when life isn't there anymore. Maybe coming back here wasn't a good idea. I flick on the TV and lie back on the sofa, pulling the blue rug that's draped over its back across me. My fingers close round Cora's ring. The sound from the TV is just noise, so I turn it down. But the changing lights add some warmth, and although I'm not really watching it, it's company. Sometime after that it blurs out of focus and I forget.

THE ROOM IS a haze of shifting lights from the TV, dancing with the shadows of twilight. Through the softness between waking and sleeping, I feel it, like a cool breeze. Someone else is here.

She's standing in front of the window, silhouetted against the night. She looks just like she used to. She's smiling at me, her head inclined a little to one side. Slowly, she lifts her hand towards me, a strong, healthy hand, not wasted and thin like it was before she...

Cold fear rushes at me and I sit bolt upright, breathing heavily, sweat gathering in the nape of my neck. The hairs on my forearms prickle and rise. The TV spills its silent colours onto the walls and the window where... I'm on my feet, waiting as a chill slithers from my neck to the back of my knees. She was there, by the window.

Shit, Robert. Calm down. Just a dream, that's all. A dream.

I take control of my breathing. It's dark outside – I must have slept for hours. I reach for the lamp beside the TV and turn it on. Then I turn on all the other lights, including the bulb hanging from a cord in the ceiling, the one we never got round to finding a light shade for.

Another coffee and a large whisky. I spend the rest of the evening trawling the internet for jobs, and finish working on the Packit Up webpage – anything to avoid sleeping.

At two in the morning, I give in and go through to the bedroom. Most of her clothes have gone and the wardrobe sits half empty. It feels like there's a stone in my chest. It feels like I could almost cut it out, but I wouldn't want to. It's all that's left of her in me. I crawl into bed and sleep.

In the middle of a dream about snow and lakes I feel it again – a trickle of cool air on my neck. The snow dissolves and the lakes melt into the stillness of the room and a gentle glow from a streetlamp outside. I don't know if my eyes are open or not. I don't know if this is part of the dream, but she's there again, her hand rising towards me. This time I reach out, I can't help it, and she's still smiling with her eyes, soft and unblinking as she looks at me, into me, pleading. As our fingertips touch, the lights go out.

"Sarah!"

I'm sitting bolt upright, entangled in the sheets, sweat dripping into my eyes. I snap on the light and see myself – alone – in the mirror against the wall. My eyes have a crazy look about them and my hair's plastered to my forehead and I'm breathing like I've run up a Munro. I slump back on the pillow and rub my hands over my face.

I need to call Cora. She's the only one who would understand.

My fingers fumble with the keys on the phone, shaking like an old man, hovering over the dial button. What am I going to say at five-fifteen in the morning? I've had a bad dream? I'm scared of the dark? She'll think I've lost it. Maybe she'd be right.

I LAST FIVE more days in the flat, surviving on pasta and Dolmio sauce, Coco Pops and whisky. I've taken to sleeping with the light on, but it doesn't make any difference. She's there, the same dream every night, where she reaches out and takes my hand until I wake up in a breathless panic.

I never used to dream much, not as an adult. But I remember a dream that used to come to me when I was young, maybe five or six years old. It was always the same: I was walking in a wood at dusk, the crows cawing, unsettled in the branches above. I'd come to a bush and stop as I caught sight of a bare foot protruding from its base, and I'd pull back the branches, slowly. There was a man underneath, who looked up at me, and I knew he was frightened. There was blood on his leg and he was breathing too fast. Then the thud of hooves on the ground coming closer. The man shook his head and raised a finger to his mouth. I let the branches fall back and stood up. When the horseman came I never told him.

It was unsettling, but not like the dreams of Sarah. The feelings they leave linger for hours before they lift. It's a low feeling: flat, lifeless, uneasy.

I call Cora a couple of times, but she doesn't answer and I don't leave a message. In a way I'm relieved; I don't know what I'd say if she picked up.

I call Chris. He's still looking for a job and hasn't heard anything from Zimmer. He comes round to see me and the first thing he says is, "You look a mess." I tell him I'm not sleeping, although I leave out the details, and he says I should see a doctor. God, do I really look that rough? "You'll never get a job on three hours' sleep a night," he says. "Not if you look like that."

On the fifth day I see the doctor. He sits in his swivel chair behind the desk and bounces a little back and forth as he listens to what I'm trying to tell him. He's middle-aged, overweight and despite the sharp smell of alcohol wipes in the room, he still smells of fags. Two babies are having a bawling competition in the waiting room as he checks my blood pressure and shines a light in my eyes. He asks me if I have any family history of any mental health issues. Not as far as I know. Why, am I going mad? He suggests I take some time off, before I tell him I don't have a job anymore or a partner. "Ah," he says, leaning over the desk to scribble, "that explains it. Stress." He hands me a prescription for some pills to help me sleep and tells me to get some fresh air and some exercise. I look at his belly and think about saying the same thing to him. When I leave I find a dustbin outside and drop the prescription into it. I don't know what I expected him to do, but pills aren't it. I go home and pack.

I GET TO the station just before eleven and call from there. "Hi, Mum."

"Robert! How are you?"

"I'm fine. Got back last week."

"So, how was it?"

"It was great – glad I went. Listen, I thought I might come up and see you."

"That would be great! When were you thinking about?"

"Now, if that's okay with you. Might as well, while I have some time on my hands."

"What time's the next train?"

"Eleven-forty – I could be up by late afternoon."

"Fine. I'll see you when you get here."

"Eh... Mum?"

"Yes?"

"Have you seen Cora?"

"I saw her last week."

"Oh."

"Listen, Robert, Jessie's waiting for me in the car, so I'll have to go just now, but I'll talk to you when you get home. Can't wait to see you! Have a safe journey."

"Okay, see you soon."

SOME THINGS NEVER change. Kildowan station is one of them. It hasn't changed since the 'seventies, apart from the newly purchased digital announcement board which hangs from the ceiling of Platform One. Two chipped wooden benches clinging to the stone walls get a new coat of white paint every few years, and it's overdue. A few red begonias struggle in their pots against the harsh north-easterly wind. There's a wire rack nailed to the wall displaying pamphlets advertising visitor attractions for the odd one or two tourists who end up here, usually by accident. Today, it's only me who disembarks.

The station is empty. As I step out into the street, I zip up my fleece and pull on my woollen beanie. It's late April, but it might as well be January. Or Siberia. I set off up the street for home. I still call it that, even though I've been away for years. Somewhere that holds in the fabric of its bricks and mortar the memories and changes and constancy which made me, even though I'm someone else now.

The sun is dipping in the sky. It slices between the buildings, dazzling brightness through the shadowy gaps. The cool, crisp air is just what's needed after the muggy train trip, and after years of working in an underground lab, I relish any time outside. Fresh air reminds me of what's real, what's tangible. Fresh air and Danny Mitchell. It makes me smile thinking about him. No doubt still bumming about in Tibet.

The road leads up from the station into the village, where the post office and bakery doors are bolted shut to mark the day of rest. Lining the street on one side are low terraced houses with small doors and even smaller windows set in thick stone walls, some whitewashed, some coloured, some grey. They look like they're huddling from the biting wind themselves. Opposite is the small museum which sits in carefully tended grounds and next to that, the kirk, built four hundred years ago, with its imposing spire and modest cemetery, now the resting place for some very old people. I've seen headstones in that graveyard which have been there even longer than the church, with their symbols of the sun and the moon faded, but still discernible, echoes of a forgotten age.

I cross the street towards the orange glow spilling from the lamps in the deep window sills of the Stone Circle pub. A familiar wave of chatter and a beery waft greets me as I approach. I glance at my watch. Time for a quick pint. Just one. The heavy oak door groans as I push it open, the chatter swells and my face tingles in the blanket of warm air. Tam, the proprietor of the Stone Circle, a rotund individual with red cheeks just visible over his large greying beard, nods to me with as much expression as he applies to everything, which isn't much.

"Robert," Tam says in his usual cursory manner of greeting.

"Tam," I reply in kind. I don't take this personally; Tam addresses all of his customers with equal indifference. Behind the bar, Tam continues to dry a glass with a cloth, inspecting it every so often against the dim lights that hang from the ceiling. An open fire crackles under the large stone mantle, spitting and hissing. Four hill walkers, in muddy boots and waterproof clothes, huddle around a small table, recounting tales of their various experiences of the harsh Scottish wilderness and unpredictable weather. Sitting on a stool and leaning over the dark wooden bar is Angus, the retired postman. Angus drinks unashamedly now that he has little else to occupy his time. His son, Alasdair, has followed in his father's footsteps and delivers the letters and parcels to the people of Kildowan, but he has seen what drink can do to a man and so he doesn't touch the stuff himself. Angus hugs his pint glass, frowning as he tries to focus on it.

"Hello, Angus," I say as I reach the bar. "A pint of bitter, please, Tam."

Angus sways a little as he looks up and his bushy eyebrows try hard to meet his hair as he registers his surprise. He claps me affectionately on the shoulder, but struggles to say anything coherent by way of conversation. I haven't had a pint since I got back. Plenty of whisky, but no beer. Nectar. Worth three days of butter tea for this one moment.

"Would that be Robert Strong?" I turn towards the voice.

"It would, Casimir. Good to see you." I join him at the table by the fire. Michael Casimir gets to his feet and I clasp the hand he holds out towards me. He's thinner than the last time I saw him, almost a year ago now, his bones more pronounced in his wiry frame, but his grip's just as strong.

"And how is it these days at the cutting edge of science?" asks Casimir, his green eyes twinkling. His voice is steady but weaker than it used to be. God, he's aged. A ripple of something in me, regret flickering. He won't be around forever. He's more stooped than before, the little hair he has left whiter and wispier, and deep lines now etch his square face, which, despite this, still shines with the strength of his character. He leans across the table and, with a voice just above a whisper, says, "Did you find it?"

He's followed the research every step of the way. In fact, he's the reason I ended up in physics. He has a telescope, and when I was young, and whenever I wasn't helping him with his bees, I'd spend hours stargazing, listening to all he knew about the cosmos, which was a vast amount for a man who never had enough money to go to university. It didn't stop him learning, though. He had books on all kinds of things – astronomy, particle physics, archaeology, philosophy. A real thinker. The idea of finding dark matter always intrigued him. A hunch, he said, that it would change everything. I wish I'd something more to tell him. "No, not yet. We came close, though. They pulled the funding at the last hurdle, so my services are no longer required." I take another gulp of beer, as bitter as my mood.

He looks crestfallen. "The bastards."

"The bastards."

"Why did they do it now?"

I shrug. "I've no idea. We were so close, Casimir. I reckon we'd have found it, if we'd had a bit more time. We had some provisional results – encouraging results – I mean, we were onto something concrete for the first time in years. We just needed to verify what we found. That was the last phase."

He rubs his thumb across his chin, his habit when he's thinking. "Maybe they didn't want you to find it, after all."

"Who knows how these things work." I turn back to my pint. I've stopped asking that question. All it does is wind me up. "Anyway, how have you been? You're looking well."

"You're lying," says Casimir. "Ach, you know, getting on with it. I'm on a health kick at the minute – you see?" He fumbles on the table to find his glass of tomato juice and holds it up.

"Where's the fun in that?"

"Aye, but the doctor says I'll live to be a hundred if I keep off the drams."

"And is it worth it?"

I don't know what he's thinking as he looks at me. Finally he says, "Life's too sweet, Robert."

"Aye."

He lets out a sigh. "And what's this I hear about you and Cora?"

The mention of her name turns the stone in my chest. "Och, I don't know. We're just too different."

"Are you?"

"Well, she's into all this New Age hippy crap and I'm... well, you know me."

"She's a free spirit." Casimir raises his eyebrows. "Maybe you could do with a little more of that."

"Oh, don't you start."

"You might see things differently when you get a bit older."

"Oh, come on, Casimir. You're a man of science. You can't buy into all that shit."

"Layman's science. Maybe science isn't the whole story." He sips his juiced tomatoes.

I lean back against the hard curve of the chair. "When did you start thinking like this?"

"It's always been there, I suppose."

"You're not going all religious on me, are you?"

"No, I'm not going back to that. Too many of man's opinions muddy the waters and obscure the point, if you ask me. But that doesn't mean I don't believe in something else."

I've never heard him speak like this. He was always comfortable in a world without a God. In his lifetime of prolific reading, he found too many other things to take its place. "Like what?"

Casimir leans forwards, his elbows resting on the

table. "Well, that's the Big Secret, isn't it? If I find out first, and I probably will, given that I've got a good few years on you, then I'll let you know."

"I'll hold you to that." I raise my pint to him.

"Aye." Casimir nods, lifting his glass of red sludge. "You know Cora's minding the pottery just now? I bumped into Frank not long ago – they're away to Barcelona for a holiday."

"Yeah, I know."

"Hmm. Have you seen your mother yet?"

"No, I'm just off the train, but I should be getting home soon."

"It's her birthday tomorrow. Did you remember to get her something?" I rub my forehead. Every year. Why is it so difficult?

"Well, maybe you should take a trip to the pottery tomorrow to get her a wee present – I'm sure Cora would be good enough to sell you something. Unless you want to get her one of those plastic sunflowers that Flora's selling in the post office." I grin, but my heart clenches at the thought of meeting Cora, even though she's the reason I came here.

Casimir reaches into his pocket. "Give this to your mother for me tomorrow, will you?" He hands me a wooden letter opener. Its smooth handle and sharp teeth are carefully carved, but with minor inconsistencies that wouldn't be made by a machine, and I know without asking that Casimir made it himself.

"Why don't you give her it yourself? We'll drop by and see you."

"Aye, and you'd be very welcome," says Casimir. "But you hold onto it, just in case." He sits back and appraises me, as he does from time to time whenever we meet, his fingers slowly twirling the glass on the table. "You've done well for yourself, Robert."

I snort. "What do you mean? Unemployment?"

"No," says Casimir. "What you've done with your life. Physics, computer science, your research posts – that's quite an achievement."

"Still hasn't got me a job, though," I reply. "If it hadn't been for all your years of brainwashing about life, the universe and all that, I'd have a real job by now."

Casimir chuckles and finishes his drink. "Maybe you'd do me a wee favour and see me home? I find it a bit tricky when the light fades."

"A pleasure." I swallow the remainder of my pint and stand up to help Casimir, waving to Tam as we leave, who nods almost imperceptibly in response.

ALTHOUGH CASIMIR HOLDS onto my arm, he strides ahead with little hesitation, oblivious to the cutting wind. The elements have never phased him. The weather was just something else to add background interest to whatever he was doing. He's just as stubborn now, even if he has aged. "How are your bees doing?" I ask.

"They died in the summer, the whole bloody lot of them."

"All of them? What happened?"

"No warning at all," says Casimir. "They just up and died one day, and that was that. It's happening all over the place. If Einstein's right, we've got about four years left." He glances at me, a faint smile in his expression. "That'll about do me, anyway."

"Och, don't talk rubbish." But I feel a stab in my chest at the thought. I don't like talking about mortality with an old person. It makes me uncomfortable. They're in a place I don't understand, edging closer, every single day. We all do, I suppose, but when we're young, we have the luxury of choosing ignorance. I'm in no rush to spoil the illusion, and Casimir knows it. He doesn't elaborate. His was a statement of fact, nothing more. It's one of the gulfs of age that will always be there.

We reach the edge of the village and make our way up the gentle incline to Casimir's cottage. It's a simple single-storey white dwelling, ablaze with climbing flowers in the summer, but unassuming and somewhat bare now, apart from a few white daffodils peeping out from pots beside the front door. The late afternoon light is fading in the eastern sky, and as we arrive at Casimir's gate, I turn to take in the sunset, breathing deeply.

You can taste the air here – it's clean and fresh, like a spring from a mountainside. The mouth of the glen reaches out towards the sea, and the village, with its spire and its hunched terraced houses, lies nestled in the basin of the ancient land. Behind us, stretching to the east, the snow-capped mountains rise like they're guarding the glen's secrets, but the younger southern sentries are smaller, rolling down to the low ground. You can see the skies to the south through the gap between the mountains and the sea. It's like a giant's mouth with a gaping hole where a huge tooth used to be. To the west, the sea is calm, glowing in the orange dusk, as it sweeps out towards the islands. A crimson sun sets behind them, stealing away what's left of the day. Just beyond the village in the western fields of the glen, a circle of standing stones stands silent and still, a remnant of a world long forgotten. I used to play there when I was a child. Most of them are broken, but a couple still stand in their full glory; towering, watching. The last of the sun's rays cast long shadows onto the land in front of the stones, like dark fingers reaching across the earth.

Casimir looks out towards the sea. "I never tire of this, you know, even if it is a bit of a blur these days. You can still feel it." He sniffs in the air, contented. "Wonderful." Turning, he unlatches the gate.

"I'll help you inside."

"Not at all, lad," he replies. "I'm fine once I'm in my own patch. Off you go and see you mother, now." He smiles in the way that someone does when they care for you. "I'm glad to have seen you, Robert. Look after yourself."

I watch him make his way up the path, fumble with his keys and open the door. I'm gripped with the urge to follow him inside, to open a bottle of whisky and embark on one of our long, meandering conversations that start in the world of science and end up way off track, some time in the small hours, in the wilderness of philosophy. He turns back and waves before quietly closing the door. Tomorrow would have to do.

A LITTLE FURTHER up the track is my home. It's like stepping into the past when I open the cottage's creaky oak door. A warmth of familiar scents, sounds and feelings wash over me: the smell of the logs freshly piled on the blazing fire, the scent of the wooden timbers sagging in the low ceilings, the clang of a cast iron pot on the range. Indistinct memories and a deep sense of refuge flood through me as I walk through the hall where my old boots still sit on the rack and my dark grey coat and baggy jumper still hang from the hooks by the door.

"Mum?"

"In here!" I walk into the kitchen, almost colliding with my mother as she throws her arms around me. I drop my rucksack onto the floor and embrace her. My mother, Marion Strong, is shorter than I am; her dirty blonde hair tied up on top of her head only just reaches my chin.

"Oh, it's so good to see you, Robert!" Her voice is muffled against my shoulder. She holds me at arm's length, her hands clasping my face, and peers at me over her half moon specs. Her eyes are warm, a little older than I remember, but have the same vitality they've always had. "Look at you!" she says proudly.

I do look, glancing sideways to the driftwood-famed mirror askew on the wall, but I don't get the same sense of pride which seems to thrill her. I'm unshaven, my hair is standing in different directions, thanks to its beanie experience. I don't look any better than when Chris told me I looked a mess. There's no getting away from it – I look rough. Still, my mother loves me.

"So how was your journey?" she asks.

"It was fine," I say, taking a seat by the old wooden table that dominates the room. "No hold ups."

"That's good. I was so pleased when you called!" She beams like a little girl. "I've made some soup, are you hungry?"

"I'm always hungry, remember?"

She grins as she lifts a bowl from the wooden dresser, stacked with assorted plates and cups and mugs. A copper pan dangles from a hook in the low ceiling and a bunch of dried, faded flowers hang upside down beside it. There was always a sense of comfortable disorganisation about the place and I'm glad that it hasn't changed.

"So how's the business going?" I ask. My mum earns a modest living making jewellery in the small workshop behind the cottage and enjoys wearing her creations. A chunky wooden necklace hangs round her neck, a pair of large, silver hoops swing from her ears and bronze bracelets jangle as she moves.

"Oh, it's fine. A little slow these days, but I don't need much to keep me going. I've got an exhibition in the museum at the end of the week." She places in front of me a bowl of soup brimming with lumpy vegetables and a slice of bread that would make a perfectly functional doorstop. Beats pasta and Dolmio sauce.

"That's good. Should get you some more clients."

"Hopefully," she says as she makes the tea. "So how was your trip away?"

"It was a difficult climb," Articulation isn't easy while chewing on the doorstop. "We got a bit lost on the descent, but it was a welcome change of scene, and Danny was good company." That's as much information as I want to give, whether it's my mum or anyone else who asks. *Tell no-one.* The monk's words echo in my mind.

She sits down opposite. "And has Danny grown up any?"

I can't help but snort. "What do you think?"

She laughs, then glances sideways at me. "How about Cora? Have you heard from her at all?"

"No, nothing."

"That's a shame," she says. "Maybe you should take a trip to the pottery to see her – it's only the other end of the glen."

"I'll see. So, when did you see her?"

"I met her in the shop a couple of times. We had a good chat. I think she's enjoying the space up here." She eyes me over her specs, in the way she does when she's formed an opinion about something, and knows that a look is enough to express it. "And how about you?"

My mouth has gone dry, despite the soup. "I think it's the right thing. We both needed the space."

She raises an eyebrow.

"So," I say, trying to steer the conversation elsewhere, "what else has been happening in the big metropolis?"

"Oh, not much. There's a new minister, who doesn't seem to have won over many hearts and minds so far, but it's early days. Michael Casimir's doing alright – I'm sure he'll be keen to see you. I told him about your job when you called to let me know. I hope you don't mind."

"Course not. I met him on the way home. He looks a lot older."

"Yes," she says, her expression sagging a little, as though she was trying to forget it. "It's such a shame he doesn't have any family at this stage in his life."

"We should go and see him tomorrow. I'd like to head up the ridge in the morning, but we could go round later on. Maybe take him out for a drink."

"That sounds fine. I've got to drop off some necklaces for Jessie first thing," she says, nodding at the bundle of coiled sparkles on a shelf, "but I'll be in when you get back. Oh, I almost forgot, a man came to the door this morning looking for you."

"Who was he?"

"I don't know – he didn't leave his name. He said he was a work associate – said he would call by later in the week. Quite a distinguished looking gentleman. Well dressed and very polite."

It doesn't sound like anyone I've worked with. "Did he leave a number or a card or something?"

She shakes her head. "He just said he would be in touch sometime later this week."

"Well, if it's important enough, he'll be back."

AFTERNOON FADES INTO evening, and then night. Darkness leaks in through my open window on a clean winter breeze. Sleep comes to me eventually. The sounds of the waves in the distance, their soft brushing on the black shores, the rustle of a few leaves on brittle branches, fading, becoming silence. For a while, there's only blissful silence.

A breath on my skin. Whispers suffuse my subconscious. She's there again, reaching out for my hand, and I want to resist but I can't. Her hand reaches closer, closer, until our fingertips touch. Darkness. It feels like I'm rising up, like she's lifting me up, and we're moving, gliding... I'm drowning in a feeling of helplessness, going under...

I jolt upright, panting, doused in sweat, and shove open the window into the empty dawn. "What do you want from me?" My voice carries out over the field behind the house.

The thud of footsteps and the door opens behind me. My mum is standing in a nightshirt, staring at me. "Robert?"

I glance at the digital alarm clock, which reads 06:47, and let out a slow breath. "Sorry. Bad dream."

I LEAVE THE house for the ridge, after raiding the fridge and cupboards for some food – Twiglets, a large chunk of cheddar and homemade bread. A lazy winter sun struggles to dispel the bleak mist that lingers over the land like a banished cloud. The glen has an earthy scent: the scent of wood and plants and rain and life: not the sterile life of the city, but the life that grows and struggles and prevails unnoticed all around. The engine room of the planet. As I walk up along the well-trodden track I listen to the sound of my boots on the rocks and soil. It makes me feel part of the land, that noise. But I'm uneasy. I feel like a guitar that's out of tune, too subtly to say which string is off, but enough to know that the whole thing doesn't sound right.

Beyond, the swell of the sea and the shrill call of the gulls, as they swoop and dive over the coastline, drift through the mist, muted a little by distance. Clouds lurk on the mountains, but I know the track well. If I stay on it, it will bring me back down to the west of the village. My mind, still blistered from that fucking nightmare, begins to sooth, surrounded by the enduring mountains and the timeless ebb and flow of the tide.

THE SUN PAYS lip-service to the sky behind the clouds as the track leads me down to the glen. At least the days are getting longer. I hate the short days of winter; it feels like you're being robbed of time. How anyone could live in six months of darkness in some godforsaken place like Spitsbergen is beyond me. It's an easy path downhill, much easier than the climb, but my pulse is picking up speed with each step. I can see the pottery from here, smoke twisting up from its fat chimney. There's Cora's car, outside, on its own. No customers. I'll have to talk to her, uninterrupted. And I still haven't figured out what I'm going to say.

What if she doesn't want to see me? I stop outside the green door, fidgeting. *God, Robert, you're not seventeen.* I take a deep breath and stoop to avoid bumping my head on the small door frame. Scottish people were evidently a lot shorter in bygone years. The pottery is a brightly lit white room with deep window sills and shelves displaying all kinds of pots and jars, jugs and plates. I tread carefully, keeping my hands in my pockets, aware that breaking something would not endear me to Cora. My fingers find the silver ring on its leather cord. Movement comes from the back of the room, beyond a stone arch in the wall.

"Hello!" It's her voice. My heart quickens as she steps through the archway. Her long dark red hair is tied behind her head and some strands have escaped over the pale skin of her cheeks. She brushes them away with a hand dusted in clay. She freezes as her eyes meet mine. In that moment, it's like I'm looking at her for the first time. I'd forgotten what drew me to her in the beginning. She has a look of serenity, a deep contentment that's settled in her eyes, as though she's comfortable with the person she is. The tension I'd grown used to seeing in her face is gone. She looks better without me in her life.

"Hello, Cora," I say, smiling as casually as I can.

"Robert, what are you..." she says, as she wipes her hands on the blue apron that covers her jeans and white shirt.

"It's alright, I'm here on business."

"Oh?"

"Yeah, it's my mum's birthday today and I need to get her a present."

"Oh, of course." She smiles, a little awkwardly. "I'm impressed you remembered." It sounds like sarcasm.

"So, how are you doing?"

"I'm... not sure yet." She frowns, ringing her dusty hands. "How about you?"

"I'm, eh – I've been better."

We stand there, looking uncomfortable. Virtual strangers again.

"Eh... I'll take this," I say, and pick up a stone-coloured jug on the shelf next to me.

"Good choice," she says. "I made that one."

"Really?" I turn it round carefully in my hands. "It's beautiful."

"Give her this from me." She lifts down a sandy, domed salt cellar. She used to insist on giving one present to people from both of us. "So how was your trip?"

"It was... well..." I take a deep breath. "I've not been right since I got back... I feel like I'm going a bit crazy, you know? I can't sleep. I keep having these dreams..."

"Look, Robert, I'm sorry you're having a hard time, but you wanted this. You know you did. You can't just..."

"They're dreams about Sarah."

She hesitates. "What?"

"Every night since I got back – she keeps trying to show me something, and I get this uneasy feeling, like I'm drowning..."

She steps closer, studying me. "Well, I'm sure you'll have a rational explanation, Robert, like you have for everything else. You're not telling me you believe them?"

"No, it's just..."

The door behind me creaks and a couple with flecks of grey in their dark hair stride in. They're wearing matching blue waterproof jackets and hats.

"Hi!" says the lady. American, eyebrows raised, grinning widely. One of those tiresomely eager and optimistic people. "Could you tell us how to get to Kilmartin, please? We've gotten lost. Oh, I love this vase! How much is it? Do you have it in another colour? Oh, I'm sorry, you're serving someone."

"No, it's okay," says Cora. "He's just leaving."

"Please, Cora. I need to talk to you."

A frost has settled over her. "Get out," she whispers.

WHAT DOES SHE think? That I'm making up some bullshit story about her sister to get things back on track? I'd have come up with something better than that, for fuck's sake, after two weeks in the sodding wilderness.

The sky is the colour of old lead as I walk back along the glen. The hushed village street stretches ahead, the squat cottages huddled against the evening chill. There's a fine drizzle on my skin, like being breathed on, and the air smells of clean cotton. *You know what, Cora? The doctor was right. It is all just stress. What was I thinking? I'll see my mum's GP and get some of those pills I should have taken in the first place and I'll not need to tell you about any of it.*

"Don't forget to give your mum my present! And wish her a happy birthday for me!" Casimir's voice makes me jump – I'd barely noticed reaching his gate. The old man is standing on the grass at the side of his house with one hand on his empty beehive. He waves at me with the other.

"I'm just off to do that right now." I feel for the carved letter opener he made, safe in my pocket. "We'll be down to see you later!"

"Aye, no doubt you will." Casimir calls back, his hand still resting on the hive. I glance back. There's something in the tilt of his head that seems unfamiliar. Wonder why all his bees died. What did Einstein say? We've got four years left, after all the bees die. The tarmac is broken under my boots. Old, splintered by the frost. There's no need to tell Cora about the dreams or what happened in Tibet. It'll go. I lock the thought in the past to stop it bleeding into the present.

WITHOUT REALLY BEING aware of getting here, I find myself in the kitchen, making a conscious effort to lose the edge of irritation that's hanging over me. It's her birthday, after all. She's stirring something on the stove, her head bowed, watching the slow arc of the spoon, lost in thought.

"Something smells good. Happy Birthday Mum." I ruffle her hair, then take off my jacket and hang it on the back of the chair.

"Thanks," she says without turning round. She just keeps stirring.

"How about we go out for a drink tonight to celebrate?"

She hesitates, then reaches for a mug hanging from a hook under the wooden shelf, her back still to me, as the kettle comes to a boil. We both speak at the same time.

"Eh, Robert..." she begins, just as I say, "Casimir was asking for you."

She inclines her head a little and says quietly, "What did you say?"

"He was asking for you, when I passed on the way home just now." I pull a piece of bread from the loaf on the worktop and munch as I speak. "Said to wish you a happy birthday. I told him we'd drop by later."

Her arm falls limp as she turns towards me and the mug smashes on the tiled floor. Her face is the pale colour of cold ashes and tears spill down her cheeks.

"Robert," she says in a whisper, "Michael Casimir died last night."

Chapter Five

THE WORLD'S GONE cold. The spring air cuts like needles into my face as I gather with the congregation to pay my last respects to Michael Casimir. Ice whiskers hang from the trees and a white down caps the rooftops of the cottages in the village. Snow fell last night and laid a white blanket softly over the glen, and the sounds of the day went under it and made the world a quieter place. Sodding snow. In April. My mother stands on my left, clutching a handkerchief to her cheek. On my right are Angus and Alasdair McLeod, the postmen, and Tam Owen of the Stone Circle. I recognise a few others, but can't recall their names. Cora is there, standing quietly near the back of the small crowd, and the sight of her distracts me from the numb, empty feeling inside.

I don't know what I saw that day. But I spoke to him – *he* spoke to *me*. Did I dream that too? The thought has needled at me over the last four days. It was there when I called the undertaker to arrange for Casimir's body to be moved. It niggled at me when I handed over the death certificate at the Registry Office. It pierced me when I looked down at Casimir's cold, peaceful face.

I glance at Cora. Some people have a heart attack one day, some people's nerves shatter suddenly, some people see things that aren't there. It was Alasdair McLeod who found Casimir the day I walked the ridge. He had been dead for hours.

I helped carry Casimir from the church in his dark coffin to the little wood clustered on the hillside behind the kirk, where he had requested he be laid to rest. The edge of the coffin dug into my neck whenever my foot slipped on the snow, but it didn't really bother me all that much. Now the minister stands solemnly before us in his raven-black robe, clutching his Bible, and says a lot of things that could be applied to anyone, but nothing that would make you think, *ah, yes, that was Michael Casimir*. He doesn't know the first thing about him. I switch off.

The sea lies quiet and shimmering in the shards of golden sunlight that have broken through the snow clouds. A large boulder crested with frost sits solid and enduring beside the dark hole in the earth, the budding branches of a larch tree dipping softly down to it. I glance up. Two buzzards circle overhead, they part for a while then come together before disappearing into the clouds.

I remember the first time I was at a grave. I was only three years old, but it's one of those memories which doesn't fade with time, even if I want it to. I had to wear black trousers and a black coat – a coat with an oversized hood and brown toggles on the front. It was raining, but a warm breeze spilled over the flat Cambridgeshire fields that stretched out from the church and the small graveyard where we stood. I held my mother's hand tightly, and looked around at all the other people gathered about the hole in the ground. Some of them were crying, some were standing with their heads bowed, and all of them were wearing black coats. A large man in a flapping black robe, looking like a great burly crow, was reading something from a book in his hands. I remember thinking it wasn't a very interesting story, so I crouched down and picked up a stick and began drawing a picture in the dark earth, glancing up at my mum every so often to see whether she would tell me off. But she wasn't looking at me – she wasn't looking at anyone – she just stared ahead, like she'd fallen asleep with her eyes open. I peeked down at the box in the ground which the men had put there. I knew my dad was inside, although I didn't know why. I just assumed he would come out again sometime soon – we had a story to finish which we read together each night, and he'd want know the end of it. When I looked back as we walked away, still holding onto my mum's hand, and saw the men in black caps shovel the earth into the hole, I came to realise that my dad might never come out of the box. For the first time I'd felt fear. My bubble of security and love had been burst. I tugged on my mum's hand to go back, to dig him out myself, but she kept a strong grip and kept on walking. The men in black caps kept shovelling and blurred into the distance through my tears as I wrestled to make sense of it. I don't know if I ever did.

This time my mum is crying. There's no noise, but her shoulders shudder a little as she clutches her handkerchief to her face. I put an arm around her. As the minister concludes his words, I step forward with the five other bearers, and take the cords holding the weight of Casimir's coffin. It's heavy and bumps into the side of the pit as we lower it down into the earth. The minister sprinkles some dirt over it and mutters, "Ashes to ashes, dust to dust..."

* * *

AND IT IS done.

All that life and now, nothing.

The crowd splinters and begins to drift down the hillside.

What's happened to you, Casimir?

I thought I had this weighed off. I thought, at this stage in my life, I had come to terms with my reasoning. We're a sophisticated collection of atoms, nothing more. And one day, the biochemical powerhouse inside us shuts down. That's all there is to it. Casimir was, and now he isn't. So why does it feel wrong?

"Hello, dear," says my mum. Cora is standing beside me. "It was good of you to come."

"I wouldn't have missed it," she replies. "He was such a fine man. Are you alright?"

My mum takes a deep breath, as though drawing in strength. "It doesn't get any easier, the older you get. But yes, I'm alright." She smiles at Cora, a sad smile, then pats her forearm. "Now, please excuse me – I must catch Flora about something." She disappears into the small crowd, leaving us together. The last of the group makes its way to the Stone Circle, where Tam has arranged some food and drinks for everyone.

"It won't be the same here anymore."

"No, it won't." Cora stares at her feet as she walks slowly down the hillside. "My folks were really upset when I phoned them." She steals a glance. "Sorry I cut you off the other day. I just found it hard to swallow."

"I can see that. Don't worry about it."

"Are you still getting the dreams?"

I haven't had the nightmare for a few days, not since Casimir died, and I don't want to let it out of its box.

"No, not anymore. I was just under a bit of pressure, but I'm alright now."

She nods and we walk side by side in silence, straggling behind the group, ambling through the soft snow. The buzzards are calling overhead. Whatever happened to Casimir, he knows the Big Secret now.

BY THE SOUND of it, the drowning of sorrows in the Stone Circle is well underway by the time we reach the street.

"You going in?" asks Cora.

Before I can answer, a car purrs to a stop behind us, and a door opens, then clicks shut. I glance back and see a man standing a little way back, next to a BMW. Black, sleek, tinted windows. I've never seen the man before – tall, lean and dressed in a long, dark, well tailored coat. A purple silk scarf is draped around his neck and his hands are hidden inside black leather gloves. Subtle but unquestionable wealth. He looks out of place in the village – composed, unflustered, certain. He holds his head level, his hands clasped in front of him, very still. He's waiting. I can't say why, but I know he's waiting for me.

"D'you know him?" whispers Cora. Her eyes fix on the stranger, and she stiffens as he walks towards us. His hair is the colour of a crow's wing and sweeps back from his slim face to the nape of his neck, glinting like a black feather. His eyes are the pale blue of a deep glacial crevasse. He has the presence of someone who is very sure of his place in the world.

"No, I don't."

"I am sorry to interrupt, Miss Martin," the man says politely, and his mouth smiles at Cora, "but I would be grateful if you would allow me a few minutes of Mr

Strong's time. I have some urgent business to discuss with him."

Cora looks to me and I nod. "I'll see you later," I say.

She holds the stranger's gaze for a moment, but doesn't return the smile. She walks away, glancing over her shoulder before she disappears into the Stone Circle. The sound of laughter swells as the door opens, and fades again. The stranger waits patiently until she's gone, then turns to me.

"Forgive the intrusion, Mr Strong. My name is Victor Amos." He holds out a black gloved hand, and I shake it but say nothing. "I called by your mother's home the other day."

So that's who it was. "Do I know you, Mr Amos?"

"I don't believe our paths have crossed until now." He pauses, watching me, comfortable with the silence. "I understand you were recently released from your employment with SightLabs and are... at a bit of a loose end."

"How do you know that?"

"I do my homework, Mr Strong. Your reputation in the field goes before you."

I snort. Is he being sarcastic?

Victor Amos smiles a little and this time his eyes smile too. "There's no need to be modest, Mr Strong. I am aware of your career progression so far. You have considerable experience in physics, your work with the Grid, in dark matter research. I was sorry that your recent submission to the *Journal of Physics* was rejected. Personally I thought your paper on ZEPLIN-III showed a great deal of promise." He nods courteously.

"What, do you work for the *Journal*?"

He gives a little laugh. "No, but I have contacts. I also

have a talent in spotting true potential, and you, Mr Strong, have a great deal of potential."

Suspicion of flattery is a true British quality which I have in plenty. People who pay you compliments tend to be after something. "What do you want, Mr Amos?"

"I am here to offer you a business opportunity."

"Oh?"

"I am the Director of a large global corporation which is committed to furthering many areas of scientific research. I regret that I cannot divulge the details of our work at this stage, but I need someone with a certain skill set to assist with our current project. And you happen to have the skills I seek."

"You're offering me a job?"

"Yes."

"What does it involve?"

Amos glances along the street, his look not furtive, but assured. "Perhaps this is not the place, but if we can arrange for you to come to my office, I can explain the nature of our project and your part in it. And I should add that I am willing to pay handsomely for your contribution."

"How handsomely?" I ask, frowning.

"One hundred thousand British pounds."

I stare at him. "You are kidding me."

"I am too busy a man for practical jokes."

"Is this some kind of government project? MI5?"

Amos shakes his head. "No, Mr Strong. This is not a government project."

"What's the catch?"

"You help us with this project, and we pay you for your time and efforts. It's a straightforward business deal."

"Why are you offering so much?"

"That's a fair question. This is important work, Mr Strong, ultimately for the benefit of the entire planet. It's a small price to pay, in the larger scheme of things." I raise an eyebrow. "If you could make some time tomorrow, I will explain things in a little more depth."

"Alright, then." The words have left my lips before I have time to consider them.

"Very good. One of my associates will meet you here at 6am tomorrow." His glacial eyes hold mine as he extends a gloved hand. "This is an exciting opportunity for both of us, Mr Strong. I look forward to our discussion in the morning. Please ensure that this offer remains between us." I find myself shaking hands with him before he walks away. He's only taken a few steps before he stops and turns. "And my condolences for Mr Casimir. He was a fine man."

The chauffeur steps out and holds open the car door, and tips his hat as Amos steps inside. He knew Casimir? The car slips past me and away from the village.

I don't know how long I stand there, looking along the empty road. Miniature snow tornados spiral around my feet as the wind blows in from the north. I've had some publications over the years, and being headhunted for the temporary lecturing post was flattering while it lasted, but a hundred grand? I'm good, but I'm not that good. What's the catch? Maybe there isn't one.

The snow falls again in large, fluffy flakes, but it's some time before I notice the cold seeping into my bones. I walk towards the Stone Circle, but hesitate as my hand rests on the door handle. I need some time to think. I'll see Cora later. Turning away, I walk home.

* * *

I SIT FOR a long time in front of the fire. The smell of burning logs suffuses the living room, with its low timber ceilings, its white walls hung with my mum's tapestries and, on either side of the fire, faded but comfortable armchairs. We didn't speak much over dinner. My mum pushed her food around the plate and I wasn't hungry.

My mind churns with thoughts that seem to go round and come back to where they started. No more conversations with Casimir. The hollowness in my chest reminds me of that. I could do with one now, more than ever. What would you say, Casimir? Would you go for it? I stare at the flames, hissing and coiling like angry, red snakes.

I thought I was one of those people who didn't care that much about money. Told myself it didn't really matter, as long as I had enough to get by. So how come I'm so excited?

It's a funny thing, money. They don't look like much, those small rectangles of paper. But they're more persuasive than religion. Money means choice. A promise of something more. The prospect of prosperity is not something I'd considered before, and now that it's on the table, I can feel my principles shifting. More travel. More time. New motorbike. Just the idea of more cash is opening doors in my mind that I didn't even know existed.

The flames are stuttering. I watch them dying. People don't just walk up to you and offer you thousands of pounds for doing what would normally earn you only a mediocre income.

But is it all about the money? I was singled out. Maybe this project is for the good of the planet, like he said, and I could help with it. I am good at what I do, so why not use it? That depends on what he wants me to do.

My mum comes in from the kitchen with two glasses of whisky and hands one to me, before settling into the armchair opposite. She sighs heavily. "Now, why don't you tell me what's on your mind?"

I say nothing at first, and she doesn't push me. I swivel the glass around in my hand; the peaty scent wafts up to my nose. "I've had a job offer that might be too good to be true."

"Then it probably is."

"The man who came to the door the other day – he came back."

"And he offered you a job?"

I nod.

"Well, that's great, isn't it? In research?"

"I don't know the details yet. I'll find out a bit more about it tomorrow, but it's the kind of offer that's hard to refuse. I don't think I'll get an offer like this again. Not ever."

She takes a sip of whisky. "Your father was once offered a job that seemed too good to be true."

This makes me sit up. "Really? What happened?" I say it before I can stop myself. God, I hope she doesn't cry. The subject of my dad has been taboo for most of my life. I know he was a physicist, I know he worked in Cambridge, I know he loved us both. But beyond that, she got upset whenever I asked. Over the years I learned to stop asking.

This time, she remains composed. "Shortly after his first job, he was offered a prodigious post in a European laboratory along with a very healthy paycheque – it was an incredible break for him. Much more than he could have hoped for, at such an early stage in his career."

"Did he take it?"

She pauses. "He... didn't get the chance."

There's a knock at the door. I get up and cup my hands to the glass, peering out into the darkness.

"Cora?" I open the door and the night brightens a little. She's standing on the bottom step. Her hair is wet with snow, her arms wrapped around her in an effort to stay warm. Large white flakes settle on her head and melt. "Come in," I say and she steps inside. "You look frozen. Are you alright?" Before I can think about it, I put my arms around her to warm her up, but she pulls herself away, gently. *Well done, Romeo. You don't get to do that anymore, remember?*

I show her into the living room. "Have a seat by the fire."

My mum stands up and kisses Cora on the cheek. "I was just on my way to bed," she says. "It's been a long day." She smiles and leaves the room. Always tactful, my mother.

"Do you want a drink?"

"Alright," Cora says, and smiles, but I can tell she's nervous.

I go into the kitchen to get the bottle of whisky and another glass. I want to tell her about Amos, but I think I know what she'll say. I check my face in the mirror and try to bring the unruly hair into some semblance of order. It doesn't comply.

"Thanks," she says, holding the glass while I pour. I sit down in the seat opposite and watch the firelight dance on her cheekbones. Her brow is creased into a frown and she bites her lower lip. I hope this isn't about Sarah. I don't need another nightmare tonight.

"So what's up?"

"That man you spoke with today…"

"Yes?"

"Who is he?"

105

"He... he runs a science project. He offered me a job. It's great isn't it? Just like you said – something would come up."

"Yeah. But there's something not right about him."

I don't say anything.

"You know how you get a feeling about some people? Like when we wanted to rent the flat on Holloway Street, and then we met the guy who owned it?"

"Yeah, there was something dodgy about him." There was. My gut feeling had been vindicated when we read in the paper later that he'd been given eighteen months for fraud.

"Exactly. You couldn't put your finger on it, but you knew there was something wrong."

"So..."

"Well, I got the same feeling about the man we met today."

"Oh, I think he's alright. He's just a businessman. They're often a bit up themselves."

"No, it's more than that. God, Robert, this is difficult, after everything."

"What do you mean?"

"Look, I never told you this." She takes a gulp of whisky and watches the glass turning slowly in her hands. "I can pick up things about people that not everyone can."

"You're just empathic. That's a good thing."

"No, Robert, I can see things that not everyone can. I can see auras."

"Auras."

I stare at her, waiting for her to tell me she's joking. But there's not a hint of it in her face. She means it. She has gone off the deep end.

And you heard a dead man speak to you.

"Yes, auras. I never told you because I knew how you'd react, and it didn't really matter before. It's just something I've always been able to do."

"You mean like lights – colours – around people?"

"Yes, that tell me something about them."

"Okay... so what's mine like?"

"Yours is..." She sits back, studying me. "Yours has changed, actually. It's darker than it used to be."

I've been flirting with madness, but at least I know the things I've been imagining are a direct result of too much pressure. She doesn't – she believes they're real. She has no insight. I feel my gut twist, but remember that it doesn't need to bother me anymore; her tenuous grip on reality isn't my problem now. So why am I feeling like I'm stepping into quicksand?

"Okay, okay. So what does this have to do with the man I spoke to today?"

"That's why I'm here. He doesn't have one. He doesn't have an aura."

"So... what does that mean?"

"I don't know – I've never seen it before. Everyone has an aura. Everyone except him. I don't know what it means" – she sits forward, her green eyes level with mine – "but be careful, Robert."

Oh, come on, Cora. Bloody auras? "Alright," I say. "I'll be careful. But it could be a really good opportunity."

"Robert, you can't trust him."

"I can't pass up a chance like this, Cora. I'll never get another one like it. I lost my job, remember? I appreciate your concerns, but I can't just walk away from this because you think he doesn't light up like the rest of us."

She watches me for a moment then stands up. "This is exactly why I didn't tell you before."

"No, wait, I'm sorry." I get up and reach out to her. "I know you're just trying to help."

She holds her head high, but a frost has settled about her. "It doesn't matter whether you believe me or not," she says, her voice measured and composed. "Just promise me you'll be careful."

She still cares. I feel a little lighter.

"I will."

She lowers her eyes and moves to the door.

"I'll walk you home if you like."

"No, it's fine. I've got the car. I'll see you later." And she leaves into the snowy, still night without looking back.

I think I still love her, even if she is wired to a Mars Bar. I close the door and go to bed.

When I get to my room, I open the top drawer in the chest of drawers. Same old clothes, a set of earphones and a walkman, a Swiss army knife. Unchanged since I moved out, fifteen years ago. I lift them aside to see if it's still there. Tucked underneath a few T-shirts is an envelope, once white, now faded by time. I open it carefully and take out the photograph. It was taken in the cloisters of Cambridge University. My dad is wearing graduation robes and my mum's in a long red dress, and they're holding me up, aged three, between them. My mum's laughing at the camera and my dad's smiling at me like I mean everything to him. I used to have it in a frame on top of the chest of drawers, but when I left, my mum put it away, like she did with all of the other photos of him. But I like this one. It reminds me that he was there, once.

Chapter Six

WHY IS IT that when you need to sleep, your mind decides that this is the best time to bring to the surface all those things you can do nothing about? It's like it's been waiting until you can hardly string a thought together to spring them on you. I toss and turn for hours, beneath a pendulum which swings between Victor Amos and Cora. Why does she have to be so bloody crazy? It's like she's beckoning me from an island I can never hope to reach.

But what if she's right about Amos?

I glance at the clock: 05:25. I get up and dress in jeans and a white shirt. Dressing for interviews was not part of the plan when I packed. I lift my mobile from the bedside table. I've got a message.

"Robert... eh, I know I've just spoken to you," says Cora, "and you're probably in bed by now, but... I wanted to ask..." Silence. I stare at the blank screen. It's run out of charge. I grab the charger from the bedside table and stuff it in my rucksack. After leaving a note for my mum on the kitchen table, which explains what she already knows, I take my grey coat from the hook in the hall and open the door quietly. It's still dark and the crisp air catches in my throat. A blackbird is singing like today is its last.

There's no sign of dawn. The stars blink down in patches through dark gaps in the clouds, blending with the mountains that loom up from the edges of the glen. I make my way down the road to the main street over the glistening, frosted ground, through the sleeping village.

As I pass the kirk, a car engine starts up across the street. Headlights from a VW Golf cut into the dark and the passenger door swings open.

"Robert Strong?" The man leaning across from the driver's seat looks about the same age as me.

I get into the car.

"I'm Peter Banks. Good to meet you." We shake hands. He has a square face, cropped dark hair and an Irish accent.

"So where are we going?" I ask.

"We're heading towards Perth."

He U-turns the car and I watch Kildowan retreat in the side mirror.

"So do you work for Victor Amos?"

"I've worked with him on a few projects. I'm a prospector."

"Is that what he does? Mining?"

Banks glances at me. "That's part of it. It'll make more sense when you speak to him. I hear you're a physicist?"

"Yeah."

"I thought about geophysics myself, but I prefer being out in the open. It's long days, but I like the travel, and I get a decent amount of time at home between jobs." He reaches behind his seat and pulls out a paper bag. "Donut?"

As we turn onto the A85, the red dawn swells in the east. It catches the scar on his left forearm, which snakes up to disappear under the sleeve of his black T-shirt. By the time we see the signposts for Perth, I'm still none the wiser about Amos. Banks is amiable, but skilled in nudging the rudder of a conversation. He talks a lot and tells me nothing. He takes the turnoff for Crieff.

CHILDREN IN GREY uniforms straggle to school along the pavements. We turn through a series of streets to the edge of the town and pull up beside an old stone, semi-detached house. A woman in a suit and holding a schoolbag and lunchbox is ushering a small girl out of the front door.

"Is this where we're meeting Amos?"

Banks turns to me, ignoring my question. "You're a business associate. Don't say any more, and they won't ask."

He gets out of the car. I hesitate, but Banks gestures for me to follow.

"I'll be home about six," says the woman.

He kisses her on the cheek. "Okay. Have a good day."

"Remember to pick up her gym kit," she says. "She always forgets. Sophie, come *on!*"

Sophie is hunkered down, selecting pebbles from the ground and putting them into the pocket of her duffle coat. Banks crouches beside her. "That's a good one," he says, handing her a small stone. She pockets it and wraps her small arms around his neck. "Love you, daddy."

"Have a good day, beautiful."

"Let's go, Sophie, we're late," says the woman, flashing a smile at me. "Nice to meet you – have a good meeting." She bundles Sophie into the other car on the driveway as Banks holds open the front door. He locks it behind me.

I WAIT IN the hall as he goes into a room that looks like an office. He calls me in a moment or two later. There's a bookcase against one wall lined with folders and rolled-up maps beside a desk with a computer.

"I'll need your signature before we go on." He hands me a pen and a document with the heading *Official Secrets Act*.

I look up at him without speaking.

"Some of what you're going to see is highly classified."

"I thought this wasn't a government project."

"It's not. But we can't go any further until you sign."

I stare down at the paper without really reading it. I could back out, but what have I got to lose? I scrawl my signature and hand it back. "Now can you tell me what this is about?"

He leads me to the kitchen. I could use a cup of coffee, but he doesn't offer. Instead he opens a door to a walk-in cupboard with a sloping roof. It's stuffed with things that look like they haven't been used for a while – a rack of old shoes, some rusty tools, a stack of pots and bowls layered with dust. He pulls back the linoleum, taps on an electronic keypad on the floor and and pulls a handle next to it. Light floods in from below.

"What's going on?"

He looks up. "This will take you to Amos."

"What? I'm not getting in there!"

"Look, I know it's unusual, but this will all make sense when you speak to him." He checks his watch.

I draw closer to the opening, expecting to see a cellar room, perhaps with Amos inside. Instead a ladder stretches down about thirty feet into an illuminated tunnel.

He steps aside. "Come on. We don't want to keep Bishop waiting."

This could be a big mistake. Unease and intrigue wash over me, and intrigue sticks. I find myself gripping the rails of the ladder and climbing down.

The tunnel is big enough to walk inside, well lit, warm and dry. Banks has closed the door above and follows me down, shutting out the world above us. No one knows I'm here.

"This way." He leads me to the left.

"What is this place?"

He stops in front of a recess in the wall, where a silver door slides open. We step into the clean white lift and he pushes the button marked Sublevel One. We descend smoothly for what feels like too long.

"How deep are we going?"

"Ninety feet."

"Is this a mine?"

"No. It's not a mine."

"What then? A military setup?"

The lift glides to a stop and the doors open. We step out into a white tunnel twice as big as the one above, lined with fluorescent panels every ten feet or so. It curves into the distance in both directions.

"Bishop will be here soon. Good luck with your project, Robert." He pulls his phone from his pocket, and something falls to the ground as he heads back into the lift.

"Bishop? Wait a minute! How do I get out?" The doors glide shut between us.

What the fuck am I doing here?

I stoop to pick up what's on the floor: a photograph of three women. Their woolly hats are dusted with snow and they're laughing. The woman in the middle has arresting blue eyes, with a hint of bridled wildness in them. It's signed on the back: *To lifelong friendship*.

A hum comes from the right. I pocket the picture as an electric buggy, driven by an older man, appears round the bend and whirs to a stop beside me. A pair of silky heeled legs swings out from the back.

"Mr Strong? I'm Dana Bishop." She extends a slender, sleeveless arm and shakes my hand. Sleek, bobbed black hair and bold red lipstick: Dana Bishop is striking and comfortable with it. She lets her gaze run over me, then meets my eye. "I'm the Project Director for Mr Amos. If you agree to assist us, you'll be working with me."

THE BUGGY TAKES us deeper into the complex, through a network of interlinking tunnels. I lose track of where I've been.

"So how long has this place been here?"

"Since the Second World War."

I glance up at the smooth white walls. It looks much more contemporary, out of character for a wartime construction.

"It's been upgraded over time," she says, watching my face. "It needs to be fit for purpose. Cigarette?"

She offers me an unmarked open green packet.

"I don't smoke."

"They're antioxidant cigarettes – meant to improve your neutrophil function. We've been trialling them for a month."

"Health cigarettes? Do they work?"

She takes a drag and closes her eyes. "They taste like shit."

The buggy draws to a halt as the tunnel opens into a wide well lit atrium fed by seven main corridors, marked Sectors A to G, and populated by busy looking staff in suits and shirts. Far from the cellar room I expected when Banks pulled back the trapdoor, this is an underground colony. Dana strides past them, ignoring their acknowledgements, apart from the occasional nod. I pause and glance back.

"You won't be going back that way," Dana draws on her cigarette with a faint look of amusement. "You really think that's the only way in and out of here?"

She leads me into G Sector, which seems quieter than the others, past a door marked 'D Bishop Director of Operations', towards the one at the end, which simply reads 'VICTOR AMOS'. Dana pauses outside and breathes in, composing herself. She knocks then opens the door.

The room is spacious, white and sparsely furnished. A wide desk sits at one end with a leather seat on each side. Victor Amos is standing in the middle of the room, facing a large balcony window, watching a flock of birds moving over the rooftops below. It takes me a moment to process that it's not a window, but a projection. He turns as we enter.

"Ah, Mr Strong, good morning. I'm delighted you decided to come. Thank you Ms Bishop, I'll take it from here."

When Dana closes the door, he asks. "Have you heard of stigmery?"

"No."

"It's a key concept in swarm intelligence." He turns back to the projection, which has morphed into a swarm of bees moving across a field. "I could watch them for hours. It's as if they are one entity, each responding to the same thought. But that's an aside." He walks behind the desk and lifts a slim silver pot as the projection becomes a view over mountain ridges capped with snow. "Please, take a seat. Would you like some coffee?"

"Yeah, thanks."

As he pours, he says, "I suspect you found your journey here to be somewhat unconventional. Given what we do here, I'm afraid it's necessary." He smoothes out his silk tie and settles into his high-backed leather seat. "So, Mr Strong. You must have been disappointed about the SightLabs closure. How long were you with them?"

"Five years."

"That's quite a long time. Your journal submission suggested that you were making some good progress with your research."

I take a drink. Proper coffee, not the instant crap I usually buy. "We were close. The last thing we were expecting was that they would pull the funding."

"It's most unfortunate. But I suppose, in the current climate of recession, it is science and the arts that are the first casualties. And I am a great believer in both. Do you like art, Mr Strong?"

I glance at the abstract picture on the wall behind him: a grey background with what looks like the silhouette of trees at the bottom and a solid black circle at the top. "I don't know a lot about it. But I can appreciate a good painting when I see one." And I don't like that one.

"Well, that's what matters. I am not a musician, but I find music touches the soul like nothing else can. Perhaps one day science will tell us why that is."

"Not if they keep interfering with research."

"Ah, yes. Indeed. Tell me about your research into dark matter. How did you go about it?"

"We were looking for evidence of WIMPs – Weakly Interacting Massive Particles. We can't see them directly, but in theory we can infer their presence when they collide with other nuclei. We were using various approaches: semiconductors, crystals, gases, xenon – as the paper outlined. We had some provisional results that we were close to verifying, only we didn't get the chance."

"It's fascinating, isn't it? To think that there is so much out there that still evades us. If I'm not mistaken, the dark universe constitutes most of what is around us."

"Ninety-five per cent of it."

"Really? Why is it so difficult to measure?"

"Dark matter isn't visible. It's not like ordinary matter. Everything around us that we see and feel and hear, it's all perceptible to us through electromagnetism. Dark matter speaks a different language, even though it accounts for most of the matter out there. The best evidence we have for it is Cosmic Background radiation, or the afterglow of the Big Bang."

"And what about dark energy?"

"We know the universe is expanding, which you'd expect after the Big Bang, but if it were down to only the gravitational effects of galaxies, the expansion should slow down.

What we're seeing is the opposite: the expansion is speeding up. Galaxies are accelerating away from each other. So either gravity is misbehaving or there's a propulsive force that's driving the expansion. Most scientists think it's the latter, and they've called it dark energy and reckon it makes up over two thirds of the universe. There are different schools of thought – some people think it's a fifth fundamental force, called quintessence, but nobody really knows yet."

"I can imagine it would be quite a breakthrough, if we were to discover what they are. You must have found it difficult to lose your position, given the implications of your work."

"It was a bit of a kick in the teeth."

Amos nods. "They say that losing your job is one of the biggest life events one can face, after bereavement and separation. But a combination, such as you have had to deal with, can make it particularly stressful."

You've no idea, Mr Amos. "I've had easier times."

"I'm sure. But it undoubtedly helps to have the support of someone close. Are you lucky enough to have a wife or a partner, Mr Strong?"

"Eh... not any more, no."

Amos bows his head a little. "Forgive me. I did not mean to pry. All I will say, through personal experience, is that there is light at the end of the tunnel."

"Oh?"

"Yes. I was in a position once, not dissimilar to yours. Many years ago I was employed as a research assistant in an environmental agency that worked to protect endangered marine species. It didn't pay much, but when I lost that job, after the agency's financial position became untenable, it put a strain on my marriage that was enough to break it. It was a difficult time. But sometimes you need to hit the bottom before you can find your way out of the pit. I knew then that I had the opportunity to invest my time in creating something worthwhile, something that channelled my passions."

"And what was that?"

"I have always been fascinated by science, but I am not a scientist. What I care about, above all, is the future of Earth and the species that inhabit it. Science is a hugely important part of that future, but it has to be the right science that will take our planet forwards, not destroy it. We have seen already the ugly face of scientific discovery, and it's something we can ill afford to see again. Whilst the physicists have given us the beauty of string theory, they have also given us the atomic bomb. So, I began with only a few like minded people to help me, and it has gone beyond anything I could have imagined."

"What exactly do you do, Mr Amos?"

Amos places his cup to one side and clasps his hands loosely in front of him on the desk. "I am the director of a global corporation, called ORB – the Observation Research Board. Its purpose is to monitor the world's scientific progress. We oversee projects ranging from nano-therapy and quantum technology to climate modification and space exploration. Our role is to ensure that progress continues, but in a controlled and measured way which will enhance rather than endanger the future of our species. We do not recognise political or geographical boundaries, but rather take a view of the planet as one."

I stare at him, feeling a twist in my gut. "So you're the global science police?"

He smiles. "I prefer to think of us more as guardians. 'Police' has connotations of enforcement that I find a little distasteful. We are more of a guiding hand in keeping our progress on the straight and narrow, as it were."

"I like to think I'm pretty well informed in my own field, Mr Amos. Why haven't I heard of ORB?"

"You are well informed – that's why I invited you here. But there is more going on around you than you know, Mr Strong, and some if it would leave you with sleepless nights for many years to come. No. No one outside of ORB knows we exist, apart from a few highly influential international advisers. It works better that way. In order to make an accurate assessment of what is really happening in the field of scientific research, scientists must be allowed to proceed without hindrance or interference or an awareness of being observed. We strive to eliminate the observer effect."

"So what do you do if you don't approve of the research?"

"We steer it in a more positive direction."

I lean forward; I want to be sure I hear his answer to this. "Mr Amos, did ORB close down SightLabs?"

He laughs. "I'm not aware of any destructive potential in dark matter research, Mr Strong. At least, not yet. I'm sure you would be in a better position than I am to comment. No, that was a political decision taken for financial reasons. Nothing more."

I sit back slowly in my chair. "What is it you want with me?"

Amos looks at me for a moment before answering. I don't know what he's thinking. He takes a sip of coffee without breaking eye contact, then sets the cup aside. "Our current area of investigation is focusing on the work in progress at CERN."

"You mean the LHC?"

"Yes. As you know, the Large Hadron Collider was constructed with the purpose of finding the Higgs boson, the elusive God Particle, amongst other things. And the initial experimental data strongly suggests that they were successful, if I'm not mistaken."

I nod. "The particle they found seems to have the spin-parity of a Standard Model Higgs boson."

"Are you aware of the other elements of the experiments?"

"The detectors are looking for different things – extra dimensions, unification of fundamental forces, evidence of dark matter."

"Have you ever been to CERN?"

"No. But when I worked with Romfield Labs, I was involved in making the Grid software compatible with the systems at our end.

"Detailed work, I expect."

"Yes."

"I understand that you were responsible for its success. That's quite an achievement."

"I was part of a team that worked on it, yes."

Amos sits back in his seat. "I had the opportunity to visit CERN recently. It is a phenomenal piece of engineering. Its achievements so far have accelerated our understanding further than we could have imagined. But there is a problem."

"Oh?"

"We have concerns about the safety of the project."

I shrug. "They've had no issues with the collisions they've conducted so far."

"Not to date. But the next round of experiments are due to accelerate and collide particles at far higher energies, virtually at the speed of light. No-one has done this before."

"That's the whole point. Finding the Higgs-like

particle proves that it works. Higher energy experiments will answer more questions."

"Provided we are around to observe it."

It's beginning to make sense now: he's a doomsday prophet. "There's been a lot of scaremongering, but there's nothing substantial in the claims."

Amos inclines his head. "That is debatable." He opens a drawer to his right and hands me a document. "This is a copy of a recent paper by the Risk Assessment Assembly to the CERN Council, endorsed by physicists, philosophers, ethicists and judges. It has only just come to our attention."

I flick through the report.

"It makes for disturbing reading, but the area that is most concerning is the production of strangelets. Do you know about strangelets, Mr Strong?"

"They're theoretical particles – a combination of up, down and strange quarks. Some people think that they're what make up dark matter."

"Correct. But if they are negatively charged and their surface tension is large enough, they have the potential to change whichever nuclei are around them into more strangelets, setting up a chain reaction."

"The Ice-nine type transition." A disaster scenario concocted by the kind of person who spends their days figuring out how the world will end.

"Which, in a matter of seconds, will convert our planet into a large hot lump of strange matter. Oblivion."

"Oh, come on. There's no evidence that strangelets exist, even in neutron stars."

"Not in the public arena. But I am party to information that comes directly from the inner sanctum." He hands me another report. "This is an unofficial document from CERN which confirms that, at these high energies, there is a greater than fifty per cent chance of finding strangelets."

I turn the pages slowly. It's written by Professor Wenton. I saw him speak at a conference last year, on another subject, and three weeks ago I read his obituary in the *Journal of Physics*. He was sixty-four and died of a heart attack. The last paragraph is what catches my eye:

Because of the inherent risk that strangelets pose, and the high likelihood of their production in the forthcoming experiments, the price of proceeding with further collisions at high energy is annihilation. The physicists at CERN must decide whether their loyalties lie in the responsible search for truth or the satisfaction of their curiosity at any cost.

"Where did you get this information?"

"Professor Wenton is no longer a CERN employee."

"I know. He died last month."

"The paper," continues Amos, "and others like it, comes directly from another lead physicist in CERN, who shares Professor Wenton's concerns."

"Well, why doesn't he take it up with the CERN Council?"

"He has done, but I regret that they have not taken his concerns seriously. There is a great deal invested in these experiments, from twenty European member states and others, including USA, the Russian Federation and Japan. No-one wants to see it stopped. Not at this stage. We have had some success in stalling events so far, but, after a recent setback, we need something more concrete."

"So what exactly are you asking me to do?"

Amos pauses and his eyes rest evenly on mine. "I need you to stop the experiments proceeding."

"How do you suggest I do that?"

"By assisting my team in creating a cyberattack on CERN. We need your expertise in identifying a weakness in the system. And we need you to release the final product from inside CERN itself."

"You're asking me to sabotage one of the greatest experiments in scientific history?"

"Do you remember the Challenger disaster, Mr Strong?"

I stare at him. White noise is ringing in my ears.

"On 28th January 1986, the Space Shuttle broke apart seventy-three seconds after lift-off, leading to the death of its seven crew members. It resulted from a failure in an O-ring seal on the right rocket booster. NASA had known about a fundamental flaw in the O-ring since 1977, but did nothing about it and would not listen when engineers warned about launching at the low temperatures on that January morning."

I rest my forehead on clasped hands. I watched the launch on TV when I was a child. I remember the build up, the buzz, the disbelief that ordinary people could be part of something like that. I remember the blaze of blinding white-yellow light on the launch pad, the clouds of steam, the unending roar as it rose into the air and I remember wondering what they were thinking, on board. I was jealous of them, of what they would feel when they looked back at the earth from up there – a beautiful, perfect blue globe drifting against the backdrop of endless space. I wanted to experience what they did. Until the flash of yellow sparks in the stratosphere, the trail of thick, white smoke that split into two and arced downwards, the wrong way. For a moment, no one on the TV said anything – no one could tell if this was part of the plan. And then the horror sank in, slowly, like fallout, burned into my memory.

Amos's voice pulls me from it. "The consequences for the crew of Challenger Space Shuttle were tragic, and it is a small mercy that no one else was harmed. But in our case, if no one listens, the consequences could be cataclysmic. The future of our planet is at stake."

A pounding pulse in my temples punctuates the white noise. "You want me to release a virus through the Grid?"

"We have connections to a Tier One Grid facility, but we are struggling to break through CERN's firewalls. The virus will have to be released from inside CERN. I can arrange temporary employment there, with all the security clearance you would need. My team here at ORB will give you any assistance you require. Clean and simple. No embarrassment, no fuss. This way, everyone wins."

"Everyone wins?" Am I hearing this? "How can you say that they win out of this? It destroys everything they've worked for!"

"But no-one is harmed. Robert – may I call you Robert? – I understand that to you this is like desecrating a temple. But we cannot ignore the genuine concerns of the people who know the facts. It takes great courage to break from one's past and stand alone against the crowd."

"You expect me to buy this on the basis of one man's opinion?"

"No. Indeed, I would be disappointed if you did." He presses the intercom on the desk. "Ms Bishop, would you show Mr Strong to the library?

"Take as much time as you need. There is not a resource in the world that we cannot access, both published and unpublished, but I would suggest CERN's unpublished work is worth exploring."

"Papers are usually unpublished for a reason."

"Like yours?"

DANA LEADS ME through the atrium down another corridor, which branches off to a dozen more. I pause as a soft rumble comes from the right and something flashes at the end of the tunnel. "You have your own train line?"

"It's a big place. So what do you think so far?"

"I'm not convinced."

She raises a slight smile as she pushes open the door marked 'Library'. I haven't been in a library like this before. It's huge, lined with white walls that slope gracefully up to become a domed ceiling. There are spacious desks around the periphery, each with large screens angled like lecterns and padded seats you could fall asleep in.

"Everything is electronic. The stations are touchscreen readers, and can access any professional database you choose for published work."

"Do you have Inspec or SPIRES?"

"As I said, we have links to all of them. You just need to type in your search."

"And what about unpublished work from CERN and other accelerators?"

"It's restricted access – I'll send you the link once you're logged on." She raises an eyebrow. "Will there be anything else?"

"I don't think so. Not at the moment."

She turns and walks away, taking a seat at a large corner desk and taps on a keyboard.

There's only one other man in the library. He's leaning back in one of the seats, reading, slowly dragging his index finger along the bottom of the screen, turning the page. He looks up, watching me as I walk past him, his small eyes dark above his greying beard. He's wearing overalls with his name on the left breast pocket: Abrams.

"Alright?" I say in passing. Abrams doesn't reply, but drops his gaze and touches the screen, then gets up and walks out. I take my place at another seat, underwhelmed by the frosty interaction. The screen's like a giant iPad and easy to use. I search on SPIRES, a good start for mainstream physics papers.

It brings up lots of the usual publications: 'Strangelets and the Quasiparticle Model', 'Effects of Surface Tension on Strangelets in the Quasiparticle Model', 'Magnetised Strangelets and Temperature Changes'... I scan through them, losing track of time. They're still speculation. Nothing concrete, nothing that proves that strangelets are real.

A box appears at the lower right hand corner of the screen. I click on it and find the link to the unpublished work from the accelerators. I open the list from the Relativistic Heavy Ion Collider in the States – the type of particles they collide there makes it more likely that they'll be the first to find any signs of strangelets, so that's a logical place to start. There are more unpublished papers on strangelets, some of which have a three sigma effect – a ninety-nine-point-seven per cent likelihood that what they found is real – but not enough to persuade the scientific community. For that, they need a five sigma effect. But they seemed to be gathering momentum. It's not quite there, but it looks like they were close. Much closer than I'd thought.

I try the CERN link. It brings up not only abstracts and papers, but proposals, initial results and even email correspondence between individuals. There aren't any unpublished papers on strangelets there, but it's not surprising, given the collisions haven't been running that long.

I eye the list of email senders. I don't feel right about it, but then a name catches my eye. Nathanial T. Thorpe. There can't be more than one physicist with that name. When I was a student, he was one of my tutors for a term. He was also interested in strangelets. A tall lean guy with a mop of black hair whose passion, aside from physics, was playing the mandolin. You could usually find him in some backstreet bar diddling away until the small hours in some session or other. He used to say that physics and music were the same thing, all one big vibrational party. A bit of a child of the 'sixties, but I liked him. I also respected him. He knew his stuff more than most. You'd see his name every other month in the journals until a couple of years ago, when he dropped off the radar. I guess that's when he must have moved to CERN. I glance round the room, feeling like I'm breaking in, which I am, and click on his email, searching for strangelets in subject and content. There are a couple of references to the unpublished papers I've already seen, but not much else.

Whoever Amos's advisor is, he must have known more than this. I get up and stretch, then walk over to Abrams' screen and maximise what he was reading, just out of curiosity. A paper on aviation engineering. He left his can of coke on his desk, filthy tramp. I drop it in the small silver bin against the wall.

I wonder…

I go back to my screen and click on Thorpe's trash bin. The first email is a polite rant about a parking permit that hasn't been delivered. The second is a draft to a PhD student who, by the looks of things, hasn't come through with his thesis on time – a gentle ticking off. Thorpe was never one for conflict.

The third makes me sit up.

From: ntthorpe@CERN.ac
To: jjavier@CERN.ac
Sent: 24th Jan, 02.47
Subject: Re
Attachment: strangeletfivesig.doc

Jose,

It's been two weeks since I resubmitted our results, and given what we've found, I would have expected a more timely response. I understand your reluctance to engage with this, but I would urge you to look beyond the immediate implications and consider your position of responsibility to the wider community. I think it's clear we cannot proceed in the light of these findings. As I'm sure you're aware, the RHIC stopped their experiments on the basis of their findings. What we have is far more significant.

I have attached the paper again for your appraisal, and await your response. I would prefer that the Council takes it upon itself to act on the basis of our findings, but you should know that I am willing to

make these results public if I am left with no other choice.
  Regards,
  Nathanial

There's a response.

From: jjavier@CERN.ac
To: ntthorpe@CERN.ac
Sent: 13th Feb, 08.47
Subject: Re

Dear Professor Thorpe,
  Thank you for your resubmission, but I regret to inform you that, while you have some encouraging results, the Council feels that there are still some queries regarding your methodology and as such we cannot endorse the course of action you suggest. If anything, the forthcoming experiments could help to validate your findings. As you know, we undertook a painstaking safety analysis before embarking on this project, and remain persuaded that the collisions are safe. Whilst we cannot comment on the decisions taken regarding other colliders, our collisions will continue as scheduled. I would remind you that, under contract, any work you produce in CERN remains copyright of CERN.
  Sincerely,
  Jose Javier
  Director of CERN Council

I open the attachment and read his paper.

The methodology seems sound. And the results, a five sigma effect.

Holy fuck. Am I missing something?

"WE NEED TO get that paper out there."

"It's too late for that, Robert. Thorpe already tried that, but his colleagues didn't want to listen. The Council didn't want to listen. They'll reach their target energies next week. We don't have time for persuasion."

"Then I need to speak to him."

Amos is sitting behind his desk. "Of course." He reaches out and taps the intercom. "Rachel, get me Professor Nathanial Thorpe's secretary at CERN."

"Of course, sir."

Amos passes me a handset. It rings, a continental tone. After a minute or so, a woman answers, her accent American, with a hint of something Mediterranean. "Professor Thorpe's secretary. May I help you?"

"I'm looking to speak to Professor Thorpe, please."

"Can I take your name please?"

"My name?" I glance at Amos, who nods. "It's Robert Strong."

"Mr Strong, I'm afraid he's not available for the foreseeable future, but I can put you on to Professor Stiller if that would help?"

"No, no that's OK. Where can I find Professor Thorpe? I was one of his students and I need to speak to him about his research."

"Erm..." Her voice tails away, as if she's considering whether she should tell me. "They flew him back to England three days ago, after he became unwell. I think he's still in hospital."

"Hospital? Which one?"

"I'm sorry, I can't give you that information."

"Okay. Thanks for your help." I hang up. "He's here in the UK. In hospital."

"If you still feel you need to speak to him," says Amos, "my staff will find him."

NATHANIAL T. THORPE is in a side room on Ward 3 in the Neurology Unit at The Royal London. Without hesitation, Amos arranged for me to get there and for Dana to go with me. We took a buggy to an exit concealed in a small substation in a field, where a helicopter was waiting. It flew us to the helipad on the roof of the hospital.

"He's in Room Three," says the nurse, who's scribbling in a set of notes. "Third on the right."

"I'll wait here," said Dana.

There's a faint smell of urine in the air and some old woman, just a bag of bones with skin stretched loosely over them, is shouting from the first room, "Help me! Please help me! HELP ME!" over and over and over.

Nathanial T. Thorpe is lying on his bed, glazed in sweat. His eyes are closed and his limbs are twitching; his mop of black hair plastered to his head. Even the muscles in his neck and face seem to be jerking. Christ, do they know he's doing this?

"Nurse?" I stick my head out and call down the corridor, over the old woman's cries for help.

"Is he fitting?"

The nurse drops her pen and hurries towards me. She pauses as she reaches the door. "No, he's not fitting; it's muscle spasms. He's been like this since he got here."

"Muscles spasms? What's wrong with him?"

"Well, the nurse who's looking after him is on her break." She reaches for a piece of paper in her uniform pocket and scans down the scribbled notes. "Mr Thorpe..."

"Can I help you?" says a voice from behind me. Another nurse, tall and Asian, with a soft accent. "He's my patient. Thanks, Ellen." Ellen goes back to writing her notes.

"I'm a friend of Professor Thorpe. We worked together." A loose association with the truth, but I didn't come all the way here to be stonewalled. "What happened to him?"

"They think it's new variant CJD. Creutzfeldt-Jakob disease."

"What does it do to you?"

"It's a disease of the brain tissue, causing dementia and muscle spasms. His case is one of the most progressive we've seen."

"When will he get better?"

"I'm afraid he's not going to get better. There's no cure for CJD."

"What?" I glance back into the room, where he's twitching and moaning like a rabid animal. I wonder if he knows what's going on. Part of me hopes he doesn't.

"Do you think he can hear me?"

"I'd assume that he can, so don't be afraid to talk to him," she says gently, before she leaves me alone with him, closing the door behind her.

I stand there for a moment, staring at the horror of it. He was a brilliant man, and now...

"Nathanial?"

He seems to turn a little towards me, and his eyes open slightly.

"Can you hear me Nathanial? It's Robert Strong... you probably don't remember, but you were one of my tutors."

He tries to speak, but only manages to spill frothy saliva down his chin. He turns away.

The door opens behind me and a wave of perfume suffuses the room. A woman in her late thirties walks in: blonde, slim, striking, dressed in jeans and high-heeled boots, carrying a large black leather handbag.

She stops and stares at me. "Who are you?"

"Eh, I'm, eh... my name's Robert Strong. I used to work with Nathanial, in Cambridge."

"Oh." She closes the door. "He won't remember."

"I'm sorry, I didn't mean to intrude. Are you his...?"

"I'm his wife." She moves over to the empty chair on the other side of the bed, sits down and takes his hand.

I shouldn't be here. "I'm sorry, I'll leave you." I turn and push the handle of the door downwards slowly, then pause. I won't get another chance.

"Can I ask you a question?" I say, turning back.

"Yes?"

"Did he ever mention his work at CERN?"

She holds my gaze. "Sometimes."

"Did he mention anything that he was worried about? Anything to do with the experiments?"

She stares at me. "Did they send you?"

"Who?"

"CERN Council? Did they send you?" She gets to her feet, and I can feel the edge of aggression in the room.

"No! No, I... I came across something Nathanial was working on. That's why I came here, to talk to him. I think he was on to something."

Her eyes slide over me, as if she's considering where I

stand. "He was," she says. "But they wouldn't listen."
She glances down at him.

"Did he believe they produced strangelets in the
experiments?"

She nods. "He couldn't tell me much about it, but
he wanted them to stop." She shakes her head and
strokes the hair away from his eyes. "He didn't sleep
for months, he hardly ate. It scared me before, but now
this has happened…"

I stare at them, the pretty blonde woman and her ghost
of a husband. It's not the answer I was looking for; it's
not an answer at all – just one unpublished paper from
a man with dementia, and his wife's testimony – but I
feel the tide beginning to turn.

AMOS IS STUDYING a shoal of fish on the projection
when I get back, watching the flecks of sapphire and
ultramarine drift and flicker.

He turns to me. "Did he speak to you?"

"He's got CJD. He can't give me anything."

"So where does that leave us, Mr Strong?"

"Look, I admit that his paper looks solid. If he's right,
then CERN's in a lot of trouble."

"If he's right, and I believe he is, we're *all* in a lot of
trouble."

I stare at the blue glow on the wall, the artificial
tranquillity. How the hell did I get myself into all this?
If Amos is wrong, I'll go down in history as the second
Judas, and no amount of money will make up for that.
How I felt when they shut down SightLabs – betrayal,
injustice, bitterness – it still burns inside me. Years of
work swept aside in one morning. Can I really do that

to them? They must have people at CERN who've looked at this, who've weighed it all up. They can't be foolhardy enough not to take it seriously. But Thorpe's paper, and everything his wife said, and what they were beginning to find at the American collider...

"I'm not a hacker, Mr Amos. That's not what I do."

"But you know the software system through your work with the Grid. I need you to identify a weakness, that's all. Our ethical hackers and programmers will take care of the rest." He walks over to his desk, sits down and gathers together a few papers.

"Look, I admit that some of the work produced in the States is persuasive, and if they're accurate, so are Thorpe's findings; but if he was your mole in CERN, who's to say he wasn't biased?"

Amos stops arranging his papers and looks up. "Nathanial Thorpe wasn't our mole."

"You mean you still have someone there, in CERN?"

"Oh, yes."

"Then why don't you get him to do your dirty work?"

Amos shakes his head. "He is an eminent physicist with a deep loyalty to CERN, borne of the many years he has invested in it. He has shown great strength of character to bring this information to light, but he does not have the computing skills for this task."

"And I do."

"And you do."

So, not just Wenton and Thorpe. Someone else believes this too. A shoal of tiny, ultraviolet fish drifts along the wall. Shimmering simplicity. I glance back at Amos, who sits calmly, watching me.

"I'm not the man you want for this."

"Robert, I believe you are."

I walk towards him. "No, I'm not cut out for espionage. I know that Thorpe thought he was onto something, and maybe he was, but I think the people in CERN know what they're doing." I lean towards Amos, my hands resting on the desk. "Tell me this. Why should I trust that your mole knows any more than they do?"

Those eyes, clear and still, study my face for a long moment before he answers. "Because, Robert, our mole is your father."

The silence rushes at me as the world shifts. Memories mug my attention, flashing a mishmash of images. The only ones I have of him. I'm on a blue climbing frame, I glance behind me to see my dad standing there, I stretch a hand to grasp the metal strut above, my foot slips from under me, I feel a rush of panic but he's there, gripping my chest, lifting me gently to the ground. Then I'm lying on my front on the floor next to him, building a spaceship out of Lego. He's reading me a story, and the sound of his voice is all that's safe. I'm safe. I try to keep my eyes open under the warmth and comfort of a blanket, waiting for the end of the story that never comes. Men in flat caps shovel earth onto his coffin, soft thuds on wood.

"My father died when I was three."

"Sit down, Robert," says Amos. He watches as I sink slowly into the chair before he continues. "Your father, Elliot Strong, was one of the leading men in physics in our country. Thirty years ago, he became involved in a highly sensitive government project, the ethics of which became increasingly difficult for him to accept. ORB had been observing this project for some time and was aware of, and supported, your father's concerns. We helped him distance himself from the programme."

"If he's still alive, why hasn't he contacted me?"

"The nature of the project made that too risky."

Is he lying? I search his face for any tiny inflection that might betray him, any shift of his gaze that suggests hesitation, but there is none. He looks back at me, still, certain. Perhaps even compassionate.

He opens a file and pulls out two photographs. The first one makes me freeze. It's a copy of the picture I've kept in my drawer, taken in Cambridge on his graduation day. I slide it behind the second. It is a close-up of a man who looks like my dad, older, greyer, thinner with deeper lines around his eyes – but the same eyes, grey-blue, behind a pair of small, round specs, the same oval-shaped face. Oh, Jesus. It's him. I hear the rushing of blood in my ears. I'm trembling.

Amos's voice sounds like it comes from a great distance. "Your father sacrificed his identity to ensure your safety. And despite what that did to him, he carried on contributing to the greater good through his work in quantum physics. Yet with all of his loyalties to his field, he still has the courage to voice his true concerns. If he's right, he knows he will be at the epicentre of the consequences, but his loyalties will not let him leave." He lifts the photograph gently from my limp grip, and stares at it for a moment. "I have the greatest respect for him and I trust his judgement. If you had had a chance to know him, I'm sure you would too." He raises his eyes to meet mine. "Perhaps, now, you can find out for yourself."

He's alive. And he believes Amos.

The tide turns.

"I'll do it."

Chapter Seven

"YOU MADE THE right decision," says Dana as we walk away from Amos's office.

I say nothing.

"I'm glad to have you on the project. Let's get started, shall we?"

"Where are we going?"

"D Sector." She climbs into a buggy and I follow.

"Do you have a map of this place?"

"You won't need it. You'll be accompanied offsite, when you go. You'll only need to find your way from the Project Hub to the living quarters. Other Sectors are off-limits. Understand?"

"Living quarters? How long am I going to be here?"

"I need your assessment in the next forty-eight hours – the collisions begin next week. There's no time to go home."

We disembark outside a glass partition leading to a corridor marked 'Subsector 4' and she taps keys on a small wall-mounted keypad. "We need a retinal scan for security. Hold your eye level with the screen."

The screen is four inches square and sends a flickering layer of yellow light over the surface of my eye. It beeps its approval and the door slides open.

At the end of the corridor is the Hub; a circular room with eight consoles stationed around it, three black podiums in the centre and an umbrella plant against the wall.

Dana introduces me to the computer operators. I don't retain their names. "We have people working on network enumeration, gathering information about the CERN systems." She walks over to the central podium, which reaches level with her hips, and presses her right hand on the black glass. It hums and spills out a cone of light fragments which coalesce into a hologram: a valley, dotted with concrete buildings, surrounded by hills.

"This is the CERN site in Switzerland. Twenty-seven kilometres of the collider crossing the Franco-Swiss border, buried one hundred meters underground." She reaches her hands into the image and opens them, like she's parting the air in front of her. The fields and buildings stretch towards us, honing in on a large rectangular building.

"Touch sensitive holography?"

She nods and spreads the air under her hands again, until the image becomes an underground chasm the size of a cathedral. Men in hard hats and safety suits are working in the chasm, some of them on a crane that reaches up to a huge flanged metal tunnel.

"ATLAS," I say.

"You need to familiarise yourself with the physical layout of the site, but you're job will be focused on vulnerability analysis of the programs running the accelerator and ATLAS detector. You can access any files you need on your console."

I take a seat at the unmanned station, feeling numb. "We'll arrange exploitation once you come up with a way forward." Dana leans in towards me. "For this to work, we need the solution to be subtle, untraceable and permanent."

She straightens up and pulls out another health fag. "If you need anything, let me know. Lambert will keep you right on any technical issues. I'll leave you to it."

"Luke Lambert." The young guy sitting next to me extends a hand. His accent is American and he looks fresh out of college. Blond hair sweeps across his forehead so that I can't see his right eye, and he has a bad dose of acne.

I shake his hand. "What do you do, Luke?"

"I'm working on privilege escalation, to allow us to release the malware through the Grid. But we all do a bit of everything – encryption breaking, analysis, looking out for security holes we can use."

"Which site are you using for Grid access?"

"We have a route into the University of Surrey. Jo Trench over in C section is managing that."

"So why do you need me to release the malware from inside CERN?"

"Surrey's a user account. We're working on upgrading it to superuser access, but Dana thinks we won't crack it in time."

"What do you think?"

"It's a headache, alright, but we'll get it. Now that you're here, we can concentrate on figuring out which part of the system to break. We've been analysing the software that triggers the hydrogen release into the source chamber, but so far we've drawn a blank." He grins. "But I love a challenge."

I turn to my console. "They're using Scientific Linux 6?"

"Yeah."

"Is that what you use here?"

"No. We use Linux 6. You want a coffee? You've got a lot to read through."

"Yeah, thanks." I stare after him as he leaves the Hub and wonder if this is a game to him.

I create a password for the console and pull up the data. Luke returns with two coffees and a cup of water. He waters the plant and brushes some soil off its leaves.

"Thanks. How long have you been here?"

"Eighteen months. Bishop found me in my final year at Harvard. It was too good an opportunity to miss. Who needs a bit of paper when they give you an offer like this one?"

"Do you have any doubts about what we're doing here?"

"Listen, man, ORB doesn't make mistakes. I've been here long enough to know that they get their facts straight. So when they say there's a real threat from the LHC, you'd better believe there is one. Don't sweat it. You're doing the right thing."

I turn back to the console, and swallow the sick feeling in my throat. Nothing is certain, not even death. My dad, Elliot Strong, is testament to that.

FIVE EMPTY CUPS sit on my desk and I've missed two meals so far. I'm not hungry. Bishop has been back four times and I've nothing to tell her. I wonder how he would do it. How would he find the loophole? I imagine, for a moment, what it would be like to have him here, working it out together. Father and son. A shared purpose, healing all those years of absence. It could be almost as though he never left.

"Come on, man, take a break." Luke places another mug and a packet of sandwiches on the desk.

"There's no way. Everything's watertight," I say without looking up.

"If you'd spent millions of pounds and years of work developing something like this, damn sure you'd make it watertight. But there's always a way."

I sit back and press my eyes. There's a dull pressure inside them, like they've become too big for their sockets. "There's got to be something simpler."

"We considered another magnet quench," says Luke, taking a bite from his bagel.

"That won't do it. Quenches are fairly routine in accelerators. They'd be onto it in no time."

"That's what we thought."

"What's your progress, gentlemen?" Dana Bishop strides into the Hub.

"Not much."

She walks towards me. Her voice is soft. "You know what's at stake here. We need you to deliver."

"The man's fragged, Dana. It's ten-thirty. He needs a break. Let him watch some TV or something."

Dana frowns at Luke as he takes a swig of Coke. "Alright. Get some rest. Come back when you're fresh."

"She's a bitch when she's stressed," says Luke after Dana leaves. He gets to his feet. "Come on. You need some sleep."

MY ROOM IS clean and functional, but airless. There aren't any windows. What did I expect in a bunker? It has light walls and light sheets on the bed. A large flat screen hangs on the far wall and displays a succession of pictures which fade from one to the other – deserted beaches and palm trees, high green mountains, waterfalls with accompanying sounds of birdsong and water babbling over rocks. Mind-soothing crap. It doesn't make up for the fact that there aren't any windows. I push a button on the black box lying on the bed and the pictures vanish, leaving me staring at a blank screen. Fumbling inside my rucksack, I pull out my phone charger. No windows, but plenty of wall sockets, at least. I plug in the phone and it pings its appreciation. I lie back on the bed and look up at the ceiling.

What the hell am I doing?

I try to push the thought from my mind.

SOME TIME LATER, I wake with my face crumpled against the pillow, drooling. I sit up through a thick fog of fatigue and balance on the edge of a bed for a moment as the surroundings filter back to me. That's right. Inside a room in a bunker. I pick up my phone and it reads two-thirty-three am. I lie down again and close my eyes until the thoughts start. What if I can't find a weakness in time? What then?

Fuck it. I get up and stumble to the bathroom, run the cold tap and splash icy water on my face, then dry it with a fluffy white towel. Better. I pick up the phone again and walk around the room, holding it at various angles to try to find a signal, to listen to Cora's message. Nothing. With all this technology, you'd think they'd have access to a bloody mobile signal. My head's too busy to go back to bed, so I get dressed.

I open the door, stepping into the deserted corridor,

but something makes me freeze. I stand there, knowing that I don't want to turn round, but not knowing why. Slowly, I force myself to respond.

To my right, at the end of the corridor, is a woman. Lean, fair hair flowing to her shoulders, loose white clothes and no shoes. Sarah.

Jesus Christ, am I still asleep?

I stare at her and she stares back, before turning and walking away, glancing back once as if I should be following.

She leads me out of the accommodation block to the far end of D Sector, turning into a deserted corridor. I follow. She's waiting by a partition marked AREA 9 RESTRICTED, her hand resting on the glass. It slides open. I stand there for a moment, blinking. I must be dreaming this.

I follow. The corridor stretches out in front of me, dark grey walls dimly lit by sickly yellow light panels in the ceiling. She moves towards a thick metal door near the end of the corridor. I've only taken a few steps when something makes me freeze. What is that?

Something like the rustle of leaves in an autumn breeze. I creep forward and the sound evolves. Whispers. I pause again and they die away. Another step, and they return. Sarah glances back, then turns and walks through the door. There's a chill in the air that makes the hairs on my scalp prickle. I move towards the door as the whispers crescendo. A sudden *clang* makes me jump. The handle of the door swings downwards. A gust of cool, blue mist sprays from the seams of the door as it swings open, and the whispers swell. I back away, but not before I catch a glimpse of what's inside. Something is swirling inside a huge cylindrical tank: a pillar of grey mist, spinning slowly on its axis. What the hell is... A shadow obscures the view. A man in scrubs and a facemask stops in front of me. He pulls the mask down as the door closes behind him. Frowning, his face ashen above his grey beard. "What the hell are you doing here?" he barks.

"I'm sorry," I say, backing down the corridor. "I was..." I hold up the phone. "I'm looking for a signal."

His eyes flash and the remaining colour drains from his chalky face. "Can't you read? This area's restricted!"

"Did you see a woman down here? Blonde, slim?"

He takes a step towards me. "Did you hear me? Get out!"

"Okay. Okay." I turn, my pace quickening. I punch the release button and the partition slides open. I don't stop until I reach my room.

I DON'T KNOW if I slept again, or if I never woke up in the first place, but when I get to the Hub at seven, I have a headache. Dana is studying the hologram, arms folded, her right thumb twitching on the end of a health fag. I consider asking her if they have a doctor I can see, to give me some of those stress pills I should have taken. Maybe later.

"Morning, Robert," she says. "Let's see if we can wrap this up today."

Luke catches my eye.

I settle into my seat and begin again.

WHEN SHE COMES back at midday, I'm holding my forehead with my fingertips. "What have you got, Robert?"

146

I don't look up. "Nothing yet."

She sighs. "This whole project is riding on you, you know that? We need something."

I get to my feet. "Yeah? Well maybe you should find someone else. I'm telling you I can't find a weakness. The systems are too tight."

"Someone else?" The pitch of her voice is rising. "The clock's ticking, Robert. Who the hell else are we going to find at this stage?" She tosses her fag in the bin and storms out. "I need a real fucking cigarette."

Lambert blows air out from his cheeks. "You made her drop a bitch bomb. Come on. Let's get some food."

"So what other projects go on here?" I ask, as we stand in the queue in D Sector canteen.

Luke refills his coffee mug and shovels some chips onto his plate. "I know they do some development work. Vaccinations and shit. They only tell us what we need to know."

"Do you know what they're working on in the restricted area?"

He laughs. "Which one? Most of this place is restricted."

"Area 9."

"No idea."

My head still hurts. "What if we can't do this, Luke? What if we can't stop the launch?"

He looks suddenly older. "That's not an option, man. Not with this."

Behind the counter there's a persistent beeping, the alarm from a fridge door that's been left open too long. The chubby chef waddles over and kicks it shut, silencing the beeps. The embryo of an idea flickers somewhere in that scene.

Luke's watching me. "What is it?" he says.

I blink, then grasp the coffee cup from his hand. "Come with me."

"What have you got?" he says as we get back to the Hub.

"Have you looked at the safety systems?"

"Which one? What are you thinking?"

"We need to change tack. The firewalls for the launch software are too tight. A quench on its own won't be enough, but what if we combined it with malware that disabled the Quench Protection System?"

Lambert smiles at his console as Dana appears at the door. "Do you have something?" she asks.

"The launch software is too well protected – we're just wasting time," I say. "The accelerator runs on superconducting magnets, cooled to cryogenic temperatures. The wires are tiny filaments, sensitive to any changes in current and temperature, and they're surrounded by liquid helium. If we change the operating temperatures or current, the wires will fracture and dump the liquid helium into the chamber.

Dana frowns. "We've already discussed this one, Lambert. You said they were prepared for a quench."

"Not if we alter the safety parameters in the Quench Protection System," I say. "They won't notice there's a problem until the structural damage has been done. Quenches are commonplace, but widespread structural damage from multiple simultaneous quenches means rebuilding most of it."

Dana Bishop smiles. "Come with me."

*   *   *

SHE OPENS A security partition in a quiet corridor of A Sector and leads me to the last door. She turns to me before we enter. "He can be a little weird. Don't take it personally."

Inside is a large room. The hum of extractor fans comes from the ceiling between white neon panels. Two large white semicircular desks take up most of the space, lined with banks of computer consoles. Inside the circle sits a man in a black baseball cap.

He doesn't look up from his console. Dana taps him on the shoulder and he spins round slowly on his swivel chair, pulling the earphones from his ears. He stares up at her through small round shades, his head inclined to one side, unsmiling. He has a matching omega sign on his black baseball cap and tee shirt, sallow skin and dark hair. Beside him is a fruit bowl piled high with cola bottle sweets.

"Robert, this is Mr Y. Mr Y is one of the most gifted programmers on the planet. If you tell him your idea, he'll find a way to make it happen."

Mr Y studies me, bouncing gently as he leans back on his chair, and reaches for the bowl of cola bottles. He pushes a handful into his mouth.

"Robert has identified a potential weakness in the CERN system." Mr Y doesn't look at her as she speaks, but just sits there, watching me, chewing. "I'll leave you two to chat." I hear the swish of the door closing.

Mr Y takes a deep breath and leans over to pull another chair from the semicircular desk opposite. He gestures for me to sit down.

"So, eh…"

He raises a finger, silencing me, then turns and taps on the keys of his computer, breaking only to grasp another handful of sweets. The software I'd been examining downstairs appears on the screen.

He turns to me. "So what's your plan?" His voice is soft, an American accent with a hint of something far-eastern.

"I need a two-layered virus that will alter the parameters of the superconductor and silence the Quench Protection System alarm."

"A man-in-the-middle attack. Are you sure it's a virus you want?"

"I need something that attaches itself to an existing program. Something that will evade detection once it's in there."

"We can do that with a good worm. A rootkit, periodically moving and changing its name to avoid detection. What's your trigger?"

"The launch of the particles from the source chamber."

He nods. "Where do you plan to release your worm?"

My worm? I shift uncomfortably in my seat.

"The Operator's Room in the Computer Centre."

He turns back to the screen, scrolling through data.

"Linux 6 Scientific and YUM. And you want in to the Quench Protection System..." He studies the screen, chewing on more cola sweets. I scan the room. There's a life-size standee of a busty, scantily-clad woman next to a wall-mounted digital display showing time zones across the globe. My foot catches against something under the desk, and I glance down to see a large clear tank. Something is sliding across the bottom, a slither of gold and black. A snake. I stare at Mr Y. Weird doesn't come close.

"What's the cut-off temperature for the magnets?"

"Nine point six degrees Kelvin, maximum."

"And the current?"

"Two thousand amps."

He continues to study the screen. After a long silence, he sits back. "I'll get you your worm. You'll have admin access from the Operator's room, but you'll need five to seven minutes there to upload the file. Have you thought of a name for your worm?"

It's not my worm. "No."

"You need a name."

"Why?"

"Because it's cool to name your worm." I want to laugh, but he says it seriously, almost reverently.

His gaze wanders to the ceiling as he chews on another handful of sweets. "How about... Kali."

"Kali?"

"The Hindu Goddess. It means she who destroys."

"Oh."

He turns back to the screen.

"What's the hardware for carrying it?" I ask.

He holds up a USB flash drive without looking at me.

"That's it?"

"D'you know the US Department of Defence banned the use of these little numbers because malware was spreading like the common cold? We did a lot of damage with them. It doesn't look like much, but it can spoil your day. Enough to wipe out an entire databank." He punches in a code on a small number pad on the desk, and the drawer to his right clicks and slides open. It's stacked with upright USB drives in foam bases. Next to each drive is a small label with a code in black typeface. "There's more destructive power in this drawer than there is in the entire US air force."

"Did you create all of these?"

He smiles.

"Wow. You must have made a few waves in your time."

He nods, looking smug, and picks through the drives, handling each one like it's made of thin glass.

"This one, for instance..." He picks up a stick from the third row. "This one shut down the International Monetary Fund for thirty-six hours. And this one... this one wiped out the software of a leading Canadian bank, just with an email. They had to replace the entire mainframe – the whole lot. It took them thirteen months to get back on their feet. It's a one-way ticket." He shakes his head. "Masterstroke."

"What language do you use for the programs?"

"C and C ++." He holds up the Canadian crippler. "This one's a generic program – you could use it against any system operating on Linux 6."

Like here? I think, but I don't say it.

He replaces it in its slot in the top right corner of the foam base and slides the drawer in. It beeps and locks with a click.

"So is this what ORB does? Shut down banks and the IMF?"

"Those were my endeavours. Nothing to do with ORB."

"Right." It makes me feel a bit better. I realise that I'm talking to someone who has operated in high-end digital crime, but we're here for the greater good – I have to keep telling myself that.

I pause while he empties another packet of cola bottles into the fruit bowl, then ask, "What about the security cameras?"

"Not a problem. When you work out how you're going to do it, email your contact. I'll tap into the cameras in the Computer Centre over the next couple of days and record some of the shifts – your contact can overlay it onto the security recordings when you make an appearance. They won't see a thing. Anything else?"

"I don't think so."

"Fine. They'll be growing mushrooms on the CERN site in a couple of years."

He leans down and opens a mini fridge under the desk, pulling out something grey and furry. I retreat back into my chair as he opens the lid of the tank and drops the dead rat inside. There's a rustle and a slither as the snake unhinges its jaws and engulfs the rodent. Mr Y watches my reaction.

"His name's Reggie," he says.

"Oh."

"Do you like snakes?"

"Never given it much thought." *Of course I don't like snakes, you fucking weirdo.*

Mr Y grins for the first time, revealing rotting teeth, the product of too many sweets. He picks up the phone on his desk and dials. "I've finished with him. You can take him away."

As THE PARTITION slides closed behind us, Dana glances at her watch and lifts her phone to her ear. "Carson, when's the last departure tonight?" A pause. "Okay. Let the pilot know to be ready in ten minutes. And bring Mr Strong's rucksack to the atrium." She turns to me. "I think you'll make the last flight."

"What do you mean?"

"Our aircraft will take you to Heathrow airport, where you can board your flight for Geneva."

"What, tonight?"

"You need to become established in the CERN community as soon as possible. The last of the tests are being conducted over the next six days, and we need you in there for as many of them as possible, starting tomorrow morning. We've arranged all the paperwork. They'll be expecting you."

"But I don't have my passport –"

"Like I said: it's all taken care of."

WHEN WE REACH the atrium, a woman at the desk hands me a large brown envelope. "You'll find your tickets and everything else you need inside," says Dana.

A man walks briskly towards us as she ushers me onto a buggy. He hands over my rucksack as the buggy pulls away.

THE SKY IS overcast and there's a cold drizzle on the air, when the substation doors open onto the field. The cab door is pulled back and the pilot's checking the overhead controls in the cockpit. Outside, an engineer is tinkering with the engine. I climb into the cabin.

"We'll forward the final product to you within twenty-four hours," says Dana. "We'll be in touch with further instructions. You did a good job, Robert. Thank you." She smiles and looks beautiful.

"It's clamped out over the whole country," the pilot says to her. "There's no IFR option, so we'll go down the east coast and refuel at Newcastle. I'll do what I can, but we may be pushing it for your flight. "

There's a thud as the engine compartment closes and the engineer steps back from the aircraft. I recognise him – Abrams – the guy from the library. He wipes a rag over a spanner and glances up at me as the engine whirs into life. Dana swings the cab door closed, then backs away as the blades begin to spin, blowing her dark hair across her face. The pilot turns to me, handing me a set of headphones. When I put them on, I hear his voice. "Switch off your mobile phone, Mr Strong."

As I reach into my pocket for my phone, something falls onto the floor of the aircraft beside me. I pick it up: the photograph Banks dropped yesterday; the woman with the dangerous eyes.

"Can you get this to Peter Banks when you get back?"

"Hold onto it until we touch down," says the pilot. "We need to keep ahead of the weather. There's a cold front coming in from the west and this cab doesn't have icing clearance."

I look out over the darkening clouds as I push the photograph back into my pocket. "Is it safe to fly?"

He turns and grins. "As safe as it's going to get today."

The helicopter lifts and banks into the cloud.

What am I doing?

I close my eyes and try to sleep the thought away, concentrating on the purr of the engine, the *thub-thub* of the blades. I drift in and out, uneasy dreams coming and going.

A SUDDEN JOLT jars me awake. I grip the seat to steady myself. "What the hell..."

"Make sure you're strapped in," comes the pilot's voice. "Things could get a little bumpy."

Another violent lurch thrusts me forwards, locking me against the harness as an alarm sounds from the cockpit.

"Shit!" comes the pilot's voice over the headset.

I grip the straps of my harness as the helicopter plummets, amidst a high-pitched whine.

"*MAYDAY! MAYDAY! MAYDAY! Alpha-whisky-two-one smoke in the cockpit forced landing position two miles east of Crail...*"

Is this really happening? The scream of the engine ringing in my ears, the stench of smoke, the harness squeezing my chest like a vice; all of it beyond my control.

"*BRACE! BRACE! BRACE!*"

I squeeze my eyes shut, gripping the shoulder straps like a lifeline, something swelling in the pit of my gut.

Impact. A meteorite striking granite, it rocks my core, every fibre bouncing with the force, which rips the air into pieces with the deafening screech of breaking metal. My head smacks the headrest, the lights go out. Water, flooding in as cold as ice... seeping up onto my shins, my thighs, my torso. My breaths are shards of glass in my chest. My fingers, numb and useless in the frozen water, fumbling at the buckle that's pressing into me. Water's rising to my neck, I'm panting like a dog, shivering, dizzy with it. I'm grappling with the catch, another lurch, forcing my head into the liquid tomb, enveloping me in watery sounds. I seize a last breath, and go under.

Groaning in the darkness, scraping and screeching – a tortured whale-song, consuming me. I'm falling into cold black... *Open the fucking harness!* The catch bursts loose. I'm fumbling in the dark... what way's up? A door... a handle. I yank at it as my lungs scream for air... *must breathe*... a tearing pain in my chest. My head pounding like it will explode... *Air... please...* my heart's splitting; it's going to burst... *air...*

Fear erupts in me – deep, visceral, wild fear. It's happening all over again – it's all coming back to me. I'm not ready, not yet.

The door glides away from me into the black. I push through the threshold and then...

...and then...

Peace.

I am still.

I float gently in the current, the urge to struggle gone, the pain, a distant memory.

I become the water, the waves, the tide, part of it all. Such stillness, such peace.

I'd forgotten.

There's light, a gentle radiance, flooding me with all the peace that ever was. It's brightening. A blizzard of silent light.

It makes sense now.

There is nothing to fear.

Chapter Eight

I FEEL AS though I'm being washed clean and all that's bad is flooding away and in its place there is warmth and refuge. My senses come alive and every particle in my body seems perfectly tuned, vibrating in unison with everything. I'm energised and alive and radiant, like nothing I've ever experienced.

The world falls away. Suspended amongst the galaxies and the gas clouds and the suns, I watch as the cosmos creates and destroys itself in its timeless cycle of birth and death. Red giants folding in on themselves, great seething furnaces of gold and crimson in their last fervent gasps. Cataclysmic explosions, scattering white light and energy and the elements of life into the darkest corners of the universe – new beginnings. Space isn't black. It's not silent or empty or cold or unchanging. It's dynamic, full of violence and turmoil and evolution, an animal continually struggling to shed its old skin to make way for the new creature inside. There's something else, between all those suns – a radiant, billowing web of myriad colour. And I'm part of it, part of that unspeakable majesty, just as it is part of me. And then, for a moment as brief as it is eternal, I know everything there is to know.

I meet myself at last.

I HAD A dream about death. It wasn't a bad dream, and, like all dreams, it made sense at the time.

There is no judgement. There is no fear, or suspicion, or criticism, because how can you feel these things towards something else when you and the other are the same thing? When you are the same thing you're part of a greater whole and you see that the 'I' that you knew before was only an illusion, a vehicle of life and consciousness. All the things that once concerned the 'I' no longer matter, because they're all just experiences. It's something beyond pain and suffering, and hardship and cruelty, it's beyond happiness and excitement and pleasure. There are no words to describe it, because it simply is all that is. But it's a wonderful thing to know you are a part of it, this ultimate communion.

We share that moment of understanding, like old friends who have long since said all that needs to be said and are comfortable with the silence between them.

SOMETHING GRASPS MY shoulder, powerful, insistent.

Leave me. Let me stay.

But it won't let go, it's wresting with me, dragging me up from the depths of my peace. I feel the stillness, that perfect emptiness, flooding from me, and the snowstorm of light goes out.

I am standing on a pebbled shore. Don't ask me how I got here, or where it is. In the distance the searchlights from the rescue boats scour the unsettled, murky waters. Heavy clouds unravel from the west and the low sun illuminates their underbellies with an eerie, orange glow. The restless gulls call and swoop in the last of the light. I turn to see a small crowd nearby, people I don't know. Standing in their waterproof jackets, hoods up, huddled around something on the shore, watching in silence. I move in to look. A man with a bushy beard and red cheeks is kneeling over a body, pumping the chest with a firm, steady rhythm. He looks up and says, "How long?"

"They say less than ten minutes," says a middle-aged woman at the edge of the crowd.

I inch closer, peering at the body.

My muscles seize as the world rushes at me in that single, nauseating vision. I stumble backwards, my legs losing their footing on the pebbles, and I hear my own voice whispering, "No, no, no..." I shake my head. My breaths come in spasms, but make no mark on the cold, coastal air.

"Robert," says a voice from behind, "it is you, lad."

I spin round. "Casimir? What the fuck!" I back away from the old man. He's standing in front of me, looking at me. He's *looking* at me. "What is this?"

Casimir watches me with a level gaze, but says nothing. I squeeze my eyes shut and when I look up again the ridiculous vision is still there. Casimir, the man I lowered into the ground only a few days ago, standing calmly before me, and the crowd huddled around the cold, pale body. I hold onto my stomach, certain that I'm going to be sick. My breaths come in slow, deep waves from the pit of my gut.

The man who's pummelling the body's chest spits through gritted teeth, "Come on!" The crowd stares on, whispering amongst themselves. I edge closer, I have to be certain.

My own face, cold and sunken and the colour of death. The lips light blue, the eyes half open and glazed with a light mist.

I collapse to my hands and knees, and retch.

I feel a hand on my shoulder. "I'm sorry, Robert," says Casimir. "It's up to you. You can hold on, or you can let go. It's up to you."

I look up at him. "I don't understand. What's happening?" I stagger to my feet, the world swaying beneath me.

"Your lifeline." He nods towards my right hand. "It's your choice."

I feel something on my palm and I stare as the thing takes form. A fine silvery cord, pulsing and fading, pulsing and fading. It feels like silk in my hand. My eyes follow it, to the corpse lying on the stones, to the middle of its chest. My fingers close round it.

"What happens if I let go?"

"You already know."

It comes back to me. That feeling I had in the dream about death. Nothing comes close. I didn't want to lose it; I resented that I did. But what if it isn't like that? What if it's not alright? What the hell do I know about this? I used to think I knew. I used to speak about it with conviction, like it wasn't something to worry about. Maybe I even thought that it wouldn't really happen, not to me. Now I know the truth: I don't know anything.

My grip on the cord makes my nails dig into my palm.

"I can't do it," I whisper. My whole body's trembling. "I can't do it."

Images flash in my mind: all those things I haven't done, I haven't even begun. Cora. The stone in my chest swells and shatters as my life with her slides out of reach. It's so clear to me now, what matters most and what doesn't. Why couldn't I see it before? How many opportunities did I squander because I always thought there would be more time? But there's no time. There's no more time. Not a minute of it now.

My fist closes around the thread. I'm not giving up, I can't give up... this is insane...

"And if I hold on?"

"Then you go back."

I look down at the sweaty red-faced man whose locked fists continue to pump my chest.

The lifeline tugs at my hand, yearning to break free.

So this is it.

I'm standing at the edge of the Big Secret. We've seen what lies beyond the solar system, we've conquered illness, we've split the atom. But death? It's a dark, uncharted land that lies foreboding in the distance, until the day it comes to you. All the certainty of a lifetime fades away when it comes to your door, because it is a visitor that will not leave.

The waves rush in and reach to take back the pebbles on the shore, as the amber dusk takes back the daylight. Everything ends. That's just the way of things.

But I'm not ready.

Not yet.

I turn to Casimir. "I've more to do."

He studies me for a moment, a smile settling on his lips. "If that's what you choose."

* * *

I HAD A dream about death.

It disentangles itself from my mind as I begin to stir, and I have that feeling that you get when you try to hold onto a dream, because something in it made sense, something you don't want to lose. But already it's fading. Bits of it come back, like the echo of a memory. Casimir was there. The rest, I think I've forgotten.

I knew someone who told me once that his best mate died of leukaemia. They were both into karate and used to spar in the dojo every Tuesday night. One night, this guy, Gerry, had a dream that they were sparring away and his best mate, the one with leukaemia, said to him in his dream, "Thanks for coming to see me when I was in hospital. It meant a lot to me." And they carried on sparring. Then the phone rang and woke Gerry from his sleep. It was the call to say that his friend had just died. Nice story, I said to Gerry. You've gone soft in the head, I thought.

What else was in this dream of mine? Something about a silver thread, letting go. Something about unity, oneness.

Oneness? For Christ's sake, Robert.

MY CHEST CAVES in over and over, like I'm being punched repeatedly on the same fresh bruise. A fierce sense of suffocation grips me – I try to breathe but no air shifts into my lungs and the pain is so intense it feels like my chest is being ripped open from the inside. Death hovers nearby, holding its breath.

Fuck you, Death.

I gasp air into my lungs, like a first breath, and it makes me cough so violently that I spit out a plug of mucus and vomit, my head swimming in a sea of nausea, the world a blur.

But I'm breathing, I'm breathing.

I'm alive.

THERE'S AN IRRITATING beep. There's the stench of plastic and something on my face, digging into my right ear and the bridge of my nose. I can hear my own breathing, like I'm in a tunnel.

Did you hear me? Turn the beep off.

I open my eyes, but it's all a blur. Two blurs, to be exact, one standing on either side of me, looking down.

"They dragged him out of the sea." A woman's voice. Young. "He had no output on scene. Some local gave him CPR and got him back. He was GCS 9 on arrival, temp thirty-two, saturations maintained at ninety-five on twenty-eight per cent oxygen. Pan CT was normal. He doesn't seem to have any focal neurology, at the moment."

Hey! Get off! A finger in my eyes, forcing my eyelids open. The blur on the right leans closer and is obliterated by a white light that slices into my brain. *Turn that light out, you bastard!*

"Any signs of aspiration?" A man's voice, ignoring me completely.

Excuse me? Did you hear me?

"No, chest is clear. He must have had laryngospasm – he's lucky..."

TURN THAT LIGHT OUT!

The light goes out.

"Any family?"

"Not with him."

The thing on my face pushes closer, digging into my cheeks, pinning me down. An alien thing attached to me... stopping me breathing... Oh, God, I'll wake up and have one of them inside me, ready to burst out. *How can you just stand there and watch this?* I reach for the alien, pulling it from my face, but its tentacles grip my cheeks and it squeezes itself back on.

"Calm down, Robert, it's alright."

Calm down? It's alright? What part of this is alright? There's a plastic alien on my face! Whose side are you on?

I struggle against the fist gripping my arm.

"He's already pulled one line out."

"I'd keep him sedated for now."

The blurs begin to fade and the will to fight washes away from me in a tide of indifference.

I WAKE UP to the scent of Dettol and alcohol wipes, the stench of artificial cleanliness. The room is white and yellow, optimistic. White walls, yellow curtains, looking onto hills and a lake. A white wooden bedside cabinet sits to my left with a tall bulbous blue glass on top, next to a blue ceramic jug. A phone and two remote controllers sit on the cabinet. There's a single white orchid in a slim white pot on the window sill. I can't tell if it's real or fake. If it weren't for the observation chart hanging by a hook beneath the windowsill, I wouldn't have said this was a hospital.

"It's good to see you awake, Mr Strong." I turn towards the voice on my right.

Victor Amos is sitting there, immaculate in his dark woollen coat and purple silk scarf, his hands clasped on his lap. "I'm encouraged to hear from your consultant that you're making a full recovery. How are you feeling?"

I sit up and the room spins. "I'm not sure, yet."

He shakes his head. "I can't tell you how sorry I was to hear of the accident."

"The pilot?"

Amos shakes his head and averts his gaze. "I have launched a full enquiry into the incident. They've recovered the black box."

"Maybe you should start with your staff. Abrams, your aircraft engineer."

"I already have. He admits he may have failed to tighten the filler cap for the main rota gearbox."

"Sounds like a fairly fundamental oversight."

Amos nods. "Abrams was misguided. A frustrated engineer who felt he knew better. He found out about our intentions in CERN, and didn't see eye to eye with our philosophy. It's the reason we're so strict about sharing information on a need-to know basis only. People make assumptions without being in possession of all the facts."

I stare at him. "He did it deliberately?"

"Robert, you're going to make a few enemies in this line of work. Very few people could ever understand the magnitude of what we're facing and why we have to do this. It's important that you realise that you're acting in their best interest. But don't expect them to thank you for it."

"What if Abrams blows the whistle?"

"He won't."

I'm about to ask why, but decide against it. I don't have the stomach for it.

He watches me for a moment. "You're a very lucky man, Mr Strong. Someone must be looking out for you."

The thought makes me uncomfortable, reminding me of the dream. Perhaps Amos senses it as he frowns a little. "Do you remember much about the accident?"

"Not really."

"Probably for the best. It's been quite an ordeal." He scrutinizes me and seems to be considering what to say next. "I think you've been through enough, Robert. I'm sure your father would be willing to work with whoever we send; I suggest we find someone else to take your worm to CERN." His choice of words makes me shiver.

I sit up and the room spins. "No. No, that won't be necessary. I'll be fine."

"It's only been twelve hours since the crash, Robert." He gets to his feet. "I think you should concentrate on recovering. You've already made a vital contribution to the project and I will see to it that your payment is delivered in full, as a mark of my apology." He turns and walks towards the door.

"Wait!" I swing my legs over the side of the bed and the room swims about me. "I want to do this – I'll be fine, really." I'll be fine, will I? I'm dizzy just sitting up. They say that the mind is a powerful thing. This must be what they mean, because right now, there's no possibility of someone else taking my place on this – it's too important. Besides, it leaves me cold to think of someone else meeting with Elliot Strong and working with him. No matter how rough I feel.

Through a spinning blur, I see Amos glance back. "I admire your commitment to the task, Robert, but we don't have much time."

"I said I'm fine." I slump back down onto the mattress and the room stops moving as Amos returns to the seat.

"I know your father would be very proud of you."

He lifts a brown envelope from the floor beside him and lays it carefully on the bed. A replacement for the one Dana gave me. "Inside is the memory stick programmed with your worm." There's that word again.

"It's Mr Y's worm, really."

"I think you should take the credit for the idea, Robert. Mr Y is a genius in his field, but this is your brainchild."

I open the envelope and find a USB stick attached to a nylon cord, presumably so that I can wear it around my neck. "Our engineers will know when it's released – they have made a little modification that keeps them informed of your progress." I put the stick back and take out an electronic notebook.

"For essential communication purposes only. Mr Lambert will be your contact – his email particulars are already programmed for you along with some of the CERN software, to continue your familiarisation. You'll also find a plane ticket to Geneva, a UK passport, your security documents for CERN, details of your Swiss bank account and enough funds to make your trip more than comfortable." He pauses. "The only thing outstanding is security access to the Operator's Room in the Computer Centre. I understand that is where you will embed the worm?"

"Yeah, that's right. There's only one person on duty there at any one time. Less chance of attracting attention."

"A wise choice. Your father will help you with access, once you are established."

Anticipation ripples through me. I am going to meet him – this is real.

Looking back into the envelope, I retrieve the small maroon book that confirms who I am, with hands that are shaking like they're someone else's. "Passport? How did you get hold of my passport?"

He smiles. "I had a new one made for you."

I open it and see my face staring back, I place the book aside and reach into the envelope again. My fingers touch something metallic that clinks as I lift it out.

"Keys for the apartment I have arranged for you in Geneva. I believe it has a wonderful view of the Jura Mountains. The address is inside, as is the security code to let you into the building."

"How long I am going to be there?"

"There are only a few days left before the launch. You can stay as long as you wish, but you may not want to linger too long in the aftermath."

I peer down into the envelope again, pushing aside the memory stick and the uneasy feeling it gives me.

"You will be collected at Geneva airport, as your motorcycle will not be delivered until later."

"Motorcycle?"

"Yes. I understand your most recent model was a BSA Lightning. I thought you might enjoy having one again." He raises his eyebrows. "But if you would prefer a car, it can be arranged, quite easily..."

"No, no. That's great. I just didn't expect all this." But I'm warming to it and the dizziness seems to be subsiding. "I'd prefer the bike. I planned to get another one. How did you know?"

Amos smiles like a gentleman. "I have a talent for anticipating desires. No, the truth is that I have asked a lot of you, Mr Strong. I just want to make this as easy as possible."

I pull out a thick bundle of euros in a clear plastic bag and the plane ticket. "What's the date?"

"The fourteenth."

My eyes flick back to his face. "This flight's today."

"Yes. A car will be waiting outside in an hour to take you to the airport. I appreciate that air travel may not be your first choice, after what happened, but as we are short of time..."

"No, that's okay. But my clothes..."

"Your clothes were cut off during your resuscitation, and the staff kept them in a bag for you, which you'll find inside your bedside cupboard, should you wish to keep them. I took the liberty of arranging some new garments." He gestures towards a neat pile of clothes folded on a shelf, next to a new black rucksack.

He's thought of everything. A place to live, transport, clothes, money. The plan is all mapped out even before I've caught up with myself. I glance out of the window to the unfamiliar hill. "Where exactly am I?"

"You're in a private facility in southwest England that offers the best medical care in the country. I arranged for your transfer here as soon as I heard. After what happened, it's the least I could do."

I stare down at the envelope. "Has anyone been to see me?"

"Your mother knows that you will be out of the country on business, but I thought it unwise to worry her unnecessarily."

Unnecessarily?

He must read my face, because he adds, "The doctors were confident of your recovery. Had they predicted otherwise, I would, of course, have made sure she saw you."

"Have there been any calls?"

"No-one knows you are here, Robert, not even Miss Cora Martin. Visitors would only complicate matters."

I reach into the cabinet beside the bed and pull out the orange bag with my belongings, feeling for something other than cloth. I find Cora's ring on its cord. Maybe she called my mobile.

"I'm afraid your phone was not on you when you arrived. A replacement is in the inside pocket of your coat."

"Oh."

Amos gets to his feet and it strikes me just how tall he is. It's not just his stature; he has a presence that seems to fill the whole room. Some people have that. I remember a teacher I had at school who never raised his voice – he didn't have to. Fletcher, his name was. He wasn't that old, although at the time I thought he was – maybe in his forties – tall, greying hair, but there was something about the way he held himself that made you look at him, and listen to whatever he had to say. An unspoken command. Amos is like that. A roomful of bickering politicians would fall silent if he walked in, just by the way he did it.

"I often pass through Geneva on business, so no doubt I will see you again soon." He extends a hand towards me. "I wish you all the very best of luck, Robert. With your track record, that is a considerable amount of good fortune."

Chapter Nine

WHATEVER VICTOR AMOS thought about my recovery, the hospital staff doesn't seem to share his optimism. I'm standing dressed in a new pair of jeans, a Ralph Lauren T-shirt and grey coat, feeling slightly odd. It's more than the residue of dizziness, it's the clothes. The leather of my boots is still new and stiff but comfortable. Everything fits perfectly, it all feels good – there's nothing wrong with the clothes at all; they just feel like they belong to someone else. The orange plastic bin bag which holds the remnants of my clothes from before is tucked away in the rucksack, along with the electronic notebook and the documents. The plane ticket and passport sit inside the breast pocket of my coat, beside my new phone. Cora's silver ring on its leather cord is in my jeans' pocket.

"You're not well enough, Mr Strong. Please." The doctor, who's in his mid-thirties and wearing blue scrubs, looks like he's taking my decision to discharge myself personally. Does he really care or is he just worried that I'll sue him if I collapse in the car park?

"I'm fine, really."

"Please, it's only been thirteen hours, Mr Strong. Your heart stopped beating. Do you understand that? It stopped. You died."

"Only for a little bit."

"All I'm saying is that you should be monitored for at least another twenty-four hours."

"I appreciate your concern, doctor, I really do. But I'm fine. I'm happy to take responsibility for anything that might happen, if that makes you feel better." I pick up the suitcase.

"Well, this isn't a prison. But I'll need you to sign here." He presents me with a piece of paper stating that it's all my fault if I go home and die. I put down the suitcase and sign it without hesitating.

"Get some medical attention if you feel anything wrong. Anything at all."

I hesitate, considering asking him about the nightmares, but decide against it. Now's not the time. "You've got my word." I lift the suitcase and walk out.

THE AIRPORT CHECK-IN line shuffles forward. I watch the people around me, but I'm detached, as though the experience belongs to someone else. A couple are in line before me. The man is in his forties in a loose linen suit and brown loafers. His wife wears a lot of gold. She's watching the grungy backpacker in front of her, failing to hide the disdain on her face. Dreadlocks and patchwork trousers mustn't be her thing.

"Passport, please," says the check-in assistant when I get to the front of the queue. An orange silk neck tie is knotted in a bow over her throat. She doesn't look at me as I hand over the document.

She flicks it open and glances up with lidded eyes. "Did you pack all your belongings yourself?"

Do you need a chisel to take off your make-up at night?

"Yes."

"Could anyone have had access to your belongings without you knowing it?"

"No."

"Are you carrying any sharps, flammable substances, or liquids?"

No, but I'm carrying a memory stick that will shut down six billion pounds' worth of engineering. Does that count? "No."

"Gate nine, boarding in twenty minutes." She hands over the passport and boarding card.

I lift my rucksack and smile broadly. "Thanks. Have a nice day."

I fall in line with the jostling queue making its way onto the escalator. It glides up to the next level, past an oversized poster of a man displaying a watch against a backdrop of a city skyline at night. The man has a look in his eyes that approaches wisdom, as though he has overcome all of life's tribulations now that he has his watch. What a lot of shit.

I go into the washroom and splash cold water on my face. The face looking back at me in the mirror is in need of some sun and a sharp razor. Will he recognise me, after all this time? I stare at the blue eyes, slightly puffy with sleep deprivation – coma isn't sleep, and neither is sedation – at the flecks of black in the irises. I feel a cool breeze trickling over my skin and I freeze. A woman is standing behind me: blonde, slim, unblinking. She raises her hand towards me and I spin round.

There's the noise of flushing and a toilet door opens. An old man in a baseball cap shuffles out and washes his hands. He looks a little uncomfortable, and I realise I'm staring at him. I drop my head, scooping handfuls of cold water onto my face.

What the hell was that? Is she messing with my head when I'm awake now? It wasn't a dream – I know I'm not sleeping. Drugs. That's what it will be; the drugs they pumped into me at the hospital. A bad trip.

I dry my face on the hard paper towels and leave, avoiding the mirror.

THE FLIGHT BOARDS on time. I have two seats to myself, overlooking the wet tarmac, far enough away from the headache-inducing perfume of the hostess, which wafts over every time she clumps past.

After takeoff, I take out the electronic notebook. I open the folder containing the software data and begin to read. I can't concentrate. Something is squirming in my gut at the thought of meeting him. What if he doesn't want to see me? Maybe everything Amos said was bullshit and he left because he didn't want to be there. It happens to lots of men. They can't deal with the reality of being a father because all it does is remind them of their unfulfilled dreams.

After forty minutes, I close the computer and look out at the sunlight over the swathe of clouds. White candy floss on a summer's day.

I take out a pen and paper and sketch absentmindedly.

"Would you like any tea or coffee, sir?" I jump at the voice. The hostess smiles down at me.

"Eh... no, thanks."

"That's an unusual picture," she says, inclining her head to get a better look. "What are those?"

I stare down. I've drawn a dark circle at the top and some stick-like things at the bottom.

She frowns at my trembling hand. "Are you alright, sir?"

"I'm fine, thanks." By the looks of it, she doesn't believe me. I see her glance back as she walks up the aisle and whisper to her colleague. I can guess what she's saying. *Watch out for the weirdo in seat 42F.*

WHEN I REACH the arrivals lounge in Geneva airport, my name is on a white board. Holding the placard is a man in his twenties, medium height with dark hair and complexion, and a broad face that looks accustomed to smiling. He's wearing a faded red shirt, hanging loosely over his jeans and a pair of scruffy trainers. A student, or someone reluctant to make the transition to anything beyond student. He raises his eyebrows as I approach. "Monsieur Strong?" His accent is heavily French.

"Yes."

"Rene Valmont." He grins and holds out his hand, grasping mine with a firm grip. "You flight, it was okay?"

"Fine. It was fine, thanks." Better than the last one. Landing on tarmac is always a bonus.

"It's good you made it. I'm parked not far from here." He leads the way through the crowds to the exit, and onwards to the second floor of the dimly lit car park, stopping in front of a small blue Peugeot. There are patches of rust on the doors and a large dent above one wheel arch.

"I heard you were with Romfield Labs," says Rene. "How long were you there?"

"About five years," I step into the car. It smells of smoke and a hint of mint.

"That's a long time," says Rene, offering me a stick of chewing gum. "And the Grid, it's working out with you?"

"It's getting there." I step across the line between truth and fabrication, and realise I'll be doing a lot of this. "We've had a few glitches we're ironing out, but it's coming together."

"It's a great time to come here. Your boss must know a few people, no? To get you in?" He grins as he turns the ignition. He pays the exit fee and drives out of the car park, the old car chugging with the effort. "A very exciting time to be around."

"Yeah... So what do you do at CERN?"

"I got a post here when I graduated three years ago. I've been working on the muon detector, on the outer shell of ATLAS."

"You enjoying it?"

"It's the best decision I ever made. And what a time to be here!" Rene slaps his hand on the steering wheel. "There's a real buzz about the place, you know? Like we're on the edge of something huge. Everyone feels it." He negotiates his way out of the airport and onto the Meyrin highway. He's not a shy driver. I tighten my seatbelt.

"I'm sure they do," I say. "When's the first run?"

"First thing on Monday. So, you don't get much time to settle in, but with your background..." – he snorts – "no problem. Actually, it's a shame, you will miss a few days."

"What do you mean?"

"The engineers, they need to do their last tests, so we will have three days when we cannot work while they do that. But don't worry, you will have a lot to do today and tomorrow. The tests have been going well so far, did you hear? After all the problems last time, it's big relief, I tell you. Everyone was going crazy!" He laughs, a sound that's too big for a small car. "It's a very good place to work, you know? I mean I get up in the morning and I am happy to be going to work, and how many people can say that, eh? Not many, I bet. And I have a lot of good friends here, and it's like we're all part of this big thing that is very important, you know? Have you ever had that? But it's not all work, no, no, we have a lot of fun too. We go out at the weekends into the city. And we do a lot of sport. Last month I was the winner of the squash championship against this guy and he is crazy, I mean *crazy* that he lost and..."

He talks like a parrot. I'm reminded of a phrase I read somewhere in one of Cora's zen books: *Do not speak unless it improves on silence.*

I make the appropriate noises of understanding at the appropriate points in Rene's monologue and look at the Swiss scenery as it whizzes past – the small settlements gathered around the neat church towers, the houses with their overhanging eves, the cows being driven by old men in flat caps in the fields, the expanse of the open countryside.

"You would not guess it was here, eh? Twenty-seven kilometres of superconducting magnets right below us. It's fantastic what we built, no? And in a few days, this will be way hotter than the centre of the sun. That's hot!"

Hotter than you could imagine, Rene, if it goes ahead. "Yeah," I say. "That's hot." I glance at the graffiti on an underpass. It's stylish, artistic. Not like British graffiti; this has flair. The Swiss even have a better class of vandalism.

"It's been an incredible time. When we found the new particle..." He shakes his head.

"Must have been some party."

"You wouldn't believe it."

"Do you think it's the Higgs?"

"I think, yes. But what would be more amazing is if it doesn't fit with the Standard Model. Then we'd have a lot more questions to answer, no? 'Back to the drawing board', is that how you say it?"

Rene babbles on like a four year old with a new toy. His enthusiasm is palpable. There will be more like him, just as dedicated, just as swept up in the excitement of what they're part of. I've been there. There's a thought that's doing its best to surface, that I'm doing my best to smother – can I really do this to them?

The entrance to CERN is a little underwhelming. It breaks from the dual carriageway opposite open fields. A medium-sized blue sign displaying the CERN emblem announces it, but you'd be forgiven for driving past. It doesn't look like the kind of place that houses a particle accelerator, but then, I don't know what would. Once you drive in, though, past the blue and grey buildings on the right, there's a large red globe standing about thirty feet high.

"What is that?"

"An exhibition hall. Donated by the Swiss government."

"It's a bit rusty."

Rene snorts. "It's not rust, it's wood. OK, this will do." He pulls up outside the reception area, leaving the car abandoned, rather than parked. I follow him up the five steps to a foyer. On the left is a small visitor shop where a few tourists browse through books and soft toys.

"We have to get your security arranged," says Rene. He walks towards the front desk, where a petite blonde lady smiles when she sees him.

"Bonjour, Rene," she says, and follows this with something in French that I don't understand. Rene laughs and glances at me then strides to a door to the right of the desk and swipes a security card through the slot beside it. He steps aside and holds the door open for me.

"She said you need a shave," he whispers and grins as I pass. He leads me though to an office where a the security man, dressed in a black and white uniform, takes my documents and a photograph of my face and in return gives me a small plastic card on a red lanyard.

"We have a briefing at two," says Rene, glancing at his watch. "We'll just make it." We leave the reception building and cross the street, past the rusty globe, to a fenced off area that leads to a car park and a large concrete building at the far end. Rene swings open the gate.

"Is this ATLAS?"

"Yes," says Rene. "This is it."

Large metal towers flank the front entrance like sentries, and someone in a hard hat stands on a cherry picker, slapping paint on a brightly coloured mural on the outside wall.

"What's he doing?"

"Students," says Rene. "They've been painting a cross section of the detector. It keeps them busy. Bonjour!" shouts Rene and waves at the man in the hard hat. "Vous avez manque un peu!"

"Tres drole, Rene!"

"Do you like my bike?" says Rene as we pass a black motorbike by the entrance.

"It's a Ducati Streetfighter, isn't it?"

"Yes. You like bikes?" says Rene, his eyes lighting up. "If I knew that I would have come to get you on it. Maybe I'll let you take it for a ride sometime."

"That'd be great."

Coming towards us is a small crowd of fifteen or so people, straggling behind a tall thin man whose head looks too large for his body. They must be visitors. "Do you get a lot of tourists?"

"Yes, most days, although only above ground now that the experiments are beginning."

Rene swipes his security card to open a door into a modest, dim entrance. A glass wall opposite looks into a large room. Inside, huge flat screens hang from the walls displaying coloured data, and banks of consoles on crescent shaped desks sit in front of them. There are maybe twenty people in the room, sitting or standing, crowded around consoles.

"Is that the control room?"

"One of them," says Rene. "But the main one is on the first floor."

A man passes us on his way towards the exit. There's something odd in the way that he walks, a kind of rolling gait, as though one leg works better than the other, and his long scruffy coat makes him look out of place. His eyes, beneath a tangle of dark hair, stay on me for a moment, and the way he looks at me makes me uncomfortable. He pushes through the door and is gone.

Rene leads the way to the next level and we stop at a vending machine.

"Who was that guy?" I ask.

"What guy?"

"The one we passed just now, on the way in?"

Rene shrugs. "Didn't notice him. You want some coffee?"

"I don't have any change."

Rene grins. "Don't worry, one of the students rewired it – you don't need money." He hands me a steaming cardboard cup.

"Thanks."

"You're on the late shift," he says as he strides along the corridor. "The B team, same as me. I can show you round later. Professor Von Clerk is taking the briefing. He's a good guy."

The control room is packed full of people, too many to count, crowded around fifteen desks, peering at a line of screens.

"It's pretty busy," I say following Rene in.

"This is nothing. Wait till you see it at the launch. I mean, there will be people everywhere! You better get up early if you want a seat. Here. Let me introduce you to Professor Von Clerk."

He squeezes through the crowd, and I follow him towards a big, grey-haired man at the front of the room. He lifts his head from the console he's leaning over and looks squarely at Rene.

"Professor, this is Robert Strong, from Romfield," says Rene.

"Ah yes. I heard you were coming." His accent is German, or Austrian. He shakes my hand. "You've picked a good time for a transfer. Just don't use any initiative. Strictly observation, okay?" He winks at me.

"I understand." *But I can't promise.*

Rene leads me towards the back of the room and stops at a desk. Four screens per computer; three seats per station. "This is the station for our sub-detector." He gestures to the seat next to him.

I drop my rucksack on the floor.

"All right, people, we have a very big day ahead of us." Von Clerk announces. "We only have five days left before the launch..." – scattered applause and whistles ripple round the room – "and we'll be out of action from Friday while the engineers run their last tests. That gives today and tomorrow to make sure we're ready, so I need everybody's full attention. Can I also take this chance to introduce Robert Strong, who has been working at the UK end of the Grid." Faces turn towards me, some smiles. I wave a little awkwardly, flushed in the spotlight. Professor Von Clerk claps his hands. "Okay, then, let's get started."

But there's one person who doesn't move. He stands at the other end of the room, tall and lean with shoulder length grey hair, a clean-shaven face and small round specs. He continues to stare at me while the others take their places. I feel the man's eyes boring into mine, but Rene doesn't notice as he babbles on, explaining the data on the screens. I nod but barely hear him.

"But just ask if you are not sure, yes?" says Rene. "We have done these tests so many times now, that... Jack!" he says as a man with a pony-tail sits down to his left. "This is Robert Strong. He comes from Romfield Labs. In England."

"It is good to meet you, Robert," says Jack, extending his hand. His accent is American, but I have difficulty placing the state. "Jack Harley. Rene's showing you the ropes?"

"He's keeping me in line." Jack turns to his console. He doesn't seem to share the buzz of the other people. If anything he looks worn out. "Rene," I say in a low voice, "who's the guy over there, with the blue shirt and the round glasses?" I nod to the man, who's pointing at his screen while a younger man beside him looks on and nods.

"That's Professor Stiller," says Rene. "He's been here a long time. Bit of a loner, you know? But he's very good at his job."

"Really?" I watch Professor Stiller. He looks older than I recall from the photograph in Amos's office, but there's no doubt in my mind that it's him. My stomach has twisted itself into a tight coil.

"Yeah," says Rene. "He has a real passion for his work – I mean more than most people. He's one of the best." I feel a flush of pride.

Professor Stiller glances at me again. It's as though an unspoken bond connects us. He knows. We both do. I want to walk up to him now, to forget the worm and the threat from the accelerator and everything else. I want to tell him what I've done with my life, to fill him in on all those years. But what if it doesn't work out like that? What if he doesn't want to know?

Professor Stiller's mobile phone rings. He steps away from his desk, frowning. He walks up the metal staircase to the mezzanine level above, then glances down at me. I drop my gaze and stare at my console, but on the edge of my vision I see him pacing back and forth, muttering into the phone. He nods and ends the call, then trudges down the stairs. He doesn't look at me after that.

I feel for the memory stick on the cord beneath my shirt. How the hell am I going to do this?

BY SIX PM, I'm hungry. Jack has adopted me, since Rene has a few things he wants to run through, and seems to think that if you need a food break your heart's not really in it. Professor Stiller keeps his distance. I walk beside Jack, whose long limbs mean I'm virtually jogging to keep up with him.

"Is Rene wearing you out yet?"

I smile. "He's keen, isn't he?"

"Never slows down. He's like that all day, every day. Lives and breathes it."

We pause to allow a car to pass on Route Marie Curie.

"I thought everyone would be like that, given what's happening."

"Well, most of us are. Don't get me wrong, it's an incredible time." Somehow his expression doesn't convey his conviction as he holds open the door of Restaurant 1. It opens into a long brightly-lit hall lined with rows of dark wooden tables. It looks like an upmarket service station. I follow Jack to the hot food queue.

"So, how long have you been here?" I ask as I ladle some fried rice onto a plate.

"Just over six months. I'm not much less of a rookie than you are."

"What did you do to get here, then?"

Jack throws a sideways glance at me that suggests it's a long story. "Let's just say, my previous employers thought that a stint in a prestigious establishment like CERN would do me some good. Don't get me wrong, it's an incredible opportunity, and a few years ago, I'd have jumped at it."

We pay for our food and find a table by the window. Outside, trees bend in the breeze, and the sky is a clear cornflower blue. "Is this where all the staff come for lunch?"

I glance round to see if I can see Professor Stiller, but he is not amongst the diners.

"Mostly," says Jack. "If they're working this end. There are a couple of other restaurants on site, but this one's usually the busiest."

"I bet there've been a lot of good ideas generated around these tables." Those 'eureka' moments often don't happen at a computer, or in the lab; they happen when you're doing something else, like doodling on a napkin in the canteen.

"Hey, Jack."

I look up. A blonde woman in her thirties, with skin like white china and dark eyes behind oblong specs, stops at our table. She lays down her tray and drains the last of the Coke from her glass. "Guess what I've just heard?"

"Robert, this is Helena Stanford. Helena works in the Computer Centre. Helena, this is Robert Strong. He's a visiting computer scientist from Romfield. Maybe you could show him around your patch."

Maybe she could give me the access code for the Operator's Room.

Helena raises her eyebrows. "Good to meet you, Robert. How long are you here for?"

"Not long – just a short secondment."

"Good timing. So," she says, turning back to Jack. "Any guesses?"

Jack shakes his head. "Blow me away, Helena." His voice is flat, a monotone.

"John Bryson just called me. There's a rumour Fermilab are onto a new particle."

Jack straightens up. "What is it?"

"It's communicating a new kind of force – not gravity,

not electromagnetism, not the weak or strong forces. This is completely new."

"It's not part of the standard model?"

"Nope. We might have to rewrite the textbooks. Maybe they found what you've been looking for, Jack. You could be working in the wrong accelerator. Nice to meet you, Robert." She lifts her tray and walks off, glancing back before she leaves.

Jack stares after her.

"That's huge news," I say.

"I think I'll wait for the press release."

"So what is it you've been looking for?"

Jack lowers his eyes, and pushes the remains of his stew around his plate. "It was nothing. Too many years spent on a wild goose chase."

"Oh, come on. It couldn't have been nothing."

He studies the space below my face then meets my eye. "I was looking for the particle that communicates consciousness."

"Oh?"

"I set up a project with a quantum biology team in the UK. I had a first class PhD student working on it – we just needed a chance to complete the work."

Right. A fringe scientist. I glance at the thin friendship band on his wrist. "Who knows? Maybe you were onto something." I'm being polite, and he knows it.

He snorts. "That's one of the more reserved responses I've had. My boss wasn't so understanding. He sent me here on a kind of rehab – to get back into mainstream particle physics."

"So how's the rehab going?"

"It's okay, I suppose." He shrugs. "It's been hard to shelve the work I believed in. I just ran out of steam."

We've got something in common – our research trashed by someone else's decisions.

I feel sorry for him, even if he is a misfit.

HE's A DECENT misfit, because he gives me a ride to my apartment. The rest of the shift went smoothly, and I didn't see Elliot Strong again. I did find his office, though, in the corridor beside the control room. Third along on the right, with the wrong name on the door. I had mixed feelings when I saw the nameplate – *Professor P. Stiller*. I wanted to hang around to see if he would come back, but Von Clerk wasn't far off and I didn't need any unwanted attention. It would have to wait until tomorrow.

"This is the address." Jack peers at the street name at the corner of the building as I glance down at the card in my hand. His eyes scan the sandstone, the black iron window railings trailing like dark rose tendrils at the base of the tall, wide Georgian windowpanes.

"Looks cosy enough," he says. "You friend's friend must be doing alright for himself."

"He must be."

"You need a lift in tomorrow?"

"I'm not sure yet." I step out of the car and retrieve the rucksack from the back seat.

"Give me a call if you're stuck." He scribbles his number of a piece of paper and hands it to me.

"Will do. Thanks, Jack."

The car horn *meeps* as he pulls away. Above me, the streetlamps flick on as dusk settles and the light fades. I climb the stairs to the double entrance doors and punch the code into the keypad on my right. The doors click open. A plush cream carpet leads down a wide hallway to a staircase ahead and, to the left, two elevators.

The elevator I take pings as it reaches the top floor and apartment number twelve.

The apartment is like something from a showroom. Pastel white decor, open plan kitchen and living space. A sleek white sofa faces a wall with two black wall-mounted oblongs. I pick up the remote controls lying on a low table in front of the sofa and experiment with the buttons. The larger oblong is a TV the size of a small cinema screen. The smaller one, below, turns out to be a gas fire whose flames come and go at the touch of a button. The floors are polished wood. The kitchen has one large granite worktop the length of the wall. Utensils line the rail on the wall above and all of it looks untouched. If someone did live here before, they didn't cook their own meals. To the right two large latticed windows open out to a view of the Jura mountains, hazy in the evening sunset.

My suitcase rumbles on the floorboards as I drag it behind me to the bedroom: a cream dream plucked from some magazine. There's an en-suite dressing room. A dressing room with ten deep shelves, two double wardrobes and a stack of drawers, stocked with clothes. I check the labels. They're all my size.

It takes me a good twelve strides to reach the kitchen again, and each one of them makes me feel like I've broken in. I make myself a coffee and stand there, alone in the large, perfect room, feeling empty. I miss our torn couch with the rug thrown over the top. I miss the messy bookcase; I even miss the bloody Buddha statue.

Before I've had time to reason it out, I'm listening to the long beeps of an international phone connection. It won't do any harm to speak to her, now that I'm here.

"Hi, Cora."

"Robert?"

"Yeah, it's me. How are you?"

"I'm okay. Where are you? I called a couple of times."

"I lost my phone," I lie. "I'm in Geneva."

"*Geneva?*"

"I'm working in CERN. Just for a few days."

"So you took the job?"

"Yeah." I press on before she can object, because it's welling up in me to tell her. "Cora, there's something I found out. Something huge."

She waits for me to continue.

"My dad's alive."

"*What?*"

"He's here. He's working in CERN."

"But I thought..."

"I know. So did I. It's complicated – I'll tell you sometime, but not over the phone. Listen, don't say anything to my mum. Not yet."

"I can't believe it."

"I know."

"Have you spoken to him?"

"Not properly. I should see him tomorrow."

"God, Robert, how do you feel about it?"

"I... I don't know yet. I want to speak to him, but I'm nervous about it, you know?"

"Yeah, I can imagine. Are you okay?"

I sit on down the sofa. "I'm not sure."

A pause. "Are you still getting the dreams?"

I hesitate. Maybe I shouldn't tell her any of this, but she did ask – she's the only one I can talk to. "Yeah, almost every night since I came back from Tibet. God, you know, today, I thought I saw her reflection in the mirror. I know it sounds crazy, but..." Silence. "Cora, look, I'm not making this up – you know I wouldn't do that, don't you?"

"What happens in the dream?"

"Nothing much happens, but..." I don't want to tell her about the feeling it leaves me with.

"Are you sure it's just a dream?"

I snort. "Yeah, I'm sure. There's been a lot happening. It's just knocked me sideways, that's all." I'm talking myself into this.

"I've been having dreams about her too."

"What?"

"At first it felt good, but now I wake up feeling uneasy. It feels like they're changing. I'm not sleeping so well, again."

I shouldn't have mentioned any of this.

"Don't you think that's weird?" she says. "Both of us getting dreams about her?"

This is beginning to creep me out. "Maybe we're both open to suggestion, Cora, and we've both been under pressure. Listen, let's not talk about it." I want to change the subject. "I, eh... I've got a good apartment."

"Oh?"

I get up and glance out of the window, to the street below. "It's near the centre – Rue de la Croix. It's got a great view of the mountains and..." Someone's standing on the pavement opposite, leaning against the wall at the edge of the shadows. Slightly hunched, a tangle of dark hair above the collar of a long coat. He's looking up. I step back and pull the curtains shut. Is it my imagination, or is that the guy I saw in ATLAS today?

"And?"

"And it's... it's great. It's like a five star hotel. Wall mounted TV." I move away from the window. "So anyway, I just wanted to call. Hope you don't mind."

"No. I'm glad you did."

It's funny, but with everything that's happened, she's feels like an anchor, a safety line to the life I used to have, and I don't want to let it go. Ironic, given that, not so long ago, I couldn't wait to cut loose.

"Listen, when all this is over..." My fingers find her silver ring in my pocket and close round it.

"Yeah?"

When all this is over. Could she ever understand why I'm doing this? What will she think of me? Maybe she won't have to know.

"Well, it would be good to meet up sometime," is all I can say.

"Yeah, it would."

"Well, I'll, eh... I'll let you get on."

"Let me know how it goes. I'll be thinking about you."

"Thanks."

"Take care, Robert."

"You too." It's on the tip of my tongue to tell her how I'm feeling, but before I can bring myself to say the words, she hangs up. I berate myself for having the moral fibre of a noodle.

I step back to the window and draw the curtain aside, just a crack. The man's still there, leaning against the wall, looking up. I pull back. Who the hell is he? He turns and walks away, blending with the darkness.

I tell myself it's probably nothing, and it probably is, but I'm on edge. I flick through the channels of Swiss television, the same stuff – soaps, docudramas, ads – just in another language. I finally settle on a music channel. I take out the notebook. The hours slip away as I trawl the CERN site and the web for anything I can find on Professor P. Stiller. The fifteen-year-old malt I find in one of the cupboards accompanies me as I'm introduced to the man my dad became. Hard working, plenty of publications on all kinds of things: 'Superbeam studies at ATLAS', 'The Expected Performance of the Muon Detector', 'Oscillation Physics at ATLAS'... the list goes on. Lots of hard facts, lots of papers. Nothing personal, not a single thing. Maybe this is all he is.

But what if it isn't? For the first time it occurs to me that he might have another family. What if he has another son? Someone else who's looked to him for guidance and direction all these years? Or a wife he comes home to every night, who never knew the whole story? I push the thought from my mind, close the notebook and go to bed.

IN THE DARKNESS, there's a soft, cool breath on my neck. I turn to see the silhouette of her slim figure. She reaches towards me with a slender hand and I'm compelled to reach out to her too, although I know I don't want to. But I can't resist. Our fingertips touch.

Darkness falls.

I'm gliding beside her, and she's taking me somewhere I don't want to go.

A mist lies low, stretching out for miles in all directions towards a grey horizon with a black sun. Something is rising out of the mist, withered and gnarled. A tree, leafless, with something tied to it. We're drifting side by side just above the mist. She leads me to the tree and shows me. The figure tied there looks up at me and I see her face, pleading...

"Sarah!" I'm gasping for breath, sitting bolt upright in the bed. My phone pings beside me – a text, from Cora.

Robert, are you awake? Just had another dream – it's getting worse.

I stare at the message. Breathless, I get up and turn the lights on. I go into the bathroom, avoiding the mirror, and splash cold water on my face. I pick up the phone and select Cora's number, but hesitate. Talking about it will only keep it going. I put down the phone, go into the kitchen and pour a whisky. I need to bury this.

Chapter Ten

I WAKE UP early with a crick in my neck from falling asleep on the couch, get dressed and go out in search of breakfast. I need the walk. The aroma of hot bread teases me long before I reach the boulangerie. The woman behind the counter is petite, middle-aged and smiley beneath her blue paper hat, and although I don't know what she's saying, it doesn't matter much. In an exchange of sounds and hand signals, she gives me a croissant and I give her some money, after she counts out the right amount from my palm.

The streets are quiet in the shadow of the mountains. I can just see the snow-capped peaks coming and going in the gaps between the buildings. A delivery man unloads boxes of vegetables to a grocer across the street. The men banter as one unloads the van and the other ferries the crates inside, a conversation that no doubt has gone on for years. A flock of sparrows gets itself in a tizzy as I pass a tree growing up through the pavement.

On the surface, my life is looking up. I'm walking back to my luxury apartment in the early morning sunshine eating a hot croissant. In a matter of days, I'll have more money than I know what to do with. If I just forgot about everything else, I could get used to all this. But in a funny way, the comfort seems to make things more unsettling. I'd trade all of it right now for a full night's sleep and a pint with my dad.

I stop at a crossing. It's a safe bet that jaywalking isn't tolerated in a country in which you can set your watch by the buses. A black Lamborghini draws to a stop as the traffic light turns to red. Maybe I should have asked Amos for one of those, rather than the bike, but that would arouse too much suspicion. A physicist who drives a Lamborghini must have a sideline in atomic weapons production, or some other prostitution of the profession. I step onto the road as the green man gives me the signal to cross, but someone grabs my jacket, yanking me backwards. "What the hell..."

There's a screech and the smell of burning rubber as the car jumps the red light, passing within inches of me. I stare after it, my heart thumping in my chest, mouth dry at the thought of what could have happened.

When I turn around, the first thing I notice is her eyes: large, the colour of the shallows of a tropical ocean, with something unbridled, barely hidden in the depths. I have the vague feeling that I've seen her before. "Thanks..." is all I can manage.

"Don't mention it."

She looks as though she'd like to smile, but she's forgotten how.

"Wait," I call as she turns away, but she doesn't look back. I stare after her – her head slightly bowed and her hands in her pockets. I stand there, dithering for a moment, debating with myself whether to follow her.

I gain on her as she turns into the next street. At the corner, an old woman stands scattering breadcrumbs to a flock of cooing pigeons, but there's no sign of her. Where the hell did she go? I toss my flat croissant into a bin and walk home.

THE BIKE IS in the car park under the apartment block, between a Mercedes SLR and an Aston Martin Vanquish. Whatever my neighbours do for a living, they're clearly very affluent.

The bike handles like a dream. Everything's tuned to perfection – it has a full tank of fuel and forty-seven miles on the clock. The drive to CERN takes fourteen minutes, nipping in and out of traffic in the city centre until I'm out on the Meyrin highway. The Jura mountains glisten in the morning light. The farmers are out in the fields in their tractors, working with the earth, while beneath it, the beginnings of everything are being recreated to satisfy our curiosity. How much time will we have before the meltdown? Enough time to figure out what's happening? I think of the grocer and the delivery man and the woman who sold me the croissant, the rhythm of their lives blown apart by our insatiable desire to know more.

When I pull past the dark, wooden globe and into the ATLAS car park, I see Rene walking towards the entrance, his helmet under his arm. He waves as I pull to a stop and blows a long whistle as his eyes glide over the bike. "This is yours?"

"Borrowed, for a little while."

"It's a beauty! Maybe I could take it out for a ride sometime?"

"Sure."

Rene's eyes are still on the bike as he walks beside me. When he tears them away, he says, "Listen, we are all going out for a drink tonight in Geneva. Why don't you come with us? Eight o'clock in Lacont's Bar, Rue De-Grenus."

"Oh, I don't know…" I'm uncomfortable about getting too close to people. It's like inviting the Grim Reaper to a christening.

"Oh, come on. It's a bit of fun. All visitors are obliged to come out on a Friday night – you can get to know the whole team."

Exactly. "Well, I'll see…"

"Oh, come on, make the most of it while you're here."

I might draw more attention to myself by not showing up. "Alright, I'll be there. Just for a while." I swipe open the entrance and hold the door for Rene.

I SCAN THE control room for Professor Stiller and see him on the other side of the room, in discussion with a woman whose back is to me. His eyes dart towards me briefly. *You're going to have to speak to me sooner or later, Professor; we've got four days left.* I lower my eyes and walk to my work station. The atmosphere is charged, even more so than yesterday – anticipation tinged with anxiety. Even Jack looks swept up in it. His eyes twinkle when I sit down at the station next to him. "Sleep well?" he says.

"I've slept better." I scan the data on my console. "Did you get any confirmation from Fermilab about what they found?"

"Not yet, but I'm working on it. I've got my own sources."

"Good morning!" Professor Von Clerk's voice rises above the chatter. "I know we are very keen to get started as this is our last chance to test, before the experiments begin on Monday." A few whistles and applause come from the crowd. "I'm sure you'd rather be here all weekend, but we have to give the engineers a chance to play."

The tests begin again. The hydrogen atoms are released into the source chamber, stripped of their electrons, and the proton packets fed into LINAC 2. The PSB acceleration goes smoothly, reaching 1.4 GeV easily. They reach the point of transition, the point when they can go no faster and so gain mass, and pass into the SPS successfully. Four minutes later, they're all travelling, clockwise, round the main ring. After a tense wait, that seems to go on too long, signals confirm that the proton packets have travelled the full length of the collider. We repeat the process, this time feeding the packets counter-clockwise into the LHC ring. A cheer goes up when the signal from the last packet crosses the finish line.

If I don't plant the worm, the next time we do this, the beams will cross and the particles will collide.

I glance at Professor P. Stiller again.

Jack leans across and whispers, "I could see if I can get you his number, if you like."

I snort and feel the heat rising in my cheeks. "I think I've met him somewhere before, that's all."

THE MORNING WEARS on and my patience wears thin. Stiller won't look at me. During a lull in activity, I see him leave the room and I take my chance. "Anyone want a coffee?"

"Black, no sugar," says Jack.

"Black, lots of sugar," says Rene.

I get up and walk out to the atrium, but instead of going to the coffee machine, I turn left into the office corridor, my heart hammering inside my chest. *Professor Rumsden* on the first door, *Professor Liebenberg* on the second. On the third, the lie: *Professor P. Stiller.* The door is ajar and creaks a little as I push it open. I pause, and take a deep breath.

A whiteboard scrawled with equations sits against one wall next to a small red armchair, a bookshelf lined with physics tomes against another. There's a group photograph on the wall, taken at the entrance of ATLAS. He's behind the desk, rifling through some files, frowning through his round specs. He freezes when he glances up, his hands poised holding a sheaf of papers.

"Professor, do you have a minute?"

He stares at me, then sets the papers down slowly. "Of course. Come in."

I walk into the office and we stand there awkwardly for a moment, facing each other, not quite knowing where to begin.

"My name's –"

"I know who you are... Robert." He swallows and I can't tell if he's going to smile or cry. "We need to talk."

Footsteps come from the corridor and a woman who looks to be in her sixties knocks at the open door and peeps round.

"Come in, Florence."

"Sorry to disturb you, Professor, but can you sign this mandate?" She hands him a piece of paper, which he scans before scribbling a signature at the bottom.

"Florence, this is Robert Strong. He's a visiting physicist from the UK."

"Oh, yes," she says and holds out a hand. "Nice to meet you. In fact, I've got some papers I'll need you to sign as well – just a few admin details – when you get a minute. I can bring them up to now if you like."

"No, that's okay," I step out into the corridor. "Where's your office? I come by later."

"Just along the next corridor on the right."

"Okay, thanks. See you later."

"Hey, Robert!" Rene's voice calls from the other end of the corridor. "Where's our coffee?"

"Just a minute!"

I look back at my father, who's leaning over the desk, drawing something on a piece of paper. He hands it to me. "Meet me there after the shift. We can't talk here."

I take the paper, glance at the map he's sketched, and fold it away.

"You better go now."

"You alright?" asks Rene when I reach the coffee machine.

"Yeah, fine," I say as casually as I can. "Just having a look around."

The tests run smoothly for the rest of the day, and I do my best to engage with them, but it's difficult to concentrate. I can hardly believe I've finally met him.

Jack leans towards me and whispers, "You okay?"

"Alright, everyone," Von Clerk's announces, before I can say anything. "That's it for the day. See you all on Monday for a 9am launch." The chatter bubbles up around the room.

I force a smile at Jack, reach down for my rucksack and join the crowd heading for the exit.

"Eight o'clock, tonight. Remember?" says Rene as we reach the car park.

"Eight o'clock."

He grins as he walks off, eyeing my bike. I take my time putting on my helmet, waiting for the crowd to clear, then check the map my dad gave me and set off.

Exit through the main gate on the French side, along the highway, then turn right up a long bumpy farm track between gentle rolling green fields. On the left, further up the hill, is a small white church, gravestones barely rising above the overgrown grass surrounding it. Beyond, a few houses are scattered around the hillside.

I pull up to the church beside a tired looking silver Volvo. He's sitting on a bench at the edge of the small cemetery, overlooking the hillside. A buzzard lands on the eaves of the church, its beak hooked, the arc of its head smooth as a shepherd's crook. It peers down at me as my boots crunch on the gravel.

My dad looks up, watching me approach. I sit down beside him and look out over the land. The grass is mossy and tufty and sprinkled with boulders. Sheep are grazing on the lower slopes, and in the distance, the buildings of CERN jar a little with the serenity.

"I can't believe you're here," he says.

"*You* can't believe it? Until last week, I thought you were dead."

"I know. We've got a lot to catch up on." He turns to face me. "You look just like her."

"Does she know?"

"No."

"Why did you do it? Why did you make us believe you were dead?"

"When I first graduated, I got a post with a private UK company working on ways of refining plutonium extraction for power. It turned out that the company was a front for the Soviets' weapons research. When I found out, I resigned. We'd almost completed the research and they weren't prepared to see me walk out. It turned nasty – they knew all about you and Marion. When the threats started, that's when Victor Amos showed up."

"What did he do?"

"He gave me a way out that kept you safe. But it was a high price. If the Soviets were to believe I was dead, I couldn't let anyone know – not even your mother."

"But what about afterwards? The cold war ended years ago."

"ORB kept telling me there were still threats. Soviet defectors, spies and scientists were being quietly bumped off for decades without anyone noticing."

"But you could have found some way to let us know you were still alive."

"Too risky. At least, the way it was, she had a chance to move on. You both did. Anyway, circumstances kind of overtook me."

"What do you mean?"

He glances in my direction, but doesn't meet my eye. "I suffered from depression. I was committed to a psychiatric unit for eighteen months after I tried to take my own life."

"What?"

"There didn't seem any point. I'd lost you and your mother, I was living a fake identity, a fake life. I was no one. Besides, I was already dead." He sighs and pushes a pebble about with his boot. "It couldn't have been easy for you, Robert. I wish I'd been there for you. I'm sorry that I wasn't."

"So am I."

We sit there together, lost in our memories.

"You really think the experiments are dangerous?" I ask eventually.

"There's increasing evidence that we'll create strangelets, although the Council would deny that they would cause any harm. But we haven't tested the ring at these high energies. If we do produce strangelets and there are any structural breaches in the ring, any at all, then they could interact with normal matter. And that would be it. Game over."

Sweat gathers in the nape of my neck. I wish more than anything that I'd never known anything about all this.

"What convinced you to do this?" he asks.

"There are a lot more papers out there with three sigma results than I realised. Then I found a paper by Thorpe which the Council refused to accept."

"Ah."

"I went to see him in hospital, to talk to him about it, but I could only speak to his wife. She told me he was convinced, before."

"How is he?"

"It's CJD. He's not going to get better."

He looks out over the tranquillity, his jaw clenching and unclenching. "Poor bastard."

He turns to me. "So how are we going to do this?"

"I need to get into the Operator's Room in the Computer Control Centre."

"Do you have security clearance?"

"Not yet. I met Helena Standford the other day –"

"Don't expect any favours from her. Leave the clearance to me. I'll see what I can do."

"There's only one person on duty there at a time, right?"

"Yeah, that's right."

"I'll need a distraction. Something to get them out of there while I plant it."

He nods, considering. "Okay. I'll meet you tomorrow to discuss the details. Not here. A friend of mine has a small fishing boat up in Versoix, and the weather's meant to be good all day. We could take the boat out on Lake Geneva, maybe catch some fish."

"Sounds good. Where is Versoix?"

"It's only about ten kilometres northeast of the city. It's easy to find. Probably best if we go separately."

"Okay."

He gets to his feet. "I'll be there about one o'clock, at the docks."

"Alright, see you then."

I watch as he gets into his car and drives away.

A gentle breeze picks up from the slopes and ruffles the blades of grass. I close my eyes and let it wash over me. A million leaves move with the wind and the birdsong hushes to stillness.

When I open my eyes, I'm not alone.

At the other side of the cemetery, beyond the moss-covered headstones, a man is sitting on a bench. A little dishevelled, in a long dark brown coat, his hair matted and black. His face is shadowed in stubble and lopsided, his mouth and eyelid drooping on the left. He gets up and walks with an odd rolling gait, making his way out to the fields.

Shit. Did he hear us? I get to my feet and cross the cemetery, but there's no sign of him. Just a buzzard, sitting on a fence post, which flaps into the air as I approach. Where the hell did he go?

I make my way to the bike, and glance back. The sweeping branches of the larch trees at the edge of the forest bob gently in the breeze.

Chapter Eleven

I THINK ABOUT going home and drinking a lot of whisky, but decide against it. I said I'd be there and I can't afford to arouse any suspicion, and I could use the distraction. At ten past eight the bar is crowded, the din of many conversations fighting against the europop that blares from the speakers dotted around the room.

"Robert! Over here!" Rene is waving at me, his arm sticking up above the crowd of heads. I squeeze my way through, apologising in pidgin French as I go. I recognise a few faces from ATLAS in the corner.

"You made it!" Rene's unbounded enthusiasm hasn't sagged an inch. "I didn't think you would come out, you know. It's a good place, no?"

"Yeah, it's a good place. Pretty busy."

"What would you like to drink?"

Everything.

"Antoine is just going to the bar. HEY, ANTOINE!" he bellows, before turning back to me.

"A Grolsch, please."

"And a Grolsch for the new team member! So, you enjoying it so far?"

"Yeah. It's great."

"Good." He turns to the man to his right. "Hey, Frank, this is Robert Strong, from Romfield Labs." Rene leans towards me and says in a low voice intended to be overheard, "Frank's the one I beat in the squash championships." He grins and Frank looks unimpressed. "I'll just give Antoine some help with the drinks." Rene bounces off into the crowd.

"Nice to meet you," says Frank, smiling. I shake his hand. "I didn't think they were allowing any more transfers in at this stage."

"I just got lucky."

"You must be. So, are you in ATLAS too?"

"Yeah. It's quite something."

"I know. I've been here for five years now and it's still exciting. After the success of the last run, this next one should be something. We've had our share of challenges too, though. I was there when we had our first major disappointment, before the switch on."

"The magnet quench?"

"Yeah," he says. "A tonne of liquid helium leaked into the tunnel."

"Didn't they have to evacuate the place?"

"No, that was 2007. A magnet ruptured during a pressure test."

"Oh, right." At least they've tested their evacuation procedures.

Rene returns, balancing a tray laden with drinks and begins distributing them. Some of mine sloshes out of the glass. "Oops," says Rene.

"That's okay," I take the glass from him and hold it

to my lips to salvage as much as I can of what's left. He grins and disappears into the crowd again.

I turn to Frank. "Does it worry you, all those safety breaches?"

He shrugs. "No, it's all part of it. I suppose there's an element of risk, but it's small and, anyway, it will be worth it."

I don't think you mean that.

"So," says a voice from behind me. "Where did you say you were based?"

I turn to see Helena, her head cocked to one side as she appraises me.

"Romfield Labs in the UK."

"That's what I thought. I worked there until last year."

Bollocks.

"How come I never saw you?"

"I only just transferred in – I was working in SightLabs before that."

"Oh, I read what happened – I can't believe they closed it."

"Tell me about it." There's a bag of worms writhing in my stomach. "So, eh... are you all set for Monday?"

"Well, it doesn't feel like it. There aren't enough hours in the day to do all the things on my list. Then again, I'm a bit of a perfectionist. Have you met Tony Maddox yet?"

"Who?"

She stares at me. "The Chief Scientist for Romfield?"

"Oh... no. Not yet."

"He's my ex-husband."

Well, that's just great. "Really? Do you two... still keep in touch?" I'm feeling uncomfortably hot.

"Yeah, every so often. He's still a prick, but he's not my responsibility anymore."

"Oh. Right. Listen, would you excuse me? I need to go and make a phone call if I want to hang on to my relationship." Another lie. It's funny how easily they trip off the tongue with a bit of practice.

She rolls her eyes. "I'm so glad I'm out of all that."

I make my way through the throng as the music changes and the crowd begins to bounce in unison. Brownian motion in action. I weave between them, suffering a few bumps and elbowings, before breaking out into the cool night air.

Rain glistens in the white glow from the streetlight. A car swishes past on the wet road and a couple scurries away, huddled under a coat spread over their heads. I pull up my collar and set off to the apartment.

Betrayal swells in my gut. This was never going to be easy.

My footsteps echo on the damp pavement as steam jettisons from a vent in a wall, smelling of grease, and a siren whines in the distance. The street is dark, mostly warehouses locked up for the night. The street lights seem dimmer than they should be, and too far apart. I glance back. There's someone behind me; jeans and a hooded top. Probably nothing, just keep walking. But the quickening pace of his footsteps and the discord in my gut tells me it's not nothing. He's gaining on me. I glance back again – he's ten feet away now. *Fuck*, he's holding a handgun.

There's nowhere to run – he'd take the shot – so I open my hands, a gesture of surrender. He's agitated, and he looks like a druggie: pale and thin, his bony hand shaking as he steps up and points the weapon at my head. Black, unblinking eyes. A trickle of sweat escapes from his temple and leaks down his cheek.

He says something in French, but I'm rooted to the spot, quivering.

He speaks again, raising his voice, his finger closing round the trigger, and the gun begins to tremble. Slowly I lower my right hand, reaching into my pocket and pull out my wallet. He's welcome to my credit card with the measly limit and my supermarket clubcard. My CERN security card and Amos's bank account details are in the apartment. I hold the wallet towards him, but he's not looking at it. He's looking past my right shoulder, his eyes widening, not just crazed, but scared. The shake in his hand gets worse. He might just kill me by accident. I have a thought then that surprises me. I don't care. I'm not afraid. For the first time since the mountaineering accident, I glimpse that feeling of certainty. A memory of calm. A flash of white light – was that lightning? He backs away, his eyes still pinned to something behind me, mumbling, before he turns and stumbles into the shadows.

What just happened? Suddenly aware of my vulnerability, I turn, slowly, not sure if I want to see what scared the shit out of the druggie with the gun. There's a man standing just a few feet away, slim, medium height, his arms by his sides, his loose dark hair falling to his shoulders. Beetle-black eyes. The rain patters on his dark T-shirt and baggy trousers, on the leather bands round his wrists and the tattoo on the side of his neck – a spider's web, from what I can make out in the dim light. I didn't hear him arrive.

I breathe out, a slow, juddering breath and start shivering, more than is justified for the temperature. "Thanks," I mumble. "Whatever you did, thanks a lot. Merci." He smiles with his eyes then turns and walks away. I watch him disappear down the street. Maybe he's a gangster and the druggie was on his patch. He must be a hard man, to scare off a druggie with a gun. I turn and head home, with a note to myself not to come this way again after dark.

THERE'S A MESSAGE on my voicemail, which I must have missed with all the noise in the pub. I hold the phone to my ear with one hand and pour a whisky with the other, something to steady the nerves. It's Cora.

"Hi Robert, I need to ask you something. Can you call me back?"

I dial her number and it rings out. I give it a few more whiskies before I try again, then stumble off to bed.

I DIDN'T SLEEP well. Odd dreams about dark streets. Death dressed up as a drug addict. And then...

I'm sitting alone on a bench by a small cemetery. In front of me, the hillside sweeps down to the valley below, where the collider lies under the fields, and at the edge of my vision, larch branches gently sway. A soft breeze picks up from the slopes and ruffles the blades of grass. I close my eyes and let it wash over me. A million leaves move with the wind, and the birdsong hushes to stillness. There's no sound, apart from the breeze, but I know something is there, to my right. Coldness sweeps through me. Slowly, I open my eyes.

She's there.

"What do you want, Sarah?"

Her lips move, but there's no sound. She turns and walks into the forest. My breathing quickens, my body feels like it's taken root, and I have to push through to get it to respond. I cross the cemetery, stepping around the broken monuments to people I never knew, avoiding the shallow grassy mounds where the dust of their bones mingles with the soil. She fades into the dimness of the trees. I stop just short of the edge of the forest, halted by a certainty. I don't want to go in there. I peer into the half-light, but there's no sign of her. I back away.

A SHARP BUZZING and painful beep, over and over and over, an assault on my ears. My senses reassemble themselves from wherever they were scattered. I emerge bleary and confused, slapping at the source of the insult until it falls and thuds on the floor. A phone. My phone. Answer it.

"Hello?"

"Robert? Can you talk?"

Not very well. "Uh-huh." I'm lying back with my hand over my eyes. Why's my head pounding? Oh, yeah. The whisky.

"Robert..." It's Cora. She sounds upset. I lift myself up onto an elbow. "Are you alright?"

"I'm sorry to call you so early, it's just..." I glance at the alarm clock. Six forty-two. Could be worse.

"No, that's okay. What's up?"

"It's the dreams, Robert."

"What?"

"They're getting worse. I can't sleep. I haven't slept properly for days."

I rub my fingers across my forehead. "Well maybe it's just because we were talking about it. I shouldn't have mentioned it."

"Have you had any more?"

The memory of Sarah walking away, and the feeling I got at the edge of the forest... "Well..."

"You have, haven't you?"

"Look, Cora. It'll go. They're just dreams, that's all. Everyone gets weird dreams sometimes. Don't worry about it."

"You think so? How come we're both getting them, then?"

"I think you got them because I talked about it." I pick up the glass of water on the bedside table. Must have had a few sensible neurons still firing last night before I poured whisky on them and they fizzled out.

"So," she says, "in your dreams, is she waiting for you at a forest, beside a cemetery? Or does she take you to where she's tied to a tree?"

The glass of water falls from my hand.

"How did you know that?" I whisper.

"Because I had the same dream."

"That's impossible."

"What did you say your address was again?"

"Eh, four-four-six Rue de la Croix."

"I think we need to talk face to face. I'll see if I can get a flight."

"What? Wait, no!" I'm on my feet, pacing. "Eh... it's just that I've got a lot of work on over the next few days."

"You've always got a lot of work on, Robert. This is important."

"Cora, this really isn't a good time. I do want to see you, I really do, but how about we leave it for a few days?"

"Please, Robert, I don't know if I can take much more of this. Something's wrong – I can feel it. I'll keep out of

216

your way and I'll sleep on the couch, but I really need your help with this."

"Cora, this isn't a good idea."

"Just for a couple of days."

I let out a long sigh. "Alright."

WHEN I GET to the docks at Versoix, I'm irritated, hungover and uptight. Partly it's Cora's insistence, or my inability to say 'no', but mostly it's the dream. Who the hell has the same dream as someone else? It would be pushing it to say 'coincidence' with *one* dream, but two?

My dad's loading the rods and a few supplies onto a small white rowing boat. I'm going fishing with my dad. It sounds like it should be a normal thing to do, but I'm so far removed from normal that it just seems absurd. Only when we row out away from the docks and the bustle of the small town fades does my mind begin to settle. I even begin to enjoy it. Overhead, the gulls are calling and the clouds are ripples of white and grey low in the sky. The lake is a mirror of them. We let the boat drift and cast off, side by side.

"Have you done much fishing?" he asks.

"I used to, when I was younger. There was a guy, Michael Casimir, who lived in the same village as us. He used to take me out. Sometimes the Crinan Canal, sometimes Lochgilphead."

"Were you lucky?"

"I usually caught a few, and sometimes we'd make a fire and cook them on the beach. It tasted great, fresh from the water." A gull dives into the lake ahead of us, disrupting the stillness. The ripples glide out from its epicentre and the boat rocks a little. "It was never about the fishing, really. What I enjoyed most about those trips was that we got to talk about physics."

"Really?"

"Yeah. I think he's the reason I got into all this in the first place." I steal a glance and see him frowning. "The first time I heard about black holes, I was eating flakes of white coley from tinfoil on a rock. I stopped chewing when he told me that the event horizon was the line beyond which our understanding of physics breaks down. I'll never forget it. I was hooked on the idea that it was out there, waiting to be figured out. My coley was cold by the time I got round to finishing it."

"Sounds like you owe Mr Casimir a great deal."

"I do. He died last week."

"I'm sorry. You must miss him."

"Yeah. He was just like a... I do miss him."

"Were he and your mother...?"

The thought makes me laugh. "God, no. He was a lot older – eighty-two when he died. He was just a good friend, to both of us. Kind of a grandfather."

"Oh."

We stare out in silence for a while. "There was never anyone else," I say. "It was always you."

He sighs and I don't know whether it's what he wanted to hear or not.

"What about you?" I ask.

"What do you mean?"

"Is there anyone else? Do you have a family?"

He lowers his gaze. "No. It was always her, and you."

It's odd to hear him say it. I still feel some bitterness that he could have done things differently, but I don't want to spoil this. I've been waiting for this day my whole life. "It must have been lonely."

"More than I could tell you." He straightens up, shaking his head. "They have these family events they run at CERN, you know; barbeques, hillwalks, picnics, that kind of thing. I used to go at the start, but it just got too painful."

We turn back to the view. Sunlight catches the tree line at the other side of the lake, vibrant green against the backdrop of the shadowy mountains. The reflection, in the stillness of the water, is another world like this one, only not quite.

"Do you think anyone suspects what we're about to do?" I ask.

"In CERN? No. Why, do you?"

"I don't know. There's a guy who I've seen a few times – the first time I went into ATLAS, and then he was there in the cemetery after we met. Dark-haired, walks with a limp, and his face is drooped on one side, like he's had a stroke or something."

He frowns. "I don't know anyone who fits that description. And I've been here long enough to pick out the new faces."

"Do you think Amos is tailing me?"

"Could be. But it's not really his style. We should keep a low profile."

"What happens when all this is over? Will you go back?"

"I dream about it, every single night. But I don't know. There are so many uncertainties. Until it's done, my plan extends only as far as leaving CERN, if I'm not escorted off the premises."

"Do you think they'll link it to us?"

"That depends on how well you've done your job."

"Well, that depends on you getting me into the Computer Centre."

"Ed Petreli is on nightshift in the Operator's Room for the next couple of days," he says. "I'll be able to get him out of there."

"How will you do it?"

"There's a store in the basement where we keep some of our old data. The daystaff don't start till eight, but you can get in overnight, as long as you have a pass and you log out what you're taking. I always have trouble retrieving data and I've known Ed for a long time. He'll come down and help me, but not for long. How much time do you need?"

"Not long. Five minutes to upload the worm."

"What about the security cameras?"

"ORB has that covered."

He reaches into his pocket and pulls out a black security fob, handing it to me. "Tonight. We'll do this tonight." Before he lets go, our eyes meet and I get a heady rush of realisation: this is real; we're doing it.

"Six am. It'll be getting to the end of Ed's shift and his mind will be on other things. Afterwards, go home. Call me from there."

"You could have done all this yourself. I don't understand why Amos needed me."

He looks away. "I'm not a programmer."

"They didn't need a programmer for the idea."

"Maybe he couldn't take that risk," he says, shrugging.

We sit in silence for a while, watching the sunlight on the water.

"How do you face your colleagues every day?" I say "I've only known these people for a few days, but doesn't it eat at you, what we're about to do to them?"

"It used to. I've passed on information for years, something I'm not proud of. No one knew anything about it. It never sat well with me, but it was easier than the alternative. Now that I've had a chance to meet you, there's no question that I'm doing the right thing."

I NEVER ASKED him what he meant by that at the time. Only later did it strike me as an odd thing to say. We stayed on the lake until dusk, going over the details of the plan again. He caught a pike and I caught something you'd find in a bowl in a pet shop. Both of them went back into the water. We weren't there for the fishing.

WHEN I GET back to the apartment, I email Lambert and give him the timings. I set my phone on vibrate and I go over the map of the Computer Centre, rehearsing the way in, swiping the fob on the security panel to the left of the main entrance, the short walk along the corridor to the toilets, third door on the left, where I'll wait until I get the text alert from my dad. When it comes, Ed will be on his way, and once I hear his footsteps walking past, the coast will be clear. The security panel is to the right of the door – I just need to swipe the fob and I'm in. Then it's up to me.

I DON'T SLEEP. Well, I get maybe an hour or so, but at least Sarah stays out of my head. It's too full of everything else. At two am I get up. Guilt is shaking its head and sneering at me. *How could you do be doing this? After everything you've worked for, they've worked for?* I feel for the memory stick carrying Kali, which hangs from the cord round my neck.

I stand at the window and look down at the street below. A couple are walking home, arms round each other. A few teenagers are shouting as they straggle along the middle of the road, bursting with cocky invincibility, ready for anything life dares to throw at them.

You'll never be one hundred per cent certain. Another voice, cold and quiet, silences the guilt: Obligation. *Think of what will happen if you don't. All of those people... everyone.* My fingers close round Kali and squeeze. *You don't have a choice.*

I PARK IN the services area and walk to the Computer Centre. It's a hazy dawn and my breath mists in the cool air. The place is quiet. Shifts change at eight and I don't meet anyone. My dad must already be in there. As I reach the entrance, my heart is thundering in my chest. I swipe the fob and the door clicks open. No one in the corridor. Above me the security camera blinks a red eye beside its black, blank face. Mr Y, you'd better have got this right. I make my way to the third door on the left and push it open. It squeaks on its hinges, making me wince. No one in here. I stand with my back to the door, listening to the drip, drip, drip of a leaking tap, and the sound of my breathing, and wait.

The phone in my pocket vibrates. I press my ear to the door, listening. Beyond the tribal drum of my pulse, I hear footsteps. I step back, hoping he doesn't decide to go for a piss first. The footsteps fade away and there's the sound of a door closing. I give it a minute, then open the door and step out into the corridor.

The entrance to the Operator's Room is twenty metres away on the right. I can see the security panel to the right of the door and reach for the fob, but stop suddenly. A door on the left is opening – *Shit*. I try the door nearest me but it's locked, I'm half way down the corridor and there's nowhere to go. I turn and walk back the way I came, trying to look casual.

"Can I help you?"

I turn. Helena fucking Stanford. "I was just here to see if I could arrange a look round."

"At six-fifteen in the morning? How did you get in?"

"They gave me a pass when I got here – I'm attached to ATLAS, but I asked if I could see what's going on in the Computer Centre." I snort. "I know it looks keen, but with the engineering checks happening in ATLAS just now, there's not a lot to do and, well, I couldn't sleep."

She's looking at me in a cold appraising way. Does she suspect something? No, I'm being paranoid. That's the look she gives everyone. *Just relax, you're doing fine.*

"That *is* keen," she says. "Well, I'd love to show you round, but I'm just on my way home. I've still got a lot to go over before Monday. Maybe some other time."

"Sure. That would be good."

She nods and walks away then stops. "You know," she says, turning back, "I spoke to my ex-husband last night. He said he doesn't know you."

"Yeah, like I said, I only just started there recently – not had much of a chance to meet people."

She raises an eyebrow. "Tony usually knows all the new starts."

"Well, I keep myself to myself." I try to make it sound light-hearted but she doesn't smile. She turns slowly and walks away.

I walk in the opposite direction, considering whether I should double back once she's clear. My phone vibrates

again, the warning text that Ed's on his way back. *Fuck.*
Fuck. Fuck. I dart into the toilets and wait till he passes,
then head for the exit.

WHEN I GET back to the apartment, I'm royally fucked
off. Of all the bloody people to bump into. I call my
dad. "No go."

"What?"

"Helena caught me in the corridor."

"Oh, shit. Did she see you go into the ops room?"

"No."

"Well, that's something." He sighs. "I'll need to create
another opportunity, tonight. I'll be in touch."

"Okay."

"And Robert?"

"Yeah?"

"Get some sleep."

When I log on to the notebook, Lambert's email is
already waiting for me.

From: llambert@ltp.com
To: rstrong@ltp.com
Sent: 14th May 06.25
Subject: re

That went well.

I reply:

Fuck you, Lambert. Have you any idea how difficult
all this is?

I take a few deep breaths and press *erase*. Then start again:

Regrouping tonight. Will send confirmation. I need proof that I was transferred in from Romfield. Get me on their staff role. What's the update on your admin access?

He responds immediately:

Staff role no problem.
   Re access – still no joy. May have to admit defeat on this one, but will keep you posted.
   Good luck.

I close it down and try to sleep.

SLEEP'S NOT HAPPENING. I try to read, but I can't concentrate. I watch some TV, I surf the net. Finally, worn out, I give in. It feels like I'm just on the descent when the phone goes. I scramble about until I find it in my jeans pocket, hanging over the back of the chair, but I've missed the call by the time I get to it.

I listen to the voicemail. "Hey, Robert! Rene here. We are off to climb at Leaz, it's an escarpment overlooking the Rhone, then we are going to Charlie's Bar later. If you wanna come, give me a call!"

I don't even consider it. I can't face another bonding session, not now. I turn the phone to silent, put it back in my coat pocket and try to go back to sleep.

It doesn't work.

Thanks Rene. Your timing sucks. I get up.

I make myself a late lunch, but hardly eat any of it, then, restless, get dressed and take a walk into town. The streets are busy. Saturday shoppers, Saturday tourists. I should feel like a tourist. Instead I feel like a criminal. It spoils the ambience.

Geneva is a stylish place. Lots of beautiful people, well dressed, well groomed, slim. In the breaks between buildings I can see the fountain, Jet d'Eau it's called. I remember reading somewhere that it's large enough that you can see it from anywhere in the city. It was once an escape valve for the dam, but now it's a tourist attraction. The wind spreads it sideways, forming a curtain of white spray. There are lots of small cafés on this street, with menus written on blackboards on the walls outside. I stop to read one of them, trying to figure out what food words I recognise from O-Level French. Anything to take my mind off what's coming tonight.

Raised voices come from inside – a couple arguing in English. "Why are you doing this?" he says.

I glance in through the window to my right. A block of sunlight illuminates half of the room. The woman has her back to me – slim, dark-haired, wiping a cloth vigorously over the surface of a table. "After what they did to me, cleaning tables gives me some sense of normality. I just want my life back." She slams the salt and pepper shakers down.

"Look, I know how you feel, but..." He's standing in the shadows and I can't see his face.

"You know how I feel?"

"I was in the same place myself once, Aiyana."

Why are we intrigued by other people's strife? I'm not reading the menu anymore; I'm eavesdropping.

She moves to another table, scrubbing its surface with

a brutality that suggests it's done her a great personal wrong, and as she turns I recognise her blue eyes. It's the woman from the other day, the woman who stopped me getting mowed down by the Lamborghini. I could say thanks. Or maybe get her phone number.

In the middle of an argument? And what about Cora? This isn't a good time.

What if there isn't another time, though?

"You can't change things, Aiyana," says the man as my eyes dart back to the blackboard. "What did you think would happen?"

"Think? *Think?* Why would I think? I was thirty-three years old – I wasn't ready!"

"Look," he says, his voice low and patient, "give it some time. You might see things differently in a while."

"I doubt that." Another slam for a pepper-pot in the wrong place at the wrong time.

"Well, you know where we are."

The door opens without warning and I'm caught loitering. I stride towards the entrance, reaching for it, as though I was on my way in. The man steps back and holds the door open for me. "Thanks," I say, but the word catches in my throat as I glance at him. "You..."

The gangster smiles at me with his beetle-black eyes, the web tattoo just visible at the side of his neck.

"You were there, when the guy held me up. If it weren't for you..."

"It was nothing." Now that I see him in the daylight, he doesn't strike me as a gangster. Then again, the only gangsters I've seen are the ones in films, so I wouldn't really know.

The woman has stopped venting her spleen on the tables and now stands watching us. They're wearing matching stone necklaces – his and hers – oval pebbles on leather threads. I was never going to get her phone number. What was I thinking?

I breathe a nervous laugh. "I was passing and I saw you and... well. I just wanted to say thanks." She smiles unconvincingly and there's an uncomfortable pause. I try to break it with something frivolous. "And to find you both here, that's eh... that's quite..."

"A coincidence?" he says.

She glances at him.

Another awkward silence and I recall that I did just burst in at the end of their disagreement.

"Well," I say, glancing at my feet. "Thanks anyway. I appreciate what you did. Both of you."

"That's alright." He has this faraway look in his eyes.

Okay, Robert, that's your cue to leave. I turn towards the door, then hesitate. I won't get another chance. I turn and ask, "How did you know?"

"Sorry?" she says.

"How did you know the car would jump the lights?" Her eyes shift towards the man again and I follow her gaze. "And how did you scare off that mugger?"

He studies me for a moment with an unblinking stare. "Do you really want to know?" he says. "Think before you answer."

I'm not asking for a rundown on Chaos Theory, for God's sake. I'm just curious. "Yeah, of course I do."

"Alright then. Why don't we buy you a drink? There's a pub round the corner." He gestures towards the door.

I step outside, feeling even more awkward than I did a minute ago. A sentence of explanation was all I was after. "No, look, I don't want to impose..."

"Well, how about you buy us a drink, then?"

I hesitate, beginning to regret the question, but it's the least I can do. "Okay, then."

"You did ask," she says, regarding me through lidded blue eyes as she walks past me into the street and reaches back to close the door. She smells of cinnamon, of Christmas.

We turn into an alley. There are cobblestones between the squat rows of shops, restaurants and cafes. We weave between shoppers ambling along in the blade of sunshine slicing between the high buildings.

"You're not local," I say. "Where are you from?"

"Originally?" he says. "London."

"Nevada," she says. "My name's Aiyana." She attempts to smile, although it still looks like an effort for her.

"Robert. Robert Strong."

I turn back to the man. "Balaquai," he says.

Is that a first name or a surname? I don't ask.

A woman pushing a pram is walking towards us, the baby inside bawling in vibrato as the pram judders over the cobblestones. Balaquai steps aside to let her past. We pass a tea shop on the right. Red and yellow flowers spill from tin buckets on the cobbles at its entrance. A jewellery shop on the left displays an array of glittery things on black cushions. We turn down a lane to the left, which is narrower and quieter, the familiarity of shops fading, becoming ones selling trinkets and old books – a little dustier, a little darker. I'm not sure about this, but I don't want to go back to the apartment yet and they did help me out.

There's a pub at the end of the alley, dwarfed by the huge deserted warehouse butting up against it. It looks old, from a time when people must have been a lot smaller, its windows and door set in thick stone walls. Dark wooden beams interlace the stonework on the outside, like an old Tudor house, and it's leaning a little to the left. A weathervane sits on the point of its eves, black iron with a bird of some kind on top. It pivots in the breeze. There's a brass sign outside which reads La Caverne, above a rose carved into the stone.

We step inside. The cave-like interior extends away into the gloom, far further than I expect after seeing the outside of the bar. The uneven walls arch up to become a low ceiling, which is propped up by curved, dark wooden beams. A bar sits in the corner to the left. I'm relieved to see a few people sipping drinks at the tables dotted about the room. Balaquai nods towards the woman pouring a beer at the bar. She has a broad, handsome face framed by an unruly mass of dark curls that seem a kind of deep purple when the light catches them. She smiles widely and nods. I move towards the bar, studying the choice of beer chalked up on the board above the cash register.

"What'll you have?" I ask them.

"A Grolsch," says Aiyana.

"Make that two. Balaquai?"

"Just water."

"I'll bring them up to you. It's on the house," says the barmaid as I reach into my pocket.

"Really?"

She grins again, her dark eyes glinting.

I follow Balaquai towards the back of the room, but he doesn't go for the empty table in the corner. Instead he opens a door that leads into a narrow corridor, dimly lit, with dark wooden-panelled walls and an old staircase. He takes the stairs to the upper level and

Aiyana follows, her expression something between irritable and resigned. Chatter drifts down from above, so at least there are other people up there.

The stairs open out into another cave of a room with low arched ceilings and long wooden tables. Candles flicker in sconces, fixed at regular intervals around the walls. It's busier here; at least half of the tables are full. I follow Balaquai towards a table in the corner. A large fireplace is set into the wall nearby. It's as wide as a two-seater couch with a lintel that would crush you flat if it fell on you. My footsteps become louder on the wooden floor, and I realise it's because of the sudden silence. Everyone in the room has stopped talking, and they're all looking at me. *Shit*. Is this some kind of weird club that I've gatecrashed? God, I hope it's not some wacko religious group. Scientologists, or something like that. I'm beginning to regret all of this.

"Have a seat, Robert," says a man who gets to his feet as we approach. He's black, older than me, although I've no idea how old, with a dark beard and clean-shaven head. He's wearing a loose black suit, only when you look at it closely, it's not really a suit and it's not really black. It's more of a bluish-black, like the colour of a mussel shell. His eyes have a certain look in them, the same look that Balaquai has. It's an odd mixture of intensity and distance. I glance around the room. They all have that look, these people, like they know something I don't. Why the hell are they all staring? And how does he know my name?

He smiles at me with his eyes as I sit down opposite. Balaquai and Aiyana take a seat.

"Glad you could join us," says the man. I feel like I recognise him, like I know his voice from somewhere. A grey oval stone hangs round his neck on a cord, just like theirs. "I'm sorry, do I know you?"

"No, not yet. My name is Gomda Sattva. Nice to meet you." He brings his palms together and bows a little.

Before I know it, I find myself reciprocating his gesture, then flush when I realise what I'm doing.

"I didn't think you'd be so willing to meet us."

My defences go up. If he wants me to join his church, he picked the wrong guy. "Look," I say, "I just wanted to buy these two a drink to thank them for helping me out, that's all."

"Of course. So how are you settling into CERN?"

I stare at him. "How did you know I'm there?"

"We know a lot of things, Mr Strong."

What is this? Does he work there? "Look. I don't mean to be rude, Mr Sattva, but today's not the best day." I turn to the others. "I appreciate what you did, but I've got a lot on just now." I turn to leave.

"We know what you're planning to do," says Sattva.

The blood drains from my face as I turn back to him.

"Please, sit down," he says, gently.

My legs are beginning to tremble as I find the seat. *Focus, Robert. This could all be a misunderstanding.* "What do you mean?"

"We know you're planning to sabotage the experiments."

Fuck. "Don't be ridiculous."

"Let's not play games, Robert. There's more going on around you than even you know." Where have I heard that before? "I suppose Amos gave you a plausible explanation. Something in writing, no doubt."

Do I walk out? What if they blow the whistle in CERN? The possibility of prison hadn't occurred to me before, but it's there now: grey walls, barred windows, stripy sheets and a cellmate with a beard who likes to be called Miriam. "How do you know Amos?"

"Let's just say we go back a few years. He can be quite persuasive, can't he?"

Don't commit to anything – he can't have any proof. "Some people believe the experiments are dangerous."

"Like your father?"

I don't answer.

"Have you considered that perhaps there is something other than belief driving his convictions? Fear, for instance?"

"Fear of what?"

Sattva's eyes meet Balaquai's briefly. "Robert, Victor Amos is not who you think he is. And as you've only just met him, I would say that your trust has been misplaced."

"If Amos is right, and I do nothing..."

"Ask yourself this. Do you believe, in the core of your being, that you're doing the right thing?"

A pool of sweat has gathered at the nape of my neck.

"You don't have to tell me. Just be honest with yourself before you do something you regret."

"What do you want, Mr Sattva?"

"I want you to let the experiments proceed as they're meant to."

I lean across the table. "And what if he's right? What if they do produce strangelets and we just sit back and let it happen? There's evidence that proves their existence. The CERN Council buried it, because it didn't have the stomach to abandon things this far down the line. But all it takes is the right conditions and we've got the Ice-nine reaction on our doorstep."

"And you're persuaded by this evidence?"

"Yes. I found a paper which proves it beyond all reasonable doubt. I even spoke to the author's wife – she validates what Amos said."

"Did you speak to the author himself?"

"No. He's not well enough to have a conversation."

"How convenient."

"What are you suggesting?"

Sattva regards me with an even stare. "Do you really believe that the CERN council would ignore evidence as persuasive as you found it to be?"

There's a buzzing sound in my ears and my palms are beginning to sweat. "Why do you care so much about them? What are you, a physicist?"

"No. But there's more at stake here than the curiosity of scientists." He sits back, and holds me with his level stare. "Those experiments will open doors to places you can't even begin to imagine."

Maybe he's just a crazy man with a bone to pick with Amos.

Sattva continues, "You came here because you wanted to find out how Aiyana and Balaquai helped you avoid a car accident and a gunshot wound."

And I wish to God I hadn't. I glance towards them. Balaquai is watching me and Aiyana is frowning at the table.

"In the same way you knew how to find your way down the mountain in Tibet. Everyone's entangled with everyone else to some extent, but some much more than others."

It's as though the temperature in the room has suddenly plunged.

"But if you don't want to know, that's your choice."

The barmaid arrives and places the drinks on the table.

"Thank you, Rosinda." Sattva smiles mildly, as though we've just been chatting about the weather.

"How did you know about Tibet?"

"Do you know the story of Ernest Shackleton, Robert?" says Sattva.

"The explorer?"

"That's right. In 1915, his ship, the *Endurance*, became trapped in ice during an expedition to Antarctica. The ice crushed her to pieces over the course of nine months, forcing the men to abandon ship. After six months of camping on ice floes, they took their small boats to Elephant Island, an outcrop of the Antarctic Peninsula. Their supplies were all but gone, so, from there, Shackleton and two other men began the trek over the glacial mountains to the whaling station in South Georgia, eleven hundred kilometres away. They made it to their destination, and the other men were rescued, but later, when Shackleton recorded his experiences, he admitted that he felt there were four men on that trek, not three."

"Maybe he miscounted. Hypothermia and dehydration can do that to you."

"Who else was with you and Danny when you came down the mountain?"

My mouth's gone dry. "How could you possibly..."

"Because I was there, Robert."

"What?"

"I was the one who told you to get up, I was the one who gave you the certainty in your stride, I was the one who showed you which was the right way down through the blizzard."

Is that where I know his voice from? I glance at Balaquai and Aiyana. "Is this a joke?"

Aiyana shakes her head. "I wish it were," she whispers.

"What, and I suppose you two stepped out just when I needed help, right on cue?"

"Funny thing, coincidence," says Balaquai.

It feels like I'm immersed in fog. "Is this some kind of Big Brother thing? Is there some satellite link where you're watching me? Chalking up my debt so that I'd help you out when you need it?" This is creeping me out.

"No, it's not like that."

"Well, what then?"

"Don't you get it?" says Aiyana. "We're not from here... anymore."

Sattva watches me, his expression unreadable. Something I overheard Aiyana say in the café comes back to me. *I just want my life back*. My arms have gone cold and the hairs on my neck are standing on end.

"Oh, come on. This is some kind of sick joke, right? A set up?"

"It's not a joke," says Sattva.

I become aware of someone standing to my right. "Hello, Robert."

The world slows down. I'm on my feet, the chair scraping on the wooden floor, clattering over behind me.

Sattva's eyes stay on me. "I believe you already know Michael Casimir."

Chapter Twelve

"CASIMIR?"

He nods slowly and smiles.

Is it him? Something's different; like the lines that gave such character and depth to his face have been erased. And his eyes – he has that look, like only part of him is here.

He offers me a handshake, the muscles of his forearms well defined, and the skin smooth, unblemished. He's younger. Christ, he's *alive*, and he's younger than he was before.

"Aren't you at least going to shake my hand?"

Slowly, I reach my hand towards his, unsure if I want to find out what it feels like to shake hands with a dead man. His grip is firm, solid, like nothing has changed.

"How are you?" he asks.

"How am I?" I laugh, struck by the absurdity of what he just said.

"Lighten up, Robert." He grins at me and slaps my shoulder, glancing at the others as he sits down next to Sattva.

I'm still standing there, staring at him, trying to process what's happening.

"Oh, come on. Sit down."

I don't move.

"Robert, are you okay?"

"You're dead." The words come out as a whisper.

"Depends on your perspective."

My fingers find the edge of the seat and I lower myself into it, slowly. "Please. Just tell me what's going on."

Sattva studies me with his dark eyes. I'm not sure how old he is; there's something about him that makes it difficult to judge. "Once I tell you," he says, "there's no going back. It will colour the way you see everything – *everything* – from now on. Are you sure you want to know?"

I'm not sure of anything anymore. The man who's sitting across the table from me should be in a box six feet underground, eight hundred miles away. I can see my sanity dribbling down the plughole unless I get some answers. Maybe it's headed that way anyway. "I need to know."

"Then you're going to have to take a step back from the way you see the world. And given how much time you've invested in studying the way things are, you might find this a little tricky."

"Just tell me."

Sattva regards me silently for a moment before he begins. "We all lived here once, the same as you. Different places, different times, but we all had a mother and father, we were all children, we all grew up. We had lives and families and occupations. We loved our children, and wanted the best for them. We had dreams and worries, ambitions and fears. We were, essentially, just like you. But at some point, those lives ran out. Whatever we learned from dying, we forgot when we were reborn. But over time, we evolved through each death, remembering and understanding a little more of what we really are.

"We've been called many things over the ages, but I think the term 'Eidolon' best describes us."

"What does that mean?"

"It means shade, or shadow. We can move between worlds."

It's sinking in, slowly, like a pebble falling through a drum of crude oil. "You mean you're all dead." I glance about the room, feeling queasy. "All these people...?"

Sattva nods and raises an eyebrow. "Does that bother you?"

Does it bother me that I'm in a roomful of stiffs? "You could say that."

"Why?"

"Because none of this should be happening, that's why. You shouldn't be here – you should be food for daffodils, nothing more. It doesn't make any sense."

"So, it's not fitting in with your idea of how things are."

"No! None of it is."

"I see." Sattva clasps his hands loosely on his lap. "Have you considered that perhaps you're working from the wrong premise?"

"No, I haven't, actually, because everything in my life experience so far tells me that my premise is working just fine."

"So," says Casimir, "how do you explain me being here?"

"I have no idea. Maybe it's insanity."

"You're not going mad," says Balaquai, as though he's said this a thousand times before. "Everyone finds it difficult to adjust at first."

"Everyone? Who is everyone? I've not met anyone who knows anything about this stuff. Apart from Cora."

"It's all semantics," says Sattva. "Death is just a word for something you've forgotten. It's not an end point; it's just a transition, that's all. Once you come to terms with that, the rest is easy."

"Easy? Why is it that we don't all know about this?"

"I think it's fair to say that a lot of people do."

"That's not what I meant. Why is it that I suddenly know about this? Why is this happening to me?"

Sattva leans towards me, resting his elbows on the table. "Ah, now that's a better question. Because your brush with death opened your eyes to what else is around you. It's not as sudden as you make out, Robert. You've always known, to some degree, that there's more. It's why you dedicated your life to looking for something no-one can see."

I stare at him. "That's different."

"No it's not. You see, Robert, life and death are fluid; they're not binary states. There's a spectrum of existence that corresponds to awareness. At one end are men and women who live their life on the understanding that that is all there is. At the other are those like us, who know our potential and use it. And in between are Sentients; who sense things others can't, but are still searching for what that is."

"Like Cora," says Casimir.

"Cora?"

"She's always known. Like you, only you're afraid to admit it."

He's wrong. That's not how I think, at all. At least, it wasn't... my objections cave in on themselves. Visions of insanity come to me – tranquilizer injections, wearing a dotted nightgown and playing Connect Four in some high security unit that doesn't allow visitors because you already have enough of your own. No-one will ever believe any of this. I know I don't. I reach up and pull my T-shirt away from my neck. I feel like I can't breathe. "How did you know about the sabotage?"

Casimir leans forward. "When I pulled you from the sea after the crash, your mind was wide open. It told me everything."

"Victor Amos is not who you think he is," says Sattva. "We need you to help us find out what he's planning."

"Why? If you know so much about everything – if you can just show up when I need help – why do you need me? Why can't you figure this out yourselves?"

"We have too much history with Amos. You are our best link to him, and for now, he is unaware that our paths have crossed."

My phone buzzes in my pocket, making me jump. There is a God, and he's giving me a way out of here.

I stand up and take the call, moving towards the fireplace. "Hello?"

"Robert?"

"Cora?" Relief floods through me. A lifeline to reality. "Thank God."

"Robert, are you alright? Why are you whispering?"

"Yeah, I'm... I'm okay. Where are you?"

"I'm at the airport – in Geneva."

"What?"

"Did you get my message? I called you three times this morning."

"No, I, eh... my phone was on vibrate – I must have missed them."

"Listen, I got a standby flight, last minute. Where are you?"

"I... I'm just heading back to the apartment now."

"Great, I'll see you there."

I hang up, and turn back to them, sitting watching me. A clash of two worlds, and I've no idea which one I'm in. "I need to go."

Sattva and Casimir get to their feet. "Robert, please," says Casimir. "You can't go through with your plans. At least speak to your father. Find out what's driving him, and you'll understand."

Sattva nods. "You know where we are."

Chapter Thirteen

I MAKE MY way hastily down the stairs and weave past a group of people coming into the pub, glancing back, wondering if they're alive or... I break out into the street, gulping in real air with the smells of the city: hops from a vent in the wall, cooking fat, fresh bread. I emerge from the alley and turn back onto the main drag, moving between the ambling consumers, all doing normal things.

When I get into my apartment, I slam the door and bolt it shut. The place is just as I left it. The wall-mounted TV, the gas fire, the perfect kitchen. I flick on the TV. Normal news, normal crap daytime TV. Normal.

The sound of the buzzer makes me jump. "Hello?"

"Robert? It's me."

She doesn't get far through the door before I fling my arms around her. I bury my face in her neck, breathing in the scent of jasmine, the scent of home. I don't want to let go.

She untangles herself from me, frowning. "Are you alright?"

"No, I'm not." I'm past pretending.

She comes inside, and I glance up and down the corridor, not quite sure what I'm expecting to see, then close the door.

"Wow. This is some place. You must be doing something right."

"You know what, Cora? I've no idea what I'm doing."

She sits down on the edge of the couch, looking uncomfortable. "More nightmares?"

Oh, God, if it that was all it was. Where do I begin? "Something like that." I pace over to the window and glance down at the street.

"So does this place belong to Mr Amos?"

"Yeah."

She nods to herself as she appraises the layout. "Well, he's certainly looking after you. Listen, I'm sorry all this happened so quickly. I didn't give you much of a choice. It's just the dreams have been getting bad recently. You're the only one I can talk to about it."

"Who'd have thought?"

"Yeah. It's the feeling that scares me more than the dream. I can't shake it when I wake up. Is that how you feel?"

"Yeah, but..."

"What do you think it means? Do you think she's trying to tell us something?"

"I don't know. Cora, I need to talk to you about something, too. Let's go out. You must be hungry."

THE LIGHT IS beginning to fade and there's a cool drizzle on the air. I glance behind me as we turn into a side street. There's a small cafe on the left with a bay tree propped outside next to a couple of empty tables and chairs. It looks quiet inside. "This'll do."

It's long, narrow and dim inside, with a counter on the left. Candles spill pools of yellow light onto the tables tucked against the wall beneath pictures of Geneva in the 'fifties. I choose a table near the back and make a point of sitting so that I can see through the door to the street. A tall, skinny candle drips wax onto a saucer in the middle of the table, beside the laminated menu.

"What would you like?"

Cora glances at the menu then folds it and puts it to one side. "Just a coffee. I'm not hungry."

The waiter takes our order, smiles and leaves.

"What's wrong, Robert? Is this about the dreams?" Cora says.

I drag my fingers back and forth across my chin and breathe a laugh. "I don't know if I'm going mad, Cora ..."

She stares at me, waiting.

"I saw Michael Casimir today."

"What?"

"In a bar. I had a conversation with him, and some other people who were... like him."

"Do you mean..."

"I mean dead, Cora. I had a conversation with people who were dead. I had a beer with them, for Christ's sake."

A ripple of scepticism crosses her face. "You had a beer with them."

"Look, I know this is hard to hear, even for you, but they knew things they couldn't have known. Things no one else knows."

"What kind of things?"

"They knew about the... job that Amos wants me to do."

She chews on the corner of her lip for a moment, then says, "What *is* it he wants you to do, Robert?"

I take a deep breath but I can't meet her eye as I speak. "He wants me to sabotage the CERN experiments."

"*What?*"

I can't look at her. The waiter arrives and places two small cups of black coffee on the table, each with a chocolate wrapped in golden foil.

"Are you crazy?" She says when he's gone. She glances around then leans closer, whispering. "You didn't do it, did you?"

"Not yet."

She has a look that's somewhere between incredulity and disgust. "You mean you're going to?"

"Listen, I know how this sounds, but there's evidence, strong evidence, that the experiments have a high chance of triggering a cataclysmic event. End of the world scenario. I didn't believe it until I read the research myself. CERN knows about this – they're burying it."

"Have you spoken to your dad about all this?"

"He knows all about it. He was the one who alerted Amos. He's convinced, like I was..." I break off, stifling the frustration that's bubbling up inside me. "Dammit, I had this all worked out!"

She sits back quietly, watching me, turning the chocolate over in her fingers, then puts it in her pocket.

"So, you're not sure?"

"I was, until Casimir and his friends showed up. Eidolon – that's what they call themselves."

"Eidolon? Isn't that a Greek concept?"

"I dunno. I'd never heard of it."

"Yeah, they believed that when you die you divide into three parts – your Psyche, or consciousness, your

Thymus, or life force, and the rest of you becomes an Eidolon – a shadow."

I don't say anything.

"So what did they say?"

"They knew all about it. They tried to talk me out of it, said Amos isn't who I think he is."

"Well, who is he, then?"

"We didn't get that far."

"Why would he want to stop the experiments?"

"I don't know."

"Do you believe them?"

"I don't know what to believe any more."

She lays a hand on mine.

"Robert, are you sure about all this? I mean, it just sounds..."

God, I really need her to believe me. If she doesn't, no-one will. But I can see in her eyes that she's struggling. "I saw them, Cora. It happened."

"You mean like I saw Sarah?"

I knew it was coming. "Yeah. Like you saw Sarah. I'm sorry. I should have believed you."

She lowers her eyes and twirls the salt pot on its base. "Did you ask them about her?"

"No... I didn't get a chance."

She nods at her coffee cup.

"Please, Cora, I'm not making this up."

She leans her elbows on the table and doesn't meet my eye. She doesn't buy it.

There's nothing else for it. "Alright then, I'll show you."

I LEAD HER down the cobbled alleyway into the quiet lane. It's dusk now, and a streetlamp flickers on and off above us. La Caverne is at the end of the lane, and light from its windows spills onto the pavement. The weathervane spins on the eaves in the breeze. Chatter, laughter, music, the muffled sounds of a bar, come from inside. Thank God it's here. Part of me was afraid it wouldn't be. I push open the door. Most of the tables are full, and no one pays any attention when we walk in. Behind the bar is a young blonde girl with a nose-stud and a tattoo and a stocky guy in a tight T-shirt. The girl says something to me in French, then, realising I don't understand, switches to English. "What would you like?"

"Is Rosinda here?" I ask.

"Who?"

"Never mind."

I lead Cora to the door in the corner, but it's locked. She stares at me expectantly.

"This was the way in..." I mumble, then go back to the bar. "Can you open the door? I need to go upstairs."

The barmaid frowns. "There's no seating upstairs. It's just a store room."

"No, there's tables and a fireplace and..."

She's looking at me like I'm crazy. "It's a store room. There's nothing up there except boxes."

Anxiety flutters inside me. "Please, I need to see it. I was here earlier today. Just let me have a look, and if I'm wrong we'll go. No problem." I slide a twenty euro bill towards her.

She glances sideways at the guy in the tight T-shirt and pockets the money. Then she lifts a bunch of keys from a hook and leads us to the door. It creaks as it open and she flicks on the light switch and steps over two boxes of beer. She gestures for us to go on up. I walk up the stairs, Cora just behind me. It's too quiet.

I feel sick. The room's stacked with crates and boxes. No tables, no chairs, no Eidolon. I walk over to the fireplace. The large lintel's still there, but it's cold. There hasn't been a fire here for a long time. Two chairs, one stacked on top of the other, where the coals should be. I turn back to Cora, slowly.

She's standing with her arms wrapped round her, watching me with a look that's something between pity and wariness.

"It was here, before. This is where I spoke to them..."

She bites her lip.

"Cora, I mean it."

"I believe that you believe it," she says.

Great.

THE BARMAID HAS a smirk on her face as we pass her. Easiest twenty euros she's ever made. I just want to get out of here. I hold the door open for Cora and let her out, when I catch sight of someone. He's sitting alone in the corner, a mop of black hair, a lopsided face. He watches me as he sips his beer.

I stride towards him, leaning over the table and into his face, keeping my voice low. "What is it you want?"

His voice is like gravel. "You already know."

"You stay away from me, you hear me? Just stay away."

His lip curls up at one end as he watches me, unperturbed.

"Robert..." whispers Cora. I feel her hand inside mine, pulling me away towards the door. I let it swing back and it clatters shut behind us.

"Who was he?"

"Amos is tailing me."

We walk on in silence. Then she says, "I'm sorry, Robert."

I can't speak.

"I don't know what you saw back there, but... I'm sorry you didn't find them."

"Don't worry about it. Let's just go back to the apartment."

"Look," says Cora when I hand her a mug of coffee in the kitchen. She wraps her hands around it, the sleeves of her jumper sitting low so that only her fingers are poking out. "I don't know what to make of the dreams I've been having, but I know I saw Sarah that day in our flat. If you say you saw Michael Casimir today, then I believe you."

"There was nothing there, Cora. We both saw that." I slam the fridge door shut and turn to her. "Maybe it's just guilt. I don't want to be the one who sabotages CERN, why would I? But if I don't... Maybe I'm just making things up to talk myself out of it."

"So what happened to you this afternoon?" she says. "Where were you?"

"Maybe I didn't go out. Maybe I dreamt it. It's just" – I shake my head – "it seemed so real." I feel afraid of myself, and it scares me.

She puts her arms around me and I feel the warmth of her embrace, and breathe in the scent of her hair. She's the only thing I understand right now. I stare at the wooden floorboards, polished to perfection. It feels like I'm stuck in twilight, that time when it's neither night nor day, just something indistinct, in between.

I can't go on like this. I need to regain control.

I have to make a choice.

My phone buzzes in my pocket. My dad's number. I walk over to the window to take the call, glancing below. It's raining and the drops drift down like golden glitter in the street light.

"Robert?"

"Yeah."

"Let's get this done."

"Where are you?"

"In my office. When can you get here?"

I glance at my watch and then at Cora. She takes out the chocolate she lifted from the cafe. She eats it as she smoothes out the foil wrapper, and wraps it around her index finger, making a little golden goblet. Her habit. "Ten p.m." I say.

"Okay. Same as before. I'll text you when you're clear."

I walk over to Cora and take her silver ring from my pocket. Lifting her hair aside, I tie it around her neck, so that it sits in the hollow between her collar bones. "It suits you," I say.

"I know." She kisses me on the lips. "It always did."

"I need to go."

She pulls away. "Where?"

"I'll be back in a while."

"You're not going through with this, are you?"

"Cora, we both saw that there was nothing in that attic today. It didn't happen. It's guilt, nothing more. I just need to get over it."

I take out the notebook and email Lambert. *Going live 22.00 tonight.*

He replies immediately. *Got that. Good luck.*

"Wait, Robert. You need to think about this. Even if it was just your imagination, it's telling you something. Listen to it."

"I was never going to feel good about this. But if I don't go through with it... I can't walk away, Cora. It's too important. There's too much at stake."

"Please, Robert. At least talk it through with your dad."

I don't reply, but go over to the window and check the street below. There's no sign of anyone. "I'll be back soon." I kiss her again and leave.

Chapter Fourteen

MEYRIN HIGHWAY IS almost clear of traffic. The bike handles well, even in the wet. The moon dips in and out of a bank of thick cloud. I turn into the main entrance, half an hour early, and consider turning back onto the highway to mark time when I see him again. The headlight sweeps past him on the bend, as he walks in the opposite direction, lurching in his characteristic rolling gate, the silhouette of his long coat flapping in the patchy moonlight. His head turns as I pass. I drive on then pull the bike to the side of the road, and glance back. He's making his way towards ATLAS. Keeping my distance, I see him walk in through the entrance. I check my watch. Twenty minutes to spare. I turn back, leave the bike by the entrance and follow him. Only two cars are parked here, and one of them is my dad's silver Volvo. I swipe my entry card and step inside.

There's no sign of him inside. I stop, listening, then hear uneven footsteps on the stairs. Glancing up, I can see the tail of his coat as it disappears onto the next level, into the office corridor. There's a sudden clatter and the sound of glass smashing. I take the rest of the stairs two at a time to the first floor. The lights are on in the office corridor, but the control room is locked up, and my dad's office sits in darkness. There's no sign of him, and it's eerily quiet. A framed photograph is lying on the floor, splinters of glass surrounding it. I pick it up, turning it over to let the remaining glass fall to the floor. Quick footsteps come from the end of the corridor and my pulse picks up. I try my dad's door, but it's locked. Florence appears at the top of the hallway.

She gasps and places a hand across her chest. "Oh, you scared me. I didn't think anyone else was in. What happened?" She fusses towards me and takes the broken picture from my hand.

"Where did he go?"

"Professor Stiller?"

I check the office doors, but they're all locked, then pace up to the end of the corridor, to where Florence came from. There's no-one there.

"No. There was a man here, long coat, dark hair, just a minute ago."

"I haven't seen anyone."

"You couldn't have missed him, Florence. He broke the picture -- I heard it when I came upstairs."

"Honestly, I haven't seen anyone else. I'm just getting some last minute things done before Monday. It's all locked up, and I've got the keys."

"Is there any other way out of here?"

"No. Do you want me to call security?"

"*No*. No. That's okay. Maybe I imagined it."

"You're in very late."

"Yeah... making the most of it."

She looks down at the photo in her hands. "It's a shame. But I'll get it fixed when I get back."

I look at the picture, a group photo. I recognise Rene, Jack and my dad and...

"It was taken at one of our family days. They're ever so much fun."

"Is that Professor Thorpe?" I point at the tall wiry man in the front row with the tangled black hair.

"Yes, that's Professor Thorpe, bless him. And his wife." She points to a small, dark haired, dumpy woman. He has his arm around her. "Poor woman. She'll never get over it."

"That's not his wife."

"Yes, that's Olivia."

"No, I've met her – she's blonde and, eh, slim."

She chuckles. "No, not Olivia. She's been battling with the bulge for years now, poor thing. It's all that pasta, if you ask me."

I stare at her. "Are you sure?"

"Of course. I've known her for years."

Holy fuck.

"Excuse me."

"You've still got those papers to sign!" she calls after me.

"I'll get to them, Florence."

I push through the door into the car park, my heart hammering. I can barely press the digits on my phone.

"It's me. We need to talk."

"Later, Robert. We're all set. Ten minutes."

"No. Meet me at the church. Now."

* * *

I HEAR THE sound of the tyres crunching and see the headlights swing into the driveway of the church. I leave my helmet on the bike and wait for him to approach, then lead him inside. I can't see who's in the shadows in the church grounds, and I don't want to be overheard.

The old dark wooden doors whine as I push them open. It's empty. Columns line the aisle and statues sit in the alcoves, looking down with blank faces, listening. The pews are old, dark wood. A shaft of moonlight slices in from the high, arched, stained glass window, dust motes dancing within in. A single red candle glows on the altar.

"Make this quick, Robert. We don't have much time."

I turn to face him. "When did you last see Thorpe's wife?"

"What?"

"Just answer the question."

"The day they took him to hospital."

"What colour is her hair?"

"Robert, is this really..."

"Tell me!"

"Black."

"The woman I spoke to, who told me she was Thorpe's wife, the woman who told me Thorpe believed that they'd created strangelets? She was tall, blonde, slim. It wasn't his wife."

"Is this why you called me here? To talk about Thorpe's wife?"

"Don't you get it? Amos set me up! Tell me this. Did Thorpe create strangelets with a five sigma certainty?"

He stares back at me.

"Answer me!"

"No."

"So... so all we've been doing is based on bullshit?"

"It's irrelevant now, Robert. We need to finish the job."

"*Irrelevant?* What are you talking about? If Thorpe's paper was fake, there *is* no threat!"

"There is to you, if we don't finish this."

"Am I hearing this?"

"Think about it! Amos has the worm – you gave him that. If we don't release it, *he will*."

"They don't have admin access off site. He needs me to release it from inside CERN."

"And when did you last speak to him? Three days ago? More? His team will be over it like a rash. He'll get his connection in time. But if we don't uphold our end of the bargain, he'll find us. And you don't want to know what he'll do to you if he does."

"I don't give a shit! I'm not doing it. I'm not selling myself for a pack of lies. And you? How can you even consider it?"

"Please, Robert, you don't know what he's capable of. I didn't mean to drag you into any of this – if I'd just done what he'd asked, none of this would have happened."

"What do you mean by that?"

"The only reason you're here is that I refused to agree to the sabotage when Amos first approached me. I've drip-fed him information for years, but I drew the line at this. Then he recruited you. It left me with no other option than to give him what he wanted." The colour drains from his face so that, for a moment, he looks like one of the statues.

"Why are you so afraid of him? What has he got over you?"

"Thorpe's illness wasn't just bad luck."

I pause. "He did that to him?"

"They create all kinds of things at ORB. I won't let him do to you what he did to me."

"What did he do to you?"

He stares past me, vacant, unblinking, and his eyes glisten.

I step closer. "Dad? What did he do to you?"

"He broke into my mind."

"What?"

"There was another part of the deal when he bailed me out. They were experimenting with something and they needed a test subject. He's so persuasive. It sounded straightforward to begin with, observing mood and linking it to action, but then it got more serious. They began to control how I felt. It was like being chained to something dark – I didn't have the will to break free. I lost six months." He looks up. "That's the reason I never contacted you. Every time I tried, he'd trigger it, and I'd be back there, in that place. I've never felt despair like it. That's why I tried to take my own life – I couldn't take it anymore. After that, the doctors locked me up."

"Did you tell them what he did?"

He nods. "The authorities looked into it, but they couldn't find any evidence that Amos existed. In the end they put it down to psychosis and kept me on depot injections until I learned to deny everything I'd said, because I knew it would get me out." His eyes focus on mine. "I won't let him do that to you. We don't have a choice, Robert."

"No. We do have a choice. I'm not doing it."

He takes me by the shoulders. "I took all this so that

you wouldn't have to! Don't make it be for nothing.
You can't fight him, Robert. He's too powerful."

"Maybe, but I'm not giving in before I've started."

Exasperated, he drops his hands and turns away,
staring up at one of the statues. "I don't think you
understand how powerful he is. Do you think it's a
coincidence that SightLabs was shut down?"

"He told me it was a political decision."

"A political decision based on his instructions to the
politicians. He has a *way* of getting what he wants. He's
not the man you think he is. He'll stop the experiments
whether we do it or not. And in the grand scheme of
things, history will forget, and science will find another
way. But if we don't do what he asks, he will find us.
Please, I can't lose you, not again."

"You won't. We'll get Cora and we'll go somewhere
where we can figure out what we do next."

"Who?"

"Cora. She's my... well, I'm not sure what she is right
now, but she's at the apartment. She arrived today."

The way he looks at me makes something plunge in
my gut.

"You left her alone?"

I punch in Cora's number into my phone. It rings out.
No answer.

We make for the doors. "I'll drive," he says.

"No, the bike's faster – I'll go on ahead. Four-four-six
Roux de la Croix."

I BOUNCE OVER potholes, too fast for a farm track in the
dark, and I'm approaching the highway when it hits me.
The flash of an image. I see Cora struggling, gagged,

arms tied behind her. A man in a suit is pushing her into the back of a black van. As quickly as it came, it vanishes and I swerve the bike, drawing it to a stop in the dust. I blink at the fields and the highway ahead. It only lasted a microsecond, but it felt like I was there, watching it happening. I feel shaken and sick. Gathering myself, I set off again into the night.

THE BIKE GROWLS to a stop in the street. I take the stairs, scrambling up them, calling her again from the mobile. No reply. *Please, let her be there.*

I fumble with the keys, dropping them once, swearing as I pick them up and force them into the lock. But I know before I step inside; it's too quiet.

"Cora?"

Nothing.

She's gone.

I BURST OUT into the street, into the drizzle and the darkness. A crowd of students stumble into the road, pissed. I scan the street for her. There. Ahead of the crowd, a tangle of long hair, the right height, moving in the right way. I take off after her, ignoring the barrage of drunken French abuse. She stops at the crossing. The lights change and she glances right before stepping out. I reach forward and grasp her wrist. "Cora." She turns, frowning; a woman I don't know.

"Pardon, Madame. Pardon." I back away as she glares at me and turns back to the road.

I'm aware of something to my right – something purring, dark. Turning, I see a black BMW inching along the kerb just behind me. A window glides down, noiselessly. Victor Amos is sitting in the back seat.

"I don't know about you," he begins, "but I am a man who operates on intuition. And I sense a weakening in your resolve." The moon's shining onto his face, but no light reflects in his pale eyes. "Tell me, Robert, is your resolve weakening?"

"Where is she?"

"She's quite safe, as is your father."

"My dad?"

"I feel you need a little more incentive to focus on the task at hand. They will both be returned to you, unharmed, once you deliver."

"I need him to get inside the Ops Room."

"Lambert will provide the distraction you need to plant the worm. We made a deal, Robert. Don't disappoint me."

The window glides up silently and the car pulls away. I stand there shivering in the moonlight.

Something draws my eyes across the road. A silhouette standing under a streetlamp. It takes me a minute to work it out. Slim, pale, unsmiling, Sarah turns and walks into the next street.

When I get there, she's at the other end, and I see her disappear into an alleyway on the left. Ahead, Sarah turns again and I follow her into an unlit lane. I stop as I realise where she's led me. She's standing by the door of La Caverne.

"There's nothing in there!" I shout.

She stares back, unsmiling, unblinking.

"Why are you messing with my head?"

I walk towards her and can almost reach out and touch her. She looks as real as she ever did, except that there's something haunted in her expression. As I approach the entrance, she fades, disappearing into the rain. My hand rests on the door, and I look up. The weather vane spins in a gust of wind, pointing north. I've already proved there's nothing in there. This is just wasting my time. I turn and walk away.

A creaking sound behind stops me. I turn to see Rosinda standing in the doorway. "Robert," she says. "They're waiting for you."

"UPSTAIRS," SHE SAYS as I come inside. "I'll bring you something hot to drink." She opens the door to the next level. There are no boxes of beer at the foot of the stairs.

Hope flickers inside me as I climb. I reach the top and see the fire blazing.

"Hello, Robert." Sattva is sitting at the end of an oblong table, leaning back in his chair with his legs loosely crossed, and next to him, Casimir. Balaquai picks a book from a shelf and glances back at me.

"Is this really happening?"

"Yes, it is."

"Why couldn't we see you before?"

Sattva replies. "Because Cora's not strong enough yet to see us."

"She can see Sarah."

"Cora can see Sarah because they're tightly entangled. You can see Sarah because you're one of us."

"Wait, what did you say?"

"Your recent brush with death has expanded your awareness, that's all. Now it's time you caught up with it."

I'm back down the rabbit hole, but I don't have time to process it. "Where is Sarah?"

"She's somewhere we can't reach, Robert. Is that why you're here?"

"No. Amos has Cora and my dad. If I don't deliver, he'll kill them both."

"He'll do worse than that," says Balaquai, without looking up from his book.

"What?"

"At the moment, I believe they're quite safe," Sattva says. "If he harms them now, he loses his bargaining position."

"We have people looking for them, Robert," says Casimir. "As we speak. We'll hear from them soon."

"Well, I want to help..."

"You'd just get in the way," says Balaquai.

Sattva smiles. "What Balaquai means is that you would do them a greater service by being here, for the moment, and learning something about what's going on."

I hear her footsteps on the stairs and Rosinda arrives with a large mug of coffee and a towel which she wraps round my shoulders. The grey pebble that hangs round her neck swings forwards as she leans over. "Take a seat, love," she says.

The coffee's sweet and hot. "So is this where you... end up when you die? A pub in Geneva?"

"We're wherever we need to be," Sattva says. "We can come and go between worlds as we choose. They occupy the same space, you see; all that separates them is their physics. Light from one world can't leak into another. But other things can – other signals get through. Gravity, for instance. Or consciousness."

"Consciousness?"

"The core of every living thing. In its more advanced forms, it is the ability to question and choose. What do you think drives science?"

"Consciousness is a by-product of the brain."

"Do you really believe that?" He knocks on the table. "The world isn't solid matter, Robert – you of all people know that. Solidity is an illusion – most of it is empty space. But what's vibrating in that space, in the Field, is consciousness itself."

"The Field?"

"The Quantum Field. Are you familiar with it?"

"The theory that particles are just excited states of an underlying physical field."

"Precisely. We're more attuned to picking up the resulting vibrational signals. It's how I heard your fear on the mountain in Tibet."

"Why did you help me then?"

"I remember a time when a young boy found me hiding under a bush in a forest. Yet he said nothing to my hunter, and in so doing, he saved my life. That act of compassion entangled us, through many lifetimes.

"In the same way Aiyana knew about the car jumping the lights. And it's why Balaquai appeared when the mugger threatened to shoot you for your wallet. They responded to your vibrational signal before you were even aware of what was going on. That's what we do. And once you come to terms with this, that's what you'll do too."

I get up and walk towards the French doors at the back of the room. They open out onto a large balcony with waist-high iron railings. A murky, dense cloud, a dirty mix of blue and purple and grey, reaches from the sky to the rooftops. Rain patters on the window panes.

"What about Amos?" I say, turning back to the room.

"He's a different story." Sattva stands up and walks over to join me. "To understand what Victor Amos is,

you need to see how he came to exist in the first place."
A moth is wriggling in the remnants of a spider's web,
caught in the corner of the window frame. Sattva places
his finger underneath it and lifts it gently clear of the
web, holding it up to eye level. It opens and closes its
wings. "What we've come to understand, from our
place in things, is the relationship between matter and
energy. What do your equations tell you about it?"

"That they're interchangeable."

He turns his finger, peering at the moth, then opens
the glass door. "Exactly. They are different expressions
of the same thing." He puffs out a breath and the
moth takes flight, flittering away on the cool night air.
"Everything at its most basic level is a form of energy. It's
no different for thoughts. Thoughts are an expression
of energy, and as such they can translate into matter."

"Oh, come on. Thoughts are just electrical impulses.
They don't create anything."

"Is that what you think?" He steps through the
open door onto the balcony. Leaning on the railing,
he surveys the rooftops. I follow him outside, looking
south, to where the river glints in the moonlight. "Point
out something, anything, in your world that did not
begin as a thought," he says.

I look out over the city, to the buildings, the cars, the
power lines.

"Yeah, but it took physical action to turn those ideas
into something real. A car doesn't just appear when you
think of it."

"That is true. But it began as a thought, and now
there it is. Can you see how powerful this is? Thought
is the sea of potentiality; the precursor of creation. All it
takes is enough attention to bring it into being."

His fingers fold around the curved handle of the umbrella that's just appeared in it. He passes it to me while he buttons up his jacket. It's real, solid, and it does what umbrellas do. "How did you do that?" I breathe.

"Many lifetimes of practice. Are you feeling alright?"

I nod, numbly.

"Once you get past the idea that things are solid and unchanging, then all of this becomes a lot easier. Does it disturb you that when you boil water in the kettle, steam comes out?"

I glance up at the inside of the umbrella. "That's a good trick. But what has this got to do with Amos?"

The sound of the rain on the umbrella sharpens from a soft patter to hard taps. "It has everything to do with Amos."

Balaquai leans through the doors behind us. "He's back."

I follow Sattva inside and stop when I see him. A minute later, I have him pinned against the wall. Some drool escapes from the left side of his mouth as his face contorts into a scowl.

Chapter Fifteen

"You're working for him, aren't you? Working for Amos?"

"Robert," says Casimir. "He's one of us."

"For God's sake, man, let go." His voice is gruff, like gravel caught in an old lawnmower.

"He's been tailing me for days."

My grip loosens and he yanks my arm away, glowering. "I have. And it's a good thing for you that I did."

"Robert, this is Arcos Crowley. He confirmed to us your intention to sabotage the experiments. He has a particular gift for hearing discord in people."

"What?"

"You stuck out like a sore thumb," says Arcos. "It's beyond me how none of your colleagues picked up on it."

I don't like the way he looks at me, like I've crawled out from under a stone.

"Did you find them?" asks Balaquai.

Crowley shakes his head. He turns to face the fire and pushes the hot coals about with the scuffed tip of his boot. The flames wrap themselves around it, but his boot doesn't burn. "I don't know what he's done with them," he mumbles. "I can't get anything from them."

"Nothing?" says Balaquai.

Crowley shakes his head. "The others are still looking."

I've had enough of this bullshit. I turn and make my way towards the stairs. "I'll take my chances with the police. This is just wasting time I don't have."

"Wait, Robert!" Casimir calls.

"Police?" Crowley practically spits the word. "What good do you think that will do anyone? There's no police force on earth that can help you now, Robert Strong."

Yeah, well, crazy man, I'm willing to let them give it a go.

Crowley continues to bark away behind me. "Sattva, I thought you were going to explain things to him. Was he not listening? Does he have any idea who he's dealing with?"

"We were just coming to that when you arrived."

I hear the thud of boots on wood behind me.

"Robert," Casimir says in a low voice. "You need to hear this."

"No, I don't, Casimir. Believe me."

"Please. We need your help. At least listen to this before you make your decision."

I turn back to him, irritated at first, but then I see something in his eyes that reminds me that I trusted him once, when he was alive. I stare at the floor for a moment, then turn and follow him.

Crowley drags his looks of disdain from me back to the fire where he warms his hands. I take the seat that Casimir pulls out from under a table. Sattva's eyes are on mine. "Try to stay with me, Robert." He's patient, like a good father is with an angry child. "Man has the ability to influence his reality with his thoughts. That is a truth you're just going to have to accept for now. Just as the culmination of positive thoughts has brought about the progress we see all around us, the culmination of negative emotions has a consequence too. Eons of those thoughts – fear, greed, cruelty, betrayal – they didn't go away. They coalesced, festered in the Field, creating an entity which, over time, grew conscious of itself. And the man it has become has a taste for life now. He was not born and he will not die. That man is Victor Amos. At least, that's what he's calling himself these days. There's no name for what he really is.

"He feeds on human fear – it's what fuels him. Over the eons, he has found new ways of cultivating men to grow inside them the thing he needs most. He moves with the times, playing on cultural whims. In the dark recesses of the past, it was myth and magic, then, for a long time, religion. And now it is science."

"Are you saying he's been around for..."

"He's far older than you can imagine, and he's growing more powerful with each passing age. The energies are changing, just like before."

Where have I heard that before? I pause for a minute, thinking, before it comes to me. "When I was in Tibet, I met a monk who said something about that. Some old legend about water flowing from one lake into another, the wrong way; 'energy was shifting between worlds' is what he said."

"Truth, not legend. You see, there are points on the planet which act like conduits for energy from all worlds. The exact locations of most have been lost over time, but we know that Lake Manasarovar and Lake Rakshastal –

the Lake of Consciousness and the Lake of Demons – are one of those points. Gateways to other realities."

I remember being at the lakeside – the flash of grey, the black sphere, the sound of whispering. The dread.

"You sensed it, didn't you? At the Lake of Demons?" Sattva says.

"I felt... something..."

"That is the world Amos is trying to create."

"So why is he so desperate to sabotage the experiments?"

"Amos knows that men fear what they don't understand, and he wants to keep it that way. He sees the experiments as a threat, because through them we will begin to decipher the nature of consciousness. And that may well unravel his existence."

"But if Amos is what you say he is, why didn't he just destroy the Collider himself?"

"That's not how he works," says Arcos. "He can't change mankind's reality of his own accord; only man can do that. But he can influence the choices men make. CERN is a fortress of united minds, all intent on the same goal, and collective purpose is powerful. That's why he needs someone like you and your father. He needs to break it from the inside."

Sattva is staring at the flames in the fireplace. "I can't help but feel this is part of something bigger. He's on the move again. All the signs point to it: the economy destabilising, climate change, the rise in fear. He's planning something."

"What?" I breathe.

"I don't know. But the experiments are a threat to his endeavours. And you are our only link to Amos." He turns to me. "What else is ORB involved in?"

"I only had access to the CERN project, and they

wouldn't tell me about the others. But there was something in a restricted area…"

"Yes?"

"I'm not sure what – I only glimpsed it. But there was this huge tank of what looked like a pillar of mist, spinning like a tornado."

Crowley glances at Sattva. "Maybe it's something to do with why we can't sense them."

"What do you mean?" I ask.

"We should have some sense of Cora and your father; a signature of their consciousness in the Field," Crowley says. "But there's nothing from them."

"Does that mean they're dead?"

"No," Sattva says. "Their imprint would still be there. It's as if something is shielding or blocking it."

Crowley turns from the fire towards me, the irritation and disdain softened in the light of the flames. "So, do you still want to call the police?"

I get up and walk to the window. The rain has stopped, the cloud has cleared the moon and a shaft of silver light illuminates the rooftops.

"As soon as Amos finds out I've reneged, it's over for them."

"We'll keep searching, Robert," says Sattva. "But if you do as Amos asks, you could be assisting him in something far worse."

"Even if I do nothing, Amos could still disable CERN. If they crack the admin access in time, they'll initiate the attack from ORB."

Balaquai joins me at the window. "Can you remember the layout of ORB? Picture it in your head?"

I remember the tunnels, the white fluorescent panels, the Hub…

There's a subtle change in the light. I turn to see the stones around each of their necks glowing like low-watt light bulbs.

Crowley shakes his head and growls. "Ach. It's not enough, I'm not getting a sense of it."

"Robert," says Sattva. "Did you bring anything back from ORB? Anything at all that connects it to you?"

"No. Amos gave me the notebook later. The only things I brought back were the clothes I had on. Why?"

"Objects carry imprints of events that happen around them in their subatomic structure. That extra focus can make the difference, when it comes to accessing your memories."

Crowley glances at Sattva. "It might be enough."

BALAQUAI AND CASIMIR, two dead men, accompany me back to my apartment. To say I feel self-conscious is an understatement, but the few people around don't seem to notice.

"Doesn't this bother you?" I say, turning to Casimir.

"What?"

"This? The way things have turned out. Doesn't it bother you?"

"Bother me?" He snorts. "Why would it bother me?"

"Well, there's never been any evidence for anything like this."

"Evidence? You still need evidence? How about what your eyes are telling you?"

"But doesn't that unsettle you? I mean you're *here*, you're talking to me. You shouldn't *be*. You're..." – I pause as a couple pass then whisper the next word – "... dead."

"Robert, I was an old man. Everything I looked at was blurred. My bones ached every time I stood up. I had to go for a piss every two hours at night, and then I'd lie awake and wonder if that was all there was to life now. This makes more sense to me than all that, so does it bother me that it wasn't what I expected? That technically, by the book, most people would consider me dead? No. The point is, I'm here. Look at me now. Why would it bother me?"

He has a point. "Can other people see you?"

"Let's see," says Balaquai. He winks at a brunette walking towards us, dressed for an evening out. "Hi," he says, giving her a sultry smile. She smiles back, coy and a little flustered. "Apparently so."

"But to answer your question, it depends on whether or not we want to be seen." Casimir says.

"What about Aiyana?" I ask.

"What about her?"

"It seems to be getting to her."

Balaquai glances at Casimir. "She's not adjusting all that well. She only transitioned last week. She's a quick learner, but she's still clinging to her life before. She keeps disappearing to do 'normal things'."

"Like cleaning tables in a cafe?"

"Exactly. It's not uncommon, particularly when you have a violent transition."

"Why? What happened?"

"She was murdered."

"Murdered?"

"Yeah," says Balaquai. "Just as she left work one night last week, and all for a flash drive. I found her wandering around Los Angeles, not long after that, in a bit of a state."

"What was on the drive?"

"I didn't ask. She's desperate to find the guy who killed her, but she's never going to settle if she doesn't let it go. If she finds him, she'll want revenge, and that just makes things complicated. She's developing the abilities of an Eidolon, but being stuck in the past is holding her back."

We pass the boulangerie on the corner, where the plump woman with the blue paper cap will be opening up in a few hours' time. And I thought life was complicated before I bought that croissant from her.

"Nice place," says Casimir when we reach the apartment block. "Is this where you've been staying?" He cranes his neck up at the whitewashed stone walls and iron window boxes.

"Courtesy of Victor Amos." I fumble with the keypad until the door clicks open.

"I'll wait here," says Balaquai. "Remember – anything that you brought back from ORB. Be quick."

When we reach the door to the apartment, Casimir puts his hand on my shoulder. "Wait here," he says. He walks through the door. He doesn't open it; he walks *through* the door, like it's made of mist. Another rule broken. Another segment of sanity down the toilet.

The door opens from the inside and Casimir steps back. He scans the corridor again before closing it. "How did you..." I begin, but he shakes his head.

"Not here. Get your stuff."

The apartment is as I left it. No signs of any disruption. Moonlight floods in through the windows. I keep the lights off and go to the bedroom, into the dressing room, and pick up the plastic orange hospital bag at the back of a shelf, the notebook and the rucksack, and place them on the bed. Opening the orange bag slowly,

Libby McGugan

holding it up to the moonlight, I see my old jeans, boots and T-shirt, and suddenly I feel uncomfortable wearing the clothes I'm in. Like they're someone else's. A shiver slithers down my spine. *He dressed you. Dressed you ready for the stage.*

"Robert?" Casimir's voice comes from the next room.

"Alright."

I turn to walk out and see the small foil goblet sitting on the bedside table, glinting in the pallid light. I pick it up gently, seeing her wrap it round her finger, forming it carefully, lovingly. I pick up a box of cufflinks, empty them out and place the goblet inside. It goes into the rucksack along with the notebook and the bag of clothes. I stand for a moment, picturing her in our bed, in our flat in Middlesbrough, her dark red hair loose on the pillow. *What has he done to you, Cora?*

Casimir appears at the door. "Robert, we need to go."

WHEN WE GET back to La Caverne, the bar is empty. Rosinda is stacking the chairs on top of the tables, and smiles at us. It's not her usual wide, flirtatious smile; it is tinged with concern, like she knows what's coming.

The old stairs creak as we climb and raised voices reach us from above.

"Why not? Is it really asking too much?" It's Aiyana; she sounds angry.

"I've told you, it won't help anyone." Crowley just as angry. "And we've got other things we have to be dealing with right now."

"Other things? Well, I'm sorry if this doesn't rank in your priorities, but it's pretty damned important to me. I was murdered. Did you get that? Murdered."

275

"So what? I was murdered once, myself. Get over it."

"Arcos is not one for dwelling on misfortunes," Sattva says, ever the mediator.

Crowley grumbles before he answers. "No is my final word on the subject."

"What does she want him to do?" I whisper.

Balaquai turns to me, his voice low. "She can respond to the unconscious signals from people – like yours at the lights – but she's not strong enough yet to tunnel unbidden, without the help of one of us."

"Tunnel?"

"It's when your focus on someone or something is strong enough to take you to them, instantaneously, regardless of where they are in space. She wants to find her murderer."

I turn to Casimir. "Can you do this? Tunnel, I mean?"

"Yeah, it was easier for me – I had no resistance to death. It was easier than I thought – I got your attention when you passed my house the day I died. After our conversations about the Big Secret, I felt I owed it to you to at least get you thinking."

"How did you do it?"

"You'd be surprised how quickly you pick things up after you die."

Balaquai coughs as he reaches the top of the stairs and when I get there I see Aiyana standing with her arms folded, glowering. Crowley shares his look of distaste.

"Success?" Sattva smiles broadly.

I place the rucksack on the table, ignoring Aiyana's stare, which I can feel like a hot thorn in my temple. The contents of the orange bag tumble out as I hold it upside down, along with the cufflink box. I open it and take out the goblet, and when my fingers make contact,

I get the flash. The same vision – Cora, gagged and bound, being pushed into a van. When it goes, I'm left gripping the edge of the table.

Sattva's eyes narrow. "Are you alright?"

"I saw her... her abduction. It's the second time."

"She's trying to communicate with you." Sattva leans forward and takes the goblet gently from my hand. "Is this hers?"

"She made this last night."

Carefully, he hands it to Crowley, who holds it by its thin stem, twirling it round. "She's still alive and she's unharmed." He frowns. "But I can't see beyond it. *Ach!*" He returns the goblet to me with more gentility that I would have expected of him. "I don't know how he's doing it. Get changed into your clothes, Robert. You'll get the best connection when you're wearing them."

I put the goblet back in its box and the box into the pocket of my jeans. "You didn't say anything about wearing them." I hold up the shirt, sliced roughly up the middle in large jagged cuts.

"Ah," says Sattva.

"What the hell have you been doing with those?" Crowley's face folds into a frown. I wonder if it's ever even tried to smile.

"It's a long story."

I lift up the jeans which are no better – two flapping strips of denim loosely attached to a few pockets. Something flitters from the back pocket to the floor, landing white side up, as Balaquai lifts the clothes out of my hands and lays them on the table. I reach down to pick up what's fallen and see him out of the corner of my eye, running his finger up the cut seam of my jeans. I freeze, half crouched. The material of the clothes is folding over and meeting, joining under his open palms as if his will is a sewing needle. A bubble of nausea swells in my stomach and my eyes linger on the jeans as I fumble with one hand to pick up whatever it was that fell to the floor. A piece of card with something scribbled on it. I flip it over. It's the photograph that Banks dropped at the ORB entrance. The faces of three women dusted in snowflakes – the one in the middle with the dangerous eyes, just like...

I stare at her.

"What are you looking at?" she snaps.

I hand the photograph to her without speaking.

She whips it out of my hand and looks down. "Where did you get this?" her voice is no more than a whisper.

"Is there something you want to share with us?" says Sattva, glancing between Aiyana and me.

Her eyes are fixed on me as she steps forward, brandishing the photograph like a knife. "*Where* did you get this?" There's something untamed in her eyes, like she's hanging on by a thread. A thread that's beginning to fray. But then, she was murdered.

"I found it on the floor at ORB when I was there – a guy called Peter Banks dropped it. I was going to give it back but..."

"This photograph was sitting on my desk the night I was killed. My friends signed it, on our last holiday, see?" she turns it over and pushed it towards me. I already know what it says. She tells me anyway. "'To lifelong friendship.' So how come it ends up with you?"

"I told you, I only picked it up."

"Bit of a coincidence, isn't it?" There's no mistaking the accusation in her mockery.

"Yeah, well there's been a lot of that lately. I don't

know what happened to you, Aiyana. It had nothing to do with me."

"He's telling the truth," say Arcos. It's not offered with any sense of appeasement – more that he's just stating a fact.

"How can you be so sure?" she says.

"Because I'd know if he wasn't."

"So this man, Peter Banks, works for Victor Amos?" says Sattva.

"Yeah. A prospector."

"Robert, put this on." Sattva reaches into his jacket pocket and hands me an oval stone threaded with a leather cord. Just like the ones they're all wearing.

"What is it?"

"It's a stone."

"I can see that. What does it do?"

"Think of it as a transceiver. It picks up and sends out signals. It focuses specific vibrations within the Field, helping us align with them. So if you were to think, for instance, of your memory of Mr Banks, the amulet can share it with us."

"But how does it..."

"Oh, just put it on!" snaps Aiyana.

I tie the leather cord round my neck. The stone is heavy and sits in the hollow between my collar bones.

"So," Sattva says. "Try to bring to mind any memory you have of Mr Banks."

I try to picture him; his dark hair, the scar on his left forearm, but it's vague and distorted and I can't get the details...

"You're trying too hard, Robert," Balaquai says. His eyes are closed, frowning. "Just think of the situation where you met him, not the details of his face."

I take a breath and close my eyes. Okay. The car ride to ORB. I remember...

There's a sudden scorching sensation on my chest, like the stone has suddenly heated up. I reach for it, but before I can lift it free of my skin something out-burns it inside my skull, like a migraine but without the pain. An intense flash. When it dims, it leaves an image. No, it's more than that. It's like I'm actually there.

I see Aiyana but not like she is now; she's in a dim office corridor, her eyes are wide and she's trying to scream, but she's held by someone's arm wrapped round her neck, a cloth pushed to her lips so that all that escapes is a muffled cry. She kicks her heels into his shins, flailing her arms behind her, reaching for his head while her chest rises and falls faster than it should, her face mottling to the colour of raw meat, blood appearing in the whites of her eyes that are growing wider. And then, like turning down a dimmer switch, the spark in them fades, softened then smothered by a cloudy haze. She stops struggling and slumps to the floor. The man reaches down and drags her body into an office, dumping it like litter beside the desk with the computer on it. He rolls up his sleeves, revealing a snakelike scar...

"Aiyana! This is not about your memory!" bellows Arcos. "This was meant to be Robert's!"

"That's him." I turn to Sattva. "That's Banks."

Sattva opens his eyes and glances at Arcos. "I think, on this occasion, a little longer spent down Aiyana's memory lane might serve us."

The image is still there when I close my eyes.

He pulls the cloth from her bloodstained mouth and stuffs it into a small plastic bag that he puts in his pocket. He starts the computer, takes out a memory stick from the pocket of his jeans, then plugs it in. Numbers count up on the screen. He taps his finger on the desk, waiting, then picks up the framed photograph by a mug of coffee that's still steaming. It's a portrait of three women huddled together, snowflakes suspended in the air around them – the same photograph Aiyana now has in her hand. Banks smashes the frame and stuffs the picture into his pocket. He leans over her lifeless body. "A little momento," he whispers. He snatches her bag from the floor and rips it open, and her phone and wallet and diary tumble out.

"Shit," he hisses as he turns the bag upside down with his gloved hands and shakes it until a red memory key drops to the floor. As he reaches down for it, the numbers on the screen stop counting and in their place is a single flashing word.

EXECUTE.

He presses the return key. The image on the screen melts into red streaks like blood running down a wall. He pulls out the key and pockets it. He takes out his phone and holds it to his ear. "It's me. I have it."

I open my eyes to see the glow fade from the amulets round the room. Aiyana's face is pearly white against her dark hair and she sinks slowly into a chair, staring at the empty space in front of her.

"I'm sorry," I say.

She glances up at me, emerging from her reverie. Crowley makes a noise that sounds like *Tchaw!* and pokes the fire with his boot.

"You're sure that was Peter Banks?" asks Sattva.

I nod.

"And you're sure that he works for Victor Amos?"

"Yes. I can't believe what he did – he has a wife. And a kid. But it was him, no doubt."

"Then, Aiyana, perhaps we need to know what it was about your work that interests Amos so much. Tell us about it."

"I, eh…" She clears her throat and begins again. "I worked with a company called Geowatch. We monitored background electromagnetic radiation for health control – you know, from mobile networks, antennae, broadcasting stations, that kind of thing. But over the past few months I was tracking episodes of oscillations which were much stronger than anything we'd seen before." She glances up at us, her face still pale. "They should have caused major disruption – blackouts, power failures, communications breakdown – but they didn't. Nothing was affected that I could pick up. It was registering as electromagnetism, but it wasn't behaving like it."

"What do you think caused it?" I ask.

"I've no idea. At first I just put it down to anomalies, or monitoring errors, but that night I detected the biggest swing in recordings we'd had. Like a solar flare without the consequences. I went over it all – there were no recording errors. So I called Liam…"

"Liam?" asks Balaquai.

"Liam Bradbury. He's, eh… he *was* a work associate." She holds her palm in the candle flame and doesn't take it away. There should be the smell of singeing flesh, a trickle of smoke; something. I wince, but she stares blindly at the flame, her hand white, unblemished. "Well, he was more than that." Finally she lifts her hand and I breathe out. "He would have known what to do."

"Where did you find the oscillations?" Casimir asks.

"Mostly around cities, big towns – densely populated areas. But it was just a sideline project – no-one really took much interest in it, because it wasn't causing any obvious effects."

"Maybe it's a good thing that you did," Casimir says.

"What does it matter now anyway? I gave my life up for that work. It wasn't worth that."

"Too early to say," says Balaquai. "You got Amos's attention."

"Indeed," says Sattva. "Robert, how likely is it that ORB will initiate the cyberattack?"

"They're confident they can crack the access code in time."

"Can't you warn security at CERN to disconnect from the Grid?" says Casimir.

"No. Not until we find Cora; ORB will work out that I've warned them. It's too risky."

"Anyway, that's only a temporary solution," says Casimir. "If we want to stop Amos, we need something more concrete."

I snort. "Like what? Sabotaging ORB?"

They stare at me.

"Wait a minute, I wasn't serious."

"Why not?" asks Casimir. "You already have a program. Why not send it to them?"

"It's not compatible with their system, Casimir. Anyway ORB will be scanning all of my communications. Amos doesn't trust me – if he did, he wouldn't have taken hostages."

"Robert," says Sattva, "if we could get you inside ORB, could you find a way to shut down their operations?"

"This isn't some school lab. It's an underground fortress eight hundred miles away. You need retinal scanning authorisation to get anywhere inside."

"There are ways round that."

"What ways?"

"Could you do it?"

"I don't know..."

"And we could pay Peter Banks a visit," says Balaquai, "to help us find the hostages."

"I'm in," Aiyana says.

Sattva reaches for the amulet round his neck, which begins to glow blue. "We don't have much time, Robert. For this to work, you're going to have to learn quickly and trust us. I'll leave you in Arcos's capable hands." He gets to his feet. "We'll meet on the warehouse rooftop at nightfall."

"I hope to God he's ready by then," says Crowley.

"He will be." Sattva smiles like he means it and walks out onto the balcony.

"Right, you." Crowley picks up a chair at the end of the table and slams it onto the floorboards. "Sit down."

Balaquai settles himself onto a sofa behind him, lounging back on the cushions like he's about to watch TV. Casimir squats on the hearth to the side of the fire and Aiyana moves to the other end of the room, slumps into a chair and lays the photo on the table, her back to us.

I lower myself into the wooden chair, feeling like I'm back at school with a teacher who's in a bad mood. Crowley sits down opposite me and drags a glass half full of water across the table between us. Some of the contents slop over the edge and splash onto the wood.

"Well, seeing as you're the physicist, this shouldn't take too long. But we don't have all day, so pay attention. If you're going to be any use to anyone, you need to start again with how you see things. Get rid of those preconceived ideas of how things are – because they're not. The best you've got is an interpretation of what's going on based on your senses. But those senses are only picking up one thing: vibration. It's the language of energy, and you need to learn how to speak it. So." He pushes the glass towards me. "What's going on in that glass right now?"

"Water molecules vibrating."

"Right." He leans towards me, his eyes narrowing. "Now. Make it boil."

I stare back at him, at the twitch in his left eyelid in the flickering light from the fire.

"It's water. You need to apply heat to make it boil."

"No! You don't! You need to make the molecules move faster, but it doesn't matter how you do it!" He lets out a harsh, irritated sigh. "See the molecules..."

"See them vibrating in my mind. Yeah, alright, I get it."

"Well, stop mincing about like a big girl, then, and get on with it."

The glass sits in front of me, like it should. An ordinary glass half-filled with ordinary water that ripples when I bump the table then settles down to form a predictable meniscus. Like it should.

I sense Crowley's impatience even before he says anything. "For God's sake, man. I thought you were a physicist! You got the hang of gravity without too much bother, didn't you? Without too much effort? Not fallen off yet, have you?" He stand up, leaning towards me, madness in his twitching eye, spraying a fine mist of spittle on my face. My blood's beginning to boil. I hate his unrelenting disdain, his irritation, the way he looks at me like I'm filth. "You should know how things look on the quantum scale – or is it all just abstract thought and equations? Hmm? How about a little applied science? Otherwise, what's the point?"

Casimir clears his throat and shuffles a little on the hearth, his way of reminding us that there's more than Crowley and me in the room. I see his shadow shift against the orange glow out of the corner of my eye.

Crowley leans closer, his mouth contorting into a snarl. His breath smells like overripe cheese. "If you cared at all about seeing Cora and your father again, you'd get over yourself and your narrowmindedness."

Something snaps inside. I spring to my feet, facing him, white rage pulsing in my blood, my fist reaching to grasp his collar. "Enough!"

An explosion; a shattering. Casimir shields his face with his arm, then peers out over his elbow, and I hear the scrape of Aiyana's chair. Beneath me, on the table, splintered glass lies strewn across the wood, and steam rises from the puddle of water spilling between the fragments and dripping onto the floor.

Crowley's voice is quiet for the first time. "Now do you believe me?" I drag my gaze from the hissing debris. His eyes are level with mine, intense and unblinking, the twitch in his eyelid gone.

Chapter Sixteen

I BREAK FIVE more glasses in the course of learning to make water boil, but I'm beginning to get a feel for it. That's what it is, really. It's not just visualising, although that's part of it, but it's also the awareness of a rising energy, of speed, like you get on a roller coaster as it tips over the crest of the drop and begins to accelerate – that feeling of exponential momentum – but taking that and applying it to water in a glass. *Shit, Robert, if you could hear yourself.* The first time the water boils it feels like I've broken through a barrier I didn't even know was there. Like I'm on the edge of something huge.

When I look at Crowley now, there's a glimmer of something approaching respect in his eyes; or, at the very least, less reproach.

We move on from water. Crowley is trying to get me to light an extinguished candle using only my will. The wick sits cold, stubborn and unlit. This is too much for me. A flame too far. As Crowley huffs and grumbles at my incompetence, the amulet round his neck begins to glow. He glances up at Balaquai, who is already on his feet, his amulet shining in the same way.

"Best you stay here," Crowley says. "Keep going on your candle for now. And get to work on thinking how to disable ORB's systems. We'll be back when we can."

I glance back at Casimir as they walk out onto the balcony. "Where are they off to?"

"They're responding to signals, like they did with you."

I get up and walk over to the edge of the balcony. There's no sign of them. "And where did Sattva go?"

Casimir, who's followed me out, is looking up at the sky. "Anyone's guess."

We go back inside and Casimir takes a seat by the fire. "You're doing well," he says. "If you're open to it, it doesn't take that long."

"What does it feel like, being, you know... dead?"

"No different, really." He runs his hand over the unlit candle and a flame comes to life. "No, that's not true. It's better. It's freer, like you're not constrained by your old assumptions. It's a perceptual difference, more than anything."

"There really are other worlds, then?"

"Right here, coexisting with this one." He blows out the candle and pushes it towards me.

"What are they like?"

"If you want to see, I'll have to kill you."

"What?"

"Just kidding. I can share my memory of when I first got through."

The amulet round his neck begins to glow, and I feel the heat at the top of my breastbone. A swell of violet light consumes everything.

Casimir is sitting on a pebble beach. A breeze carries the scent of the earth and the smell of minerals. It's dawn, and in the distance a shard of gold appears behind the islands, defining the boundary between sea and sky. Light burns the water as the sun clears the horizon, but it's no ordinary light. The sea and the air and the grassy bank behind the shore; everything glows with colours that don't have a name. The light unveils their essence. He gets to his feet and breathes in. I feel the connection he feels, the seamless blending with the vibrancy around him and the power that gives him. Casimir turns and begins to run. Certainty, strength, ease. Where his feet strike the grass, it glows with the contact, energizing him with every stride. Effortless, empowering. *Free*.

It's just the beginning…

When I open my eyes, he's watching me with his piercing gaze. "It's more incredible than I can tell you, Robert."

I come back to reality as Aiyana makes a noise that sounds like *Tcha!*

"You don't agree?" asks Casimir.

She gets up and stalks towards us. "No, actually I don't." She glances at me with a worn look. "It's overrated."

"What about all the things you can do?"

"What, you mean like this?" She stares at the candle, which flickers to life, then turns to warm her hands by the fire. "Cheap tricks."

Casimir rolls his eyes and blows out the candle, gesturing with raised eyebrows for me to have a go. "You need to let all that bitterness go, Aiyana. All it's doing is holding you back."

She throws him a dangerous look. "What do you know?"

I stare at the candle while they bicker. There's a sizzle as a flame flutters into life, and I feel a rush of pride at the achievement. Casimir grins. "It's a whole new world, Robert."

Aiyana snorts and stomps off down the stairs.

"Where's she away to?"

"Probably to clean some tables," says Casimir.

I change into my newly repaired clothes, and throw the designer ones in the fire. I feel lighter, like a small weight has been lifted, and it gives me a sense of satisfaction watching Amos's clothes combust in a shower of red and orange sparks.

Casimir hands me a pad of paper and a pencil from the bookshelf. "You'd better get thinking. I'm going to get some fresh air."

I sit in front of the snapping flames, alone with my thoughts. Every idea meets a stone wall.

"You're trying too hard," says Balaquai as he walks through the open balcony door some time later. Where did he come from? "Come on. We're going for a walk."

"But I've not got this worked out yet."

"And you'll be here all week if you carry on in that frame of mind," he says.

"What's that supposed to mean?"

"What were you thinking before we walked in?"

"Just that I couldn't work this out."

"Exactly. So what did you expect? Next time, line up with the idea that you'll succeed before you begin. Feel what it will feel like when you're done. It will save you a lot of time.

"Let's go for a walk."

*   *   *

WE'RE HEADING TOWARDS the river and the Jet d'Eau. The neon blue fountain stands out against the red dawn that's quivering across the lake.

Balaquai leads us along the jetty out to the river where the fountain rises; a long strip of concrete drenched in water from the spray. From a distance, the fountain's like the tail of a giant horse; up close, the most striking thing is that it's wet.

"What are we doing here?" I turn to Balaquai, who's watching the spray and the sky.

"If we're going to get into ORB, you're going to have to learn how to keep out of sight. Being unseen is a useful trick."

"Something else to add to the freak list," mumbles Aiyana.

"So what do I do?" There's a flicker of anticipation in my gut. Am I actually beginning to enjoy this? I squint up at the fountain, shading my eyes.

"Think of light," says Balaquai. "It's energy, like everything, one of the purest forms of energy. It's a messenger, taking information from one thing to another. If you don't want to share information, say, that you're standing here, on this jetty, then you've got two choices. Switch off the messenger or switch off the message. The first one is probably a bit beyond you for the moment, so let's start with the second."

"How can you do that?"

"What does light look like to you?"

"It's... well, nothing. You can't see it unless it's reflected from something."

"Okay," He glances up at the sky, as the sunlight

strikes the fountain, and as it does, a rainbow of colour sweeps from the edge of the spray; the mist dances in a perfect arc of red through to violet. "So sometimes it's white, sometimes it's colour."

"What are you driving at?"

"A subtle change is all you need to see things differently. All you need to do is bring about that change within you."

"Oh. Is that all."

"Just get on with it, Robert," says Aiyana.

Balaquai walks towards the fountain as the sun comes out again and shows its other self in the mist; he fades away with each step until there's almost nothing. Just the faintest hint of a shadow that you wouldn't see if you didn't know it should be there.

"He really did it," I breathe.

Aiyana glances up through lidded eyes and speaks in a monotone. "Incredible."

"Yeah, but he just disappeared."

"Well done, Einstein. Gold star." She turns to Casimir. "We're wasting time. I don't know why don't we just leave him here and get on with it ourselves. We've got the link."

"And who's going to disable ORB's systems? You?" Balaquai has appeared beside her, making her jump a little. "This is not about finding your killer, Aiyana, as much as you might want to think so. We need Robert if we're going to redress the balance. Which means you're just going to have to be patient until he knows what you know."

"And how long's that going to take?"

"A lot longer if you keep interrupting," says Casimir.

"Robert?" Balaquai turns to me. "Take a walk and disappear."

I begin to walk, trying to ignore the voice in my head. *Don't be so stupid. Do you really think you can disappear?* Logic is invisible, but it makes itself heard alright.

"Remember – just switch off the message. Think of the light in your body pouring down a plughole."

It's not working. I'm still completely visible. Casimir catches up with me. "Robert, think of it this way. What you're doing here is altering the subatomic structure of your atoms with your intention. You know supersymmetric particles?"

"Yeah?"

"You know how they don't have electrons orbiting the nucleus?"

"Theoretically, yes."

"That's how this works. You're switching yourself off from electromagnetism. You're flipping from ordinary matter to supersymmetric particles. It's how I walked through your apartment door – if I don't have electrons round the nuclei of my atoms, there's nothing to stop me passing through. And there'll be virtually nothing for light to interact with if you want to be unseen."

"But how do..."

"Just try it. Keep your intention pure."

I walk on, pondering what he said. I can visualise this a little better now. I'm aware of an odd feeling, like getting lighter. It's similar to the inaudible hum that you're only just aware of feeling when you drive fast down the motorway, the hum that's transmitted from the small bumps on the road through the car into your body. Glancing down, I can see the concrete moving along beneath me.

Are you deluding yourself? Logic again. *Do you think that maybe this is all in your head and everyone else out*

*there can see you walking down the jetty, plain as day?
Emperor's new clothes, by any chance?*

My legs are fading, like a poorly transmitted hologram, patchy and incomplete.

"Keep your concentration," calls Balaquai.

The sprays of water are upon me now, showering prisms of colours like confetti. They fall through the space where I'm standing. *Now look what you've done*, says Logic. I'm not just unseen, I'm just not. Nothing other than the vaguest suggestion of my presence. *Fuck!* Fear jolts me out of it, delusion or otherwise, and I stand there, sopping wet in the rainbow mist.

I did it.

"How come it took so long with the candle?" says Casimir.

BY THE TIME we get back to La Caverne, an idea has come to me. I know what I'm going to do at ORB.

I borrow a towel from Rosinda. The cufflink box is a bit damp on the outside, but Cora's goblet is still inside, intact. I look at it but don't touch it, afraid of what I might see.

Aiyana tries to burn her palm with the candle flame again.

I lie down on one of the couches. I haven't slept in more than twenty-four hours, and not properly for I don't know how long. I close my eyes, just for a moment.

"ROBERT, TIME TO GO." Casimir shakes me awake. There's a blanket over me and a crick in my neck. Outside, the light is fading.

"How long was I asleep?"

"Long enough."

BALAQUAI CLOSES THE book he's reading and places it back on the shelf. He walks to the side of the balcony and climbs the metal ladder attached to the wall of the warehouse, disappearing onto the roof. So this is where the others went.

The metal rungs are cold, and soft green moss is growing in the cracks in the wall. It must be a good sixty feet off the ground and it's blustery up here. Pigeons flap up from the concrete and scatter, their shapes dark against the inflamed sky. Balaquai heads for the opposite side of the roof and looks down onto the busy streets. The wind gusts against me, testing my sense of balance. It's a long way down. A sprinkling of pale lights appears below as the city prepares for night. All the noise and strife and struggle, so evident from the ground, are absent up here. Sattva stands with his back to us, the wind whipping his blue-black jacket, watching the setting sun. It sinks below the Jura mountains, sending shards of amber light over the grasslands that shroud the accelerator.

He turns towards us. "Quite a view."

"Yeah."

"Are you keeping up?"

"I'm trying not to think about it too much."

"Probably best." He turns back to look at the bleeding sun, now only a slash of crimson above the hills.

Aiyana is kicking a stone about on the roof behind me, frowning, like she does most of the time. Balaquai and Casimir are scanning the skies. I follow their line of sight and see five dark shapes circling above, birds of some kind.

"I hope you're comfortable with heights," says Sattva.

I was, until he mentioned it, but it makes me look down again and this time the street sways up towards me, distorting for a moment in a blur of light. I feel a hand on my arm, steadying me.

"Careful, now."

The birds are calling, circling lower. "Are they crows?"

"Buzzards," says Sattva. "And an eagle. He's mine."

"Yours?"

"He's been around for a long time. Taught me how to fly, in the beginning."

I think I've been taking things quite well, all things considered, but if he means what I think he means... "I'm sorry?"

"One of the skills you learn as an Eidolon is shape-shifting. Buzzards have the easiest frequency to lock on to, so it's a good place to start."

"Shape-shifting?"

"Yes. Are you familiar with it?"

"I've heard of it." Cora has this book. I found it one day, misfiled, in between *The Dummies Guide to Poker* – Danny's book – and *Touching the Void*. It was about shamans – medicine men, witchdoctors, that kind of thing. I flicked through it, wondering why in the hell she read this stuff, and found a passage about shape-shifting. These old shamans would get themselves bombed on the brewed root of some plant or other, and the hallucinations it gave them made them think they could become animals. And the rest of the tribe believed them. Drug fuelled crazy trips, I thought. I hope he's not going there. "I'm not taking any drugs."

Sattva snorts. "I'm pleased to hear it. They'd just cloud your head when you jump. Could end up in a bit of a mess."

"Jump?" I back away from the edge, suddenly uncomfortable with the whole thing. What am I doing? Regardless of what I think happened today, here I am on a rooftop at dusk with a bunch of people who believe they're dead. Only one of them, I can say with any certainty, actually is. And now they're talking about jumping.

The birds descend in an elegant spirals towards the roof.

"Put your arm out," says Balaquai.

"What?"

"Now, Robert. He'll need somewhere to land."

Its wings beat heavily, the downdraft they create ruffling my hair. This thing is huge. I begin to back away.

"Keep your arm out!"

I turn to Balaquai to see a buzzard perched on his forearm and, beside him, Casimir is supporting another.

"Shouldn't we be wearing gloves for this?" My buzzard is flapping, stretching out talons that look strong enough to tear my flesh wide open. It reaches out for a hold, aiming for my shoulder. I raise my arm and the bird changes direction as I pull my head back to avoid its wings flicking my face. I've never been this close to a bird of prey. My forearm slumps with its weight as it makes contact, but my skin doesn't break. The bird shifts position, then settles, heavy but motionless. The wind ruffles the soft brown feathers on its chest as it stares out over the city, before turning its eyes towards me.

"Now," says Sattva, his voice calm and steady. "Listen."

I can't help but stare at it – its sleek, arched head, its smooth, tawny feathers, its curved, hooked beak. It gazes back at me, and for a moment it's like our two disparate existences connect. *What's your world like?* Maybe the bird is thinking the same. There's something magnetic about it, that won't let me tear my eyes away. And something else... a clear sound, like a chime that rings on after it's struck and doesn't fade, one single note swelled by softer harmonies of itself. My eyes are still locked with the buzzard's, and it feels like the chime is ringing inside me and that's all there is... All other sounds fade. Those eyes, what they've seen...

The buzzard drops its gaze and the chime dies away. Lights flash across my vision. The feeling of that hum, that vibration, still pulses inside me.

"What just happened?" I whisper.

"You found its frequency," says Sattva. "When you learned to become unseen, you found the frequency of nothing. What we're about to do now is an extension of that. An exercise in the fluidity of things."

"So why are we doing this?"

"Casimir, would you be good enough to show Robert?"

Casimir comes forward, his eyes smiling, his buzzard propped on his arm. "Don't worry," he says. "It'll be alright, whatever you might think." He steps to the edge and closes his eyes.

"Casimir..." There's not enough time to fully register the dread that's swelling in my gut as he leans forward. "Casimir!" I reach out to grasp his shirt, my buzzard flapping into the air above me.

A hand grips my wrist. "No," says Sattva.

Casimir trembles in a burst of blue-white light and when my vision returns, he isn't there. I peer over the edge of the roof, afraid of seeing the gathering crowd, the upturned faces, the crumpled form on the concrete. But there's nothing.

"What the hell happened? Where's Casimir?"

Sattva glances up at the buzzard above us.

"*That's* him?" I stare at Sattva, then the others, before turning my face to the sky again. The bird's calling, a high pitched *eee* that falls away. "How did he..."

"They blended. The buzzard absorbed him into its own form. Don't worry, it's only temporary. Just a convenient way to get around, until you learn how to tunnel."

"Can the bird tunnel?"

"Oh, yes. It has no resistance."

The bird swoops down towards the rooftop and I back away, uncertain of what it might do next. As its talons strike the concrete, there's the blue-white flash again and Casimir's standing there, next to the buzzard, grinning.

"Alright, Robert," says Sattva. "You next." He gestures to the edge. I shuffle forwards, my brain frozen between thoughts.

"A little further," says Sattva. "And lift up your arm. The bird needs the kick of the drop to draw you into it, at least the first time."

I'm aware of the wind, blustering against my chin. A siren somewhere in the distance. The flap of feathers and air, and the weight that makes my forearm dip. And my thundering heartbeat. *What are you doing?* says Logic. *Have you lost your mind? You're a man – not a fucking bird!*

But what if you could do this? Another voice, this time Curiosity. *What if you really could rearrange*

*yourself at the quantum level into something else? You
did it before.*

Well, says Logic to Curiosity, *you'll have plenty of
time to think about that when they scrape you off the
pavement and put the bits that are left in the morgue.
Stop being so stupid and step back.*

Curiosity peeks out over the edge.

As I lean forwards, my hand feels warm, tingly – that
feeling you get when you lie on your arm for too long
at night and wake up with a dead limb. I turn to see not
skin and muscle but something translucent, fine threads
of blue-white light racing from my shoulder to the bird,
which is still perched, its talons spread as though it's
clinging to something that isn't there.

"What the..."

"Lean into the fall," says Sattva "Quickly, now."

It's spreading into my torso, this tingling heat,
dissolving what's left of me, consuming my chest,
inching closer to my neck, and I lift my chin, my muscles
straining to stop me drowning in nothing until it takes
my face... I can't do it!

"Oh, for God's sake," I hear Aiyana's voice at the
same time as I feel the push between my shoulder
blades, and I'm falling.

A rush of light consumes me, a roaring in my ears,
and then the chime, clear and steady, the only sound.

Something flaps on either side of me and the ground
falls away. The rooftop shrinks beneath and the streets
diminish. Now the wind is the only sound, rushing with
each beat of wings. Banking to the left, a tower block
looms, then withdraws, the thermals bring the dome of
the sky closer, darker now that the sun's gone, sprinkled
with a few diamond stars. Below, the world is sharper,

still as far away, but I can see the details like I never could before. It's easy. It's effortless. I'm free.

See? says Curiosity. *I told you.*

Fuck you, says Logic.

"You pushed me!" It's the first thing that comes out when I touch down, as soon as I've established that I'm back in my own skin.

"You'd still be dithering if it weren't for me. I did you a favour." Aiyana turns to Sattva. "Now can we get on with it?"

"I'd like to hear what Robert made of his experience first."

"Yeah, how was it, Robert?" Casimir's eyes are wide with anticipation, as though he's been waiting to ask me this for a long time.

"I... it was incredible."

"Any fear?" asks Sattva.

"No, it was... it was like I've always known how."

"That's good," says Sattva. "Then you're ready."

He glances up as the stars begin to show themselves.

"Are you happy that you know what you're going to do when you get there?" asks Balaquai.

"Yes." I've been rehearsing the programming in my mind.

"We'll give you any help you need."

"Robert," says Sattva, "do you still have Cora's goblet?"

I reach into the pocket of my jeans and take out the small box. My thumb glances the foil as I click it open. With no warning, it hits me again, that sudden flash of light inside my brain – this time her hands are tied awkwardly behind her, her face shrouded by her hair. She lifts her head slowly, almost as if she knows I can see her, but something's changed. Her eyes aren't pleading. They look like they've lost the fight – they're resigned. Her lids close and she drops her head.

I find myself on all fours, retching, and feel a hand on my back. Distant voices speak above me.

"Did you see it, Sattva?" It's Balaquai.

"Yes," replies Sattva. "They must be on the move. Go with Robert to ORB. Arcos and I will try to find them."

It brings me to my senses. "No. I'm going with you." I stumble to my feet, my legs still trembling.

"Robert," says Sattva gently, his hand grasping his glowing amulet, "we don't have much time. Cora's signal has too much interference and we have only a small window. Even now, it's fading. You're not strong enough yet. You deal with ORB. We'll do what we can to find them."

"But…"

There's a flash of blue-white light and a small spiral of dust whips up from the place where Sattva stood.

I feel gored by the image in my head. Impotent.

"Robert," says Casimir. "We need to go." He helps me to my feet like I'm an old man; the irony isn't lost on me.

"Aiyana," says Balaquai. "Do you have the photograph?"

She walks towards us, reaching into her back pocket, her eyes lingering on the picture as she hands it to Balaquai.

"How do we get there?"

"Just like you did before," says Balaquai. "Let the bird take you." He stares at the picture for a moment then hands it to me. "Ready?"

He leans from the edge and disappears in a flare of blue-white light.

Chapter Seventeen

WE BREAK THROUGH the clouds above an empty field. The air rushes at me as I head towards the flash of light on the ground where Balaquai has transformed, and then I'm standing there next to him. Within seconds, Aiyana and Casimir are by our sides. The birds flap off into the sky. A concrete bunker sits in the corner of the field surrounded by an electric fence.

"Where are we?" asks Casimir.

"The ORB helipad. I thought it would have taken us to Banks's house."

"He must have come this way recently," says Balaquai. "How do we get in?"

I lead them to the trapdoor inside the bunker and kneel down, opening the cover on the electronic keypad beside it. "I don't know the code."

"You don't need the code," says Balaquai. He steps through the trapdoor and disappears. Aiyana follows.

"Remember, you're mostly empty space," Casimir says. "Supersymmetric particles, okay?"

Empty space, that's all. Empty space. I press my hand

against the metal, and feel a change in its substance, a springiness that wasn't there before. I push my foot through its fabric with a feeling like squelching through soft putty. A wave of nausea washes over me as the rest of me follows. It subsides when I get through to the other side.

"Make sure you're unseen," says Balaquai.

We're standing in a white corridor. Me and three other ghosts. I can just see their forms like the shadow of steam on a wall.

"Which way, Robert?" asks Casimir.

"Wait. I can still make you out."

Balaquai's shadow turns to me. "It's alright. No one else can."

We make our way along the empty corridors to the main atrium.

"Where now?" asks Casimir.

I head for the corridor marked A Sector.

Aiyana lingers by the C Sector entrance, clutching her photograph. "I think Banks is down here somewhere."

"I need you with me, Aiyana," I say.

"Why?"

"You're my distraction."

"We'll look for Banks," says Balaquai, taking the photograph from Aiyana. "You can come for him when you're done."

Casimir and Balaquai disappear into C Sector, and we're on our own.

I HOLD MY breath as we pass through the door into Mr Y's office. What if he sleeps here? Reggie's brown and golden scales are just visible at the bottom of the tank, but there's no sign of his weirdo owner.

"A *snake*?" whispers Aiyana.

"I know."

I walk over to the security drawer and reach inside, feeling for the edges of the foam base, the top right corner, and retrieve the USB stick next to it.

There's a rustling as Reggie slithers through the leaves at the bottom of his tank. Aiyana takes a step back. I turn the USB stick over to read its label. Canadian Crippler. Bingo.

"Let's go."

On the way out, I toss a couple of cola bottles into the tank for Reggie. He hisses as he slithers towards them.

We make our way back to D Sector, pausing as a buggy hums past us; the driver shows no sign of seeing us. I catch Aiyana by the arm as we approach the Hub corridor. "Okay. Here's what I need you to do."

WE PASS THROUGH the glass partition leading to the Hub, pausing half way along. Voices come from inside.

"You can inform the others, but not Robert Strong." Dana Bishop.

"I told him I'd update him." Luke's voice.

"And I'm telling you not to. Nothing changes until I get confirmation that we have access control. Understood?"

We press ourselves into the wall as Dana exits the Hub. She touches the earpiece of her headset. "Get Banks to my office in thirty minutes. He has some explaining to do."

I feel a warm ripple in my arm as she walks thought it, and catch the scent of her perfume breezing past. Her pace slows as she reaches the partition at the end of the corridor. She glances back, her hand hovering on the release button for the door for a moment that goes on too long. I freeze as her eyes narrow. She punches the button, the door slides open and she walks out. I exhale a long breath.

"We'll get to Banks." I breathe. "Remember, seven minutes."

Aiyana steps forward to the Hub entrance, fully visible. "Excuse me?"

Lambert looks up from his console.

"Hi. Sorry to interrupt, but could you help me?"

"How did you get in here?"

"Eh, through the door."

"D'you have clearance for this project?"

"Your scanner let me in. I'm trying to get back to Area 9 – it's my first day here. Can you show me where it is?"

"Well, I can't leave my station, but I can tell you how to get there."

"Would you mind just showing me? We're in the middle of something and they expected me back fifteen minutes ago. I've already got lost twice and I don't want to screw up on my first day." She bites her lower lip a little and inclines her head. "Please?"

Lambert blushes. "Oh, okay. It's not far.

"So what do you do in Area 9?" he asks as they walk past me.

She smiles mischievously. "You know I can't tell you that."

The partition slides closed behind them.

I minimise the pages on Lambert's screen, pull up the Grid programs and begin the changes. I slide the Canadian Crippler into the USB port and link it to the trigger – the detection of Linux Scientific software uploading to the Grid. It's cutting it fine, but will buy the most time for Cora. The scene unfolds as it has done in my mind over countless rehearsals. Haste will cost me time and mistakes, so I'm methodical, focused. A circle of dots chases itself on the screen.

Footsteps echo in the corridor. I rearrange the pages as the dots keep circling...

Lambert crosses the threshold of the room. *Fuck*.

He passes his console, walks to the umbrella plant and tips in a cup of water.

The dots disappear as he throws the cup in the bin. I tease the memory stick from the port and silently slide out of the chair.

BALAQUAI IS WAITING when I reach the atrium, studying Aiyana's photograph.

"Well?" he asks.

"It's done."

"No sign of Banks." Casimir's shadow appears beside us.

Balaquai glances at the photograph again. "This Imprint should take us right to him. He's nearby, but it's as if something's scrambling the link here."

"Never mind. I know where he'll be in twenty minutes. He's meeting Dana Bishop in her office."

"You know where that is?" asks Casimir.

"Yes."

"Where's Aiyana?" asks Balaquai.

"What, she's not back yet?" I start back the way I came. "We'd better find her."

THE CORRIDOR TO Area 9 is as I remember it – dim, grey, sinister. The whispers strike up as we pass through the glass partition. Balaquai and Casimir freeze.

"Something's very wrong here," Balaquai breathes.

There's no sign of Aiyana. We move towards the metal door at the end of the corridor, pausing outside before passing through it.

Inside is large dark open space. In the middle is the transparent cylindrical tank reaching from beneath the floor to beyond the ceiling. Grey mist spins around a beam of light that seems to come from deeper underground. Surrounding the tank at intervals on the floor, are blue domes of varying sizes. Their surfaces swirl and shimmer, glimmering with a peculiar inner light. Aiyana is standing staring into one of the domes. I breathe a sigh of relief when I see her.

"What are they doing here?" Casimir whispers.

Aiyana doesn't take her eyes off what's inside. Beyond the murk is a rat, sitting perfectly still and blinking rapidly. I walk between the domes. Another rat, a dog, three monkeys, all unmoving, some staring ahead, others blinking. Beside each dome is a console displaying data: heart rate, respiratory rate, serum norepinephrine, serum cortisol, neutrophil function…

"Stress responses," whispers Aiyana.

Balaquai walks to the rear of the vast room, behind the tank. We follow him towards a dome much larger than the others. Inside is a man; naked, lying on his side, staring ahead. His ribcage is moving rapidly; making it uncomfortable to watch it. I crouch down, eye level with his gaze. A jolt of recognition hits me: it's Abrams, the aircraft engineer. I can tell from his eyes that he's suffering. I reach for the surface of the dome and I become aware of something pushing back, like an unseen force repelling my palm. I glance up at Balaquai.

"It impenetrable."

Balaquai's shadow-hand hovers over the dome but does not pass through. "I can't sense him."

Casimir moves closer. "Neither can I."

"What do you mean?" I ask.

"I can see him, but I can't sense his mind. The dome is some kind of shield. It's blocking the signature of his consciousness in the Field; cutting him off."

"We have to get him out," says Aiyana.

"No. It would jeopardise Robert's efforts," Balaquai says.

Behind us, a door opens. A man in scrubs and a facemask walks in carrying a digital tablet. He stops beside Abrams' monitor; Abrams' stress responses are in the red. I move behind him until I can see the screen of his tablet over his shoulder. The title 'MINDSCAPE' heads the pages as he scrolls through the data. I feel Balaquai's hand on my arm, pulling me back. Silently, we leave the room.

WE REACH THE corridor of G Sector just before Peter Banks strides down it. Aiyana bristles as he passes. He walks into Dana Bishop's office and we filter in silently behind him.

"Don't you knock?" Dana is sitting at her desk, her fingers poised above the keyboard of a laptop.

Banks ignores her and takes a seat at the other side of the desk. "What do you want, Dana?"

"One of our Californian sources informs me that police are investigating the murder of a Ms Aiyana Wolfe."

"And?"

"Did you kill her?"

"She'd have talked if I didn't."

Aiyana edges towards Banks. "Not yet," I breathe in her ear.

"Oh, for God's sake, Peter." Dana lights up a cigarette. "It's messy."

"Messy? She was a smart little bitch. I got you what you needed, plus insurance that she'll stay silent. That's a clean outcome. It's what Amos would want, given what's at stake."

Dana puffs out a ring of smoke and holds up a red memory stick. "This is the only one you found?" She slots it into the USB port.

"That's all. Do you think she was onto Mindscape?"

Dana studies the screen. "No. I think she stumbled on the side-effect of the medium, that's all. The electromagnetic fluctuations are a by-product, but I doubt she would know what they really represent."

"You look tired, Dana. When did you last get some sleep?"

She snorts. "Sleep's not an option until this is over."

"When will that be?"

"In just a few hours. Lambert's team have cracked admin access to CERN. We're just waiting for Trench to run some final checks on Surrey's firewalls to make sure they won't interfere, but he's confident we'll be ready before CERN launch. Relying on Strong was always a gamble, but we had no other option until now."

"I thought he'd have caved when we took his family."

"Would you?"

"Probably."

"Are they secured?" she asks.

"I'm told they are."

Dana's headset bleeps and she picks it up. "I'll be right

there." She takes a drag and stubs out her cigarette, pausing as she passes him. "I won't be long."

"Take your time." He runs a hand down the side of her thigh. "I'm not going anywhere."

He leans back in the leather chair, his hands clasped behind his head as Dana closes the door behind her.

Aiyana leans forwards and breathes out a long slow breath on the back of Banks's neck. He springs forward, staring over his shoulder, then snorts and settles back in the seat. Aiyana grips the chair and spins it hard. Banks yelps and stumbles to his knees.

"Who's there?" He scrambles to his feet.

Aiyana takes the photograph from Balaquai and tosses it onto the floor, where it becomes fully visible.

Banks mumbles something, his face the colour of wet clay, and darts for the door.

Aiyana pulls the memory stick from the laptop before following Banks out of the room.

He's in one of the washrooms at the end of the corridor, his face in his cupped hands over the sink, water dripping through his fingers. Casimir guards the door as Aiyana's shadow turns on the hot tap. Steam rises and settles on the mirror above. She draws her finger across its surface. Banks glances up, his gaze fixed in the letters emerging through the steam. 'YOU'VE BEEN BAD.'

"Who's there?" Banks is quivering.

Letters write themselves in front of him. 'SMART LITTLE BITCH.'

Beads of sweat prickle on Banks's forehead. His knees crumple beneath him and he grasps the edge of the sink.

Aiyana leans closer and whispers, "What is Mindscape?"

Banks shakes his head. I grab the back of his shirt as he tries to get to his feet, pulling it tight across his throat

311

and throwing him off balance and onto his knees again. Aiyana strikes him in the face.

"We can do this forever," she says. "What is Mindscape?"

"A Thought Management Project. It identifies perceived fears in subjects and enhances them."

"Why does CERN have to do with it?" asks Balaquai. Banks jumps at the new voice. "I... I don't know the details."

Aiyana strikes him again and he whimpers.

"Something to do with the scatter from the collisions disrupting Mindscape. That's all I know. Please..."

"Where are the hostages?" I whisper.

He swallows and my grip tightens making him gag. "Geneva, somewhere on the outskirts. Amos had them moved. I don't know where. Honestly."

I twist his shirt collar and Banks' arms flail. "Who does?" I whisper.

His face is purpling. "A... Amos."

I relax my grip a little but pull him back towards me. "Go home, Peter Banks," I whisper. "Breathe a word of this to anyone, *anyone*, and we'll know. We'll find you and your little girl. We're watching."

Aiyana kicks him hard in the groin. He groans and crumples to the floor, striking his chin on the sink on the way down.

"Are we going watch him?" asks Aiyana as we steal back to the field exit.

"No. But he doesn't know that."

"QUIET," SAYS BALAQUAI. He pauses at door of the concrete bunker leading to the field. Light that wasn't there when we arrived spills in under the door. Silently, we pass through to the outside.

A helicopter is sitting in the field and a tall man in a long black coat is walking towards it. He pauses as he approaches the cab door and glances back.

I shrink back into the shadow of the bunker. As Amos studies the building, I hear Casimir draw breath.

The engine whines to life and Amos climbs on board.

We watch the aircraft take off, it's lights diminishing into the night sky.

"Let's go," says Balaquai.

Casimir doesn't move. "It's him."

Chapter Eighteen

I FOLLOW CASIMIR as he walks across the empty rooftop of La Caverne. The darkness is thick now that cloud obscures the moon.

"What did you mean back there?" I ask.

He stares out over the city towards the neon fountain. The only sound is the occasional swish of a passing car and the breath of the breeze. "It was a long time ago."

"What was?"

"When I was eleven years old, I lived in Michigan with my parents. A man visited a few times, discussing things with my father. I heard them talking through the crack in my bedroom door. One night, just after he left, another man came in. He shot my parents in the head."

"What? I never knew any of this."

"I tried to forget. I managed to forgive the man who shot them, but not the man who gave the order. I saw that man tonight, for the first time in seventy-one years." He turns towards me. "He hasn't aged a day."

"Amos?" I let it sink in. A man who doesn't age. Not really a man at all. "Why did he kill your parents?"

"My father was a journalist. He was about to go public with a piece that highlighted corruption in the media industry. It would have been the end of his career and he knew it, but it was too important for him to bury. He claimed that journalists were pawns for the government, that the whole thing was rotten from the top down. All the public were getting was what the politicians wanted them to believe."

"And who do you think persuades the politicians?" says Balaquai.

"Is that why you came to Scotland?" I ask.

Casimir nods. "I was sent to stay with my grandparents. It was a different generation. When I asked them about it, all they said was that it was God's will. You just had to accept it and one day it would make sense." He stares out over the rooftops. "I wonder if they ever figured out that man's will and God's will are the same thing."

A dog barks in the next street as a flash of blue draws my eye skyward. Two birds soar down, wings outstretched, their talons reaching for solid ground, and as they strike, Sattva and Crowley stride towards us. Their faces tell me it's not good news.

"They're close, Robert," Sattva says. He hands me the small box with Cora's foil goblet. I stare down at it, feeling like someone who's been handed their wife's wedding ring when they get bad news. It's all that's left. "We know they're alive, but we can't pinpoint their location."

"Now we know why," I reply. "Mindscape."

"Mindscape?" Crowley frowns.

"It's a project Amos is developing at ORB. They're mining people's fears."

"Incubating them," Balaquai continues, "inside some kind of shield that isolates them from the Field.

They're afraid that the CERN collisions will disrupt Mindscape."

"That's what doesn't make sense," I say. "The scatter's minimal. Any particles created shouldn't escape the detector."

"Unless," Sattva begins, "they're referring to a particle that we cannot yet detect."

"There's something else," says Aiyana. She's sitting on her own, turning the red memory key over in her fingers. "They said that what I found was a medium for Mindscape."

"Medium?" Sattva glances at Crowley. "He's incubating fear and now he's found a way of dispersing it?"

"Your work uncovered clusters, Aiyana," says Crowley. "Around densely populated areas, is that right?"

Aiyana nods.

Sattva walks to the edge of the rooftop. "This is worse than we imagined."

"Robert," says Crowley, "are you certain that ORB cannot release their worm? Because those experiments may be our only way of finding Cora and your father."

I've already decided. "I'm not leaving anything to chance. I'm going back to CERN."

I TRANSFORM AS I touch down in an empty patch of ground behind a service building at the back of ATLAS. Crowley is just ahead me; I'm not practised enough to tunnel on my own.

"You'd better give me Cora's goblet."

"Just…" The words swell up in my throat as I hand over the box.

"We'll do everything we can, Robert. Do you still have your amulet?"

I pull down the neck of my T-shirt to show the oval stone.

"Then you'll know if we find them. I'll be back for you. Good luck." There's a brief flash of light and he's gone. I glance up to the buzzard circling overhead.

The ALTAS car park is full and Rene's bike is beside the entrance. He probably slept here last night.

The control room is buzzing. People are sitting on the floor, on the desks, standing in the spaces in between. All in the way. I push through the crowd.

"Rene, where's Professor Von Clerk?"

"He must be up in his office – he'll be here any minute."

Shit. I fight my way back through the crowd.

A few stragglers make their way into the control room from the corridor, leaving it empty. I run past the offices, scanning the names. A voice comes from the next corridor and I follow it to the office next to Florence's.

"No-one's seen him. I tried calling yesterday, but got no answer. Okay. Let me know if you hear anything." He puts down the phone as I open the door.

"Professor..." I begin.

"Robert, this isn't a good time." He glances at his watch.

"This is important."

"I'm sorry, it will have to wait. We're about to launch."

I step in front of him as he moves towards the door. "Listen to me, Professor. The Grid's infected. Romfield Labs have picked up a problem with their system overnight. They think it came from the Grid, so they may not be the only ones."

"Why didn't they inform us? They know the protocols..."

"I don't know. But if you stay connected to the Grid, you could wipe out the data gathering mainframe."

"We can't afford another failed launch..."

"Share the data later. You don't have to stop the experiments, but don't run them live with the Grid. How are you going to explain to the CERN Council that you knew there was a threat, and they have to reinstall an entire mainframe?"

His eyes hold mine, unblinking, and I can see the thoughts churning in his head. Behind him, the clock notches up another minute. He lets out a long breath, his lips a tight line, and picks up his phone.

"Albert, it's Jorgen. We have information that there's a security risk with the Grid – disconnect all external Grid users immediately. No live Grid connections, understand? Send me confirmation when it's done. And find the source." He drops the phone on the desk.

"How long will it take to disconnect?"

"A few minutes." He opens the door. "You'd better be right about this."

I step aside, letting out a long breath as his footsteps fade down the corridor. I reach for the amulet round my neck – cold and heavy, an ordinary stone – put it back into my T-shirt and head for my dad's office.

Silence descends on the control room as I push open the office door.

"Not watching the fireworks, Robert?"

I freeze. Victor Amos is sitting in the armchair.

Chapter Nineteen

AMOS CLOSES A book, entitled *In Search of Dark Matter*, puts it on the desk. "I'm disappointed."

"Really."

"I reunited you with your father. I gave you the chance to be part of history. Yet you chose to squander it all. And for what? To satisfy an insatiable scientific curiosity?"

I say nothing.

"Some things are better left unknown, Robert."

"Where are they?"

"We made a deal."

"Taking them hostage wasn't part of that."

"And neither was your failure to deliver your end of the bargain." Cracks appear in his composure; something threatening lies beneath. "You left me with no choice. But that's irrelevant now." He glances at the clock on the wall. "Our security specialists have rectified the problem."

"Then you've got what you wanted. Tell me where they are."

Slowly, he gets to his feet and crosses the floor towards me, but it's not the movement of an ordinary man. It's like he glides rather than walks. The door closes.

He leans in towards my right ear and somewhere underneath the cologne, I catch the stench of singed flesh on his breath. His eyes blaze, but he speaks softly. "Do you really want to know?" Another sound, a faint whispering, slithering beyond the words.

My vision shatters. The world around me splinters and suddenly I'm somewhere else, lost in a grey mist, before me colourless trees, gnarled and leafless, people tied to the trunks; and, among them, Cora Martin and Elliot Strong. The sun is a black, writhing orb on the horizon, mining my core for its spirit. Through the haze is a small church, with an overgrown cemetery. I crumple to my knees on the floor of the office as the world realigns.

"Ah." Amos closes his eyes and inhales, as though relishing the scent. "You see it, don't you? You're a Sentient?"

"Just let them go. Do what you want with me, just let them go."

I feel his eyes stray over my face as he draws near, his voice no more than a whisper. "You don't understand, do you? I gain far more from your suffering in life than I ever would from your death. I *need* your suffering." He leans closer still until I feel his breath on my cheek. Fear seizes me, chaining me to the spot. A hot, clammy tongue slides slowly from my jaw to my temple. Amos closes his eyes, savouring. "I can already taste it."

"Please..."

"I let you live, Robert Strong, so that you can watch her breathe but never hear her voice again; look on her, but know she does not know your name; think of her and appreciate what you made her sacrifice. And you will know where she really is. Where her mind and her spirit will reside forever."

"No..."

He straightens to his full height, taller than he seemed before, inclining his head to one side. His eyes close again. The black sun flashes in front of me, obliterating the room. I blink and gasp, and it vanishes. Amos is gone.

I TEAR FROM the office, past the entrance to the control room, as cheers erupt from inside. They've launched. The first particles are on course for collision. The amulet grows warm on my neck, but I already know where she is.

Crowley is not outside and I can't tunnel without him. Cursing, I go back inside, pushing through the control room crowd until I find Rene.

"I need your bike, Rene."

"What? We're just getting started –"

"Please, it's an emergency. Just give me the fucking keys."

THE BIKE ROARS from the car park, scattering a crowd of students, and out onto the highway. It's raining and the road has a sheen on it that threatens to slide the bike as I push through ninety. I cut out past a truck, narrowly missing an oncoming tanker. Horns and angry gestures from the driver are just background distractions.

My amulet burns in the hollow of my neck, a hot spot against the cold rain driving at me. The turnoff is ahead, on the right, the single track road. The back wheel slides out as I brake to make the turn, and the bike leans low towards the ground in the spin, billowing a cloud of dust. A few hard revs and it regains its grip on the track, clods of dirt scuffing up from the earth. Ahead is the church, where I last saw my dad. His car is still parked outside, abandoned where he left it. I pick up speed. The fence posts whip past, the fields a green blur and something else at the edge of my vision. Glancing sideways, I see an eagle, soaring level with me, its enormous wings rigid. It's there as I bounce over the potholes in the road, always just a little ahead, leading the way. It veers off to the left, over a grass track, and I follow it, past the low stone wall surrounding the small cemetery behind the church.

Ahead is the wood. Balaquai and the others are standing there as I dismount. A flash of blue-white light announces Sattva's transformation, and he's there next to me as I run towards them. Casimir is crouching down next to the base of one of the trees.

Sattva catches my arm. "Robert. We found them, but not in time. I'm... I'm sorry."

Casimir looks up at me as I approach, his eyes like Sattva's, full of pity and pain. My pace slows. An arm is wrapped awkwardly round the trunk. A slender, pale arm, a hand with a silver thumb ring. Another step and I see her auburn hair, straggled down over her face, her head drooping towards the ground, where she's kneeling on the dirt. *Oh, God, Cora, what has he done to you?*

I'm on my knees, my hands clasping her head, lifting it, sweeping the red strands away from her face. Her eyes open, and she looks at me. She's alive. "Cora... I'm so sorry." I press my lips against hers, but she doesn't respond. "Cora? It's me." Her eyes stare out, but there's nothing inside them. Just blank hollow pits.

"They won't recognise you, Robert," says Balaquai. He's crouched by my dad, who's kneeling by another tree in the same awkward position, his hands tethered behind him, like he's waiting for the guillotine.

Why are they just standing there? "Cut them loose!"

"There are no ties, Robert," Sattva says. "They're free to leave."

"Well, help me get them up!" I reach under Cora's arms and try to lift her, but she's a dead weight, her arms still stretched behind her, clinging to the tree. Sattva and Balaquai exchange glances, but don't move. "Do something!"

Sattva crouches down beside me and steadies my hand as he meets my eye. "Robert, we can't reach them. They're inside Mindscape."

My eyes are drawn back to Cora's face, to its emptiness. A sudden flash of grey disconnects the world again, like a strobe in a nightclub that dislocates reality into segments, only this segment is different and it lasts. I'm still where I am, crouching next to Cora, and she's still tied to a tree, like my dad, but the space in between has changed. There's no colour. None at all, only shades of grey and black. Where there was grass, there's only dry dusty earth. The tree she's tied to is dead, blackened, its gnarled branches reaching up to the grey sky. A mist the colour of lead hangs low in the air, despite the incessant howling of the wind. It clears momentarily to reveal a man tethered to the tree next to my dad. He lifts his face – it's Abrams. The mist closes around him, but beyond, dark shapes emerge from the grey, strewn across the colourless earth like an endless dead crop. They look like crosses. No, not crosses; they're trees, their lifeless branches black against the ashen sky. People are tied to each of them, arms clinging to the trunks. Jesus, there are thousands of them. Cora lifts her head, her eyes staring past me, and I follow her gaze towards the horizon, towards the dark orb that seethes in the place where the sun should be. Like a black hole, it sucks any memory of hope from me. I feel like my core has turned black.

IN A WHITE room deep underground, Dana Bishop is watching a screen over Luke Lambert's left shoulder. She picks up a headset. "Get me Jo Trench." She pauses while they connect. "This is Dana Bishop, Director of Operations. What the fuck is going on?"

"Surrey's been disconnected from the Grid."

"What? You told me our backdoor was safe."

"It is – it's not coming from this end. CERN must have switched off the Grid."

She turns to Luke Lambert. "Find a way round it. Now."

She lights a cigarette with a trembling hand, narrowing her eyes against the grey smoke. Luke Lambert taps on the keys of his console, pulling up the firewall programs. He hesitates as the screen goes blank and the room goes quiet. Five seconds later, the word 'UNLUCKY' runs across the screen. He glances round. It's on every screen in the Hub.

Dana Bishop breathes into the headset. "Get me Mr Y."

"Ms Bishop," says a woman carrying a mobile. "Mr Amos wants to speak to you."

Without looking up, Bishop draws deeply on her cigarette and grinds it out on the corner of Lambert's desk.

* * *

"ROBERT!" SATTVA SHAKES me and I stumble back on the green grass as his face comes into focus.

"I saw it... what they see..."

"You saw it?"

"Amos... he wants me to know. He let me in."

"What did you see?"

"They're tied to dead trees – Cora, my dad, Abrams and thousands of others."

Crowley's eyes flicker across the forest then he crouches down beside me. "There's more than Cora and your dad?" He glances at Sattva, who's standing very still, watching me.

"What's happening, Sattva? What was that place?"

Crowley turns to Sattva. "He's linking their consciousness."

"What?" I ask.

"He's harvesting their collective fear and incubating them inside it. He's making his own Field."

"What do you mean?"

"It means, Robert," says Crowley, "he's creating Hell."

"What? But you told me they weren't dead!"

"They're not. Hell isn't a place; it's a state of mind. You don't get there by dying. You get there by living it. To be in that place means you've forgotten you can choose."

"When are the first collisions, Robert?" says Balaquai.

I glance at my watch. "Four minutes."

Sattva is staring at the middle distance, realisation dawning in his eyes. "The collisions recreate the beginnings of the universe, the first particles in existence, is that right?"

"Yes, but –"

"That's what he's afraid of."

"Of course," says Crowley. "Why didn't we see this before?"

"What?" I ask. "What are you talking about?"

Sattva turns to me. "The basis of creation is thought. Amos is afraid that that the energy released from the collisions will create new consciousness that will disrupt his Mindscape."

"So it should release them?"

"It's the best chance they have, but they will still have to choose. And for that, they need a reason to hope. Do you think you can get back in?"

I glance down at Cora. A flash of dark mist splinters my vision. "Yes."

"And what if he gets stuck there?" Crowley interrupts. "Do we just leave him? It's too risky, Sattva."

"I'll do it," I say.

Sattva hesitates. "Alright. There will be a focal point in there somewhere, something that drains your spirit." I nod. The black sun. "It will take all your effort, but whatever you do, don't look at it. Not if you want to come back."

I feel a hand on my arm. Casimir is standing next to me. "Be careful, Robert. I'm counting on you coming back."

"Remember," says Sattva, "you can choose. Keep hold of your hope, no matter what."

Two minutes to go. I look into Cora's blank eyes, seeing through to the inside, to that place where she's suffering. The world I know shatters and becomes her Hell.

*   *   *

THE FIRST THING I feel is the wind. Cold, biting, unrelenting wind, whipping at my back. Cora is kneeling on the dark dirt, my dad tethered next to her. Glancing up, I see the field of trees, stretching on for miles – forever, it looks like – beneath a leaden mist. And kneeling by each one is a person, thin and resigned, facing the eternal wind. Their eyes are glazed beyond caring, no hope left in them. An endless crop of hollow minds.

"Hold on, Cora."

She lifts her eyes, but I can't tell if she sees me.

"Dad?" I reach out and lay a hand on his shoulder and he raises his head, his eyes deep, hollow tunnels.

It can't be long now. There's a pull on my head, like a compass to magnetic north, a strange fascination for what lies behind me. It's compelling me to look, and I don't know if I have the strength to resist. It's like it's calling me, like it has answers to all my questions. My head inclines towards my left shoulder. It's there, just behind me. I can see the black curve of its edge, writhing against the slate sky. I know what Sattva said, but there's a burning curiosity to see for myself. Just one look...

A sudden burst of light and heat shatters the darkness, an explosion that judders through me. Above, sapphire fireworks spray out over the grey, sprinkling blue light that doesn't diminish, but intensifies as it arcs towards the earth. Cora's face, and my dad's, jolt upwards. Their eyes flash with life, then fear. They're remembering.

"Cora! Dad!" Their eyes find me, bewildered, afraid. The first shower of light touches the black earth and is extinguished. "Move! Get up!"

They wrestle with their arms, trying to free them from the unseen chains as more spears of neon blue touch

down and extinguish. There are only a handful left in
the descent – minutes until the darkness returns. Dark
blood trickles down Cora's arms with her effort, and her
struggling slows, her gaze returning to the black sun.

I get down on my knees, level with them. "Look at
me. That's it – keep your eyes on me." Around me, the
candles are going out, one by one. "You have a choice.
You can choose to stay here, or you can choose to leave.
You have a life, people who love you. But you have to
choose."

They stop struggling and stare at me. "You have to
choose!" Something gets through. Cora nods. My dad
pulls his arms forward, one at a time, freeing himself
from the trunk, and stands up. Cora's on her feet now,
but she's running into the mist, away from me.

"Cora!" What the hell is she doing?

We follow her through the fog, between the bolts of
blue, between the dead trees and the dead minds. Ahead
of us, she drops to her knees, her hands clasping a face.
Its long fair hair moves aside as the face rises towards us.

As the last blue arc reaches down and connects with
the floor of Hell, Sarah opens her eyes.

The brightness fades and the wind drops. It's darker
than it was before. Whispers trickle in around us,
indistinguishable voices from everywhere and nowhere,
testing, teasing.

And then silence.

It hangs on the air, poised, breeding something worse.
Slowly, I get to my feet. The wind has dropped. In the
distance, a rumbling, something dark growing on the
horizon. Time slows down.

Then, like the blast wave of a nuclear explosion, a ring
of black fog tears across the field towards us, flattening

the trees in its wake, forcing the hollow minds chained to them onto their backs to stare straight up at the sky as the fog rips overhead. I turn to shield them, and wait for it to hit.

Chapter Twenty

AN OWL HOOTS. I'm trembling uncontrollably, clinging to Cora and my dad. I don't want to open my eyes. A soft breeze ripples across my face and I feel a hand on my back.

"Robert?" Sattva's voice.

I can't coordinate my hands to wipe the strand of hair from Cora's face. She does it for me, then presses her lips against mine. Warm, soft lips. The scent of jasmine. I'd forgotten.

My dad is on all fours, retching. Sattva and the others help us to our feet. Sunlight trickles in through the gaps between the pine needles, casting a lacy pattern on the dark earth. When we reach the edge of the forest, my dad's knees buckle.

"I'm fine. I just need to sit down for a moment. Go on, I'll catch you up." He sits down on the grass and drops his head.

Sattva nods. "He'll be alright. Just give him time."

Beside me, Cora stops. Ahead, Sarah is standing on the crest of the hill overlooking the valley. Cora frees herself from my arm and walks towards her, pausing by her right shoulder. A breeze lifts Cora's hair, but Sarah's doesn't move.

Sattva and Casimir guide me to a fallen log a little further on.

"Are you alright?" asks Casimir as I sit down.

"There were so many people there, Casimir. Hundreds... thousands... The collisions weren't enough."

"Not for all of them, no. And unless we stop Amos spreading Mindscape, there will be more." He hands me Aiyana's red flash drive. "You know he'll come after you now?"

He's right. I've known for some time now. "Then I might as well make it worth his while." The red casing glints in the sunlight as I take it from him. "What happened back there?"

Sattva glances up at me. "You witnessed the creation of new particles, new energy."

"But what was it?"

"It's what you've spent your life looking for. What the physicists created all over again when the particles collided. Call it what you like – consciousness, the Field, dark energy; it's all the same." He stares at me. "You still don't you know what it is?"

"No."

"It's the human spirit, Robert. The piece of the universe that you and everyone else are searching for. And those of us who exist within it, just a breath away in those unseen worlds, we are dark matter."

I'm trying to process his words as something draws my eyes to the hill. The light's changing – no, Sarah is changing, becoming brighter, almost iridescent.

"What's happening to her?" I whisper as she raises her right hand towards Cora.

"She's moving on."

I can see Cora trembling as she reaches out and their hands meet, one made of flesh and dusted with soil, the other made of light. She closes her eyes and smiles, her cheeks wet with tears. Sarah turns, looking over her right shoulder, and I follow her gaze. I get to my feet. Something's happening to the air behind her. It's shifting, almost imperceptibly, like the shadow of steam on a wall, becoming an opening, an archway. But it's not what it looks like that grips me; it's what it makes me feel. I feel longing, like everything I want to be and know and understand is there, through that arch.

Sarah turns back to her sister, who nods and smiles.

Sarah lowers her hand and walks towards the shifting air, glancing back at Cora, now smiling and crying, before she steps through. The air swells and brightens and she blends into it, as a dream becomes a memory.

"The coin of grief has two sides," says Sattva. "On one is the pain that will lessen but never quite leave you. On the other, the knowing that the one you love is home."

The archway still shimmers against the horizon and my eyes are drawn back to it. "It feels like..." My voice fades, unable to find the words.

"Home?" I feel Sattva's eyes on me. "You can go too, if you want. It's your choice."

"Why do I feel this way?"

"Robert, there's something we have to tell you." Sattva pauses until I look at him. "It's waiting for you."

"You mean..." I breathe the words. "The helicopter crash...?"

Sattva looks at me with eyes that have seen a million sunsets. "If we'd told you before, you wouldn't have found the focus to do what you had to. But you had to die to rediscover who you really are."

I feel my throat closing as my eyes slide back to the shimmering arch. It's waiting for me.

"It's your choice, Robert," says Sattva. "You can go now, or you can stay, if you can keep your focus in the physical. And that's something you already know you can do."

My right hand feels warm. I look down at it and find it changing, lightening, like Sarah's did. I turn it over, seeing the blades of grass beneath it. "How? How do I do that?"

"There are two incentives, right in front of you," says Sattva. "You're holding one of them." I look down at the flash drive in my left hand. "The other is standing over there." He glances at Cora. "But it's your choice. Everything is your choice."

My eyes find Cora, her slight form silhouetted against the sky. Only a few steps away, but now a universe apart.

As she turns back to me, her eyes still glistening, I feel the light in my hand fade. "What do I tell her?" I breathe as she walks towards me.

"Nothing," says Sattva. "If you want to stay focused."

As Cora stands quiet and still in my arms, it feels like we're not two people at all. It feels like we've become one person, something that goes beyond the confines of the flesh with all of its limitations, its beautiful imperfections. I breathe in the scent of her skin, the scent of jasmine, and close my eyes. Above, five buzzards circle, gliding with the clouds. They stay with us for a while, then fade away into the blue.